THE DEVIANT FUTURE SERIES

WASTELAND TREASURE

NEW YORK TIMES BESTSELLING AUTHOR

EVE LANGLAIS

Produced in Canada

Published by Eve Langlais ~ www.EveLanglais.com

eBook ISBN: 978 177 384 101 4

Print ISBN: 978 177 384 102 1

PROLOGUE

IT TOOK DECADES FOR THE EARTH TO RECOVER from a catastrophic event that not only reshaped the surface of the world but also took a chunk out of the moon—which turned out to be a really bad thing. The tides in the oceans kind of needed it whole. It was amazing the ripple effect something like that had. Add in meteor showers, a few nuke strikes, and BAM!

Once the worst of the destruction ceased, meaning the craters only smoldered and the shuddering waves from the impacts had subsided, the planet was never the same. The Ancients, as some called them—although could a few centuries really make them so old?—had done a number on the planet. It wasn't the plastic pollution that did it in—as so many predicted. The Earth had a way of breaking things down when given a chance. There were other less natural things that did it. Toxic waste from nuclear bombs. Biological hazards that, when released, killed, not just humans but huge chunks of life, animal and insect alike. The meteor showers brought shit to an extinction level event.

But humans, like the rats and roaches of the world, knew how to survive and adapt.

New Earth needed them to change because, while some of the poisons in the ground eventually dissipated, others remained, requiring a stronger constitution. Evolution of the fittest ensured life on the planet didn't die out.

Humanity lived, but they weren't the same people as the Ancients. They were wilier. Stronger. And also very divided.

In that nothing changed.

There were a few disparate groups, the most prominent being the Enclave and its citizens. Ruled by the members of specific families—a strange process that involved breeding and testing to ensure a certain quality—the Enclave lived for the most part in the Cities. One major city per kingdom. Everything else was considered a satellite to it and existed to serve.

There were five kingdoms on the continent, with some being more divided from their neighbors than others because of natural barriers. The Emerald domain consisted, for the most part, of a barren wasteland with mountains running along part of it, an impenetrable forest on another, and a chasm to complete the lopsided triangle. The Sapphire City and its satellite towns were past the encroaching marshlands and bordering the Savage Sea.

There was Ruby—where debauchery ran rampant—Diamond, and Lazuli. Those five kingdoms—with a sixth emerging from the boggy lands vying for status—were ruled by the Enclave, two kings, three queens, and their various courts under them. The Enclave regulated every inch of their citizens' lives from creation, to placement, to punishment if someone objected to their lot in life.

They provided a direct contrast to those who chose to ignore the Enclave's rules, sworn enemies known as Wasteland Rats, Marauders, Deviants. They preferred the term survivors. They managed to live outside the domes in dangerous places like the barren Emerald and very wild Ruby. It wasn't easy, but they were free. However, they did long for something a little safer, more permanent. A real home.

Rumors spoke of a fantasy place, a city with the highest walls, perfect for repelling monsters. Trees in tended gardens that didn't try to capture and digest the unwary. Clean running water, food, justice. A city where everyone was treated equally. Every traveler passed on a story about Eden from someone who'd heard it from someone else.

It was ruled by a man who refused the title of king. Who forged a kingdom out of the Wasteland. Who ruled fairly. A true leader and savior who might be able to save them all.

Or so they said.

Now if only someone could find him.

ONE

*M*ANY YEARS AGO, IN A CITY RULED BY A QUEEN...

"You there, behind the counter, pay attention. You have business to conduct if you can be bothered to do your job."

The acerbic tone and words might as well have been a slap. Staring at the jars she dusted, Sofia bit her lip lest she speak out of turn.

The customer is always right.

Not always. Only once had she dared mutter that back to her teacher.

She still remembered that lesson, and the stinging on her knuckles from the spoon he'd used to smack them. *Never tell them they're pompous jerks.*

With a fake smile pasted on her face, Sofia turned to greet Jezebelle, a regular customer—and pain to deal with. She was always quick to verbally abuse. Insulting those she considered inferior. Which included Sofia.

The older woman, her blonde hair pulled into an intricate series of knots, had a sneer on her lips. "About time you did your job. It would seem you need lessons on promptness."

If they insult, do not respond. Do your job. Serve the client.

"Can I help you, Citizen Jezebelle?" Sofia used her most polite tone, the one that required her grinding her teeth lest she scream something else. She knew some choice words, since she'd moved from apprentice to assistant. It meant she got to leave the shop more often and that she was allowed to handle the shop on her own. It was as if Jezebelle knew when the master left on business and visited on purpose.

The woman always arrived determined to taunt, firing Sofia's temper. A temper she never realized she owned until recently.

The master had been gone for more than a week, felled by an illness, with no one available to take his place. A week during which Sofia had no one to tell her what to do. Or what to eat. Was it any wonder she skipped that disgusting shake he fed her each morning that he claimed was full of vitamins? Perhaps she should have been more diligent about drinking it, because she felt quite out of sorts.

She couldn't have said why her emotions toward people like Jezebelle had turned fierce of late. She felt quite rebellious. Inside at least. On the outside, she pretended servitude and mouthed platitudes.

"Do I look like a person who requires anything from you?"

Knowing how this game was played, Sofia kept her pasted smile as she murmured, "Of course not, citizen. You are perfection yourself. None of my wares are obviously worthy or needed."

It was the same stupid game each time. Jezebelle pretended she wasn't going to get anything, but she knew the Red Rosy was the place to go when it came to certain remedies. Especially the one to keep skin supple and young.

"I dislike giving business to one so obviously ill-bred, but at the same time, one should encourage the local merchants," she said with a resigned sigh.

The urge to roll her eyes resulted in Sofia fisting her hands so hard that her nails left marks on her palms. "Perhaps as a gift, a soothing lotion, not that your skin requires aid. But one can never be too careful about the toxins in the air."

"If you insist on atoning for your rudeness, then I shall accept." The haughty air deserved a slap.

Instead, Sofia offered a bob of her head and a short curtsy. "Of course, citizen. I will prepare it immediately."

Sofia turned to the display of jars lining the wall. As recently promoted assistant apothecary, she prepared fresh salves and powders for the rich of the city who could afford to shop. They happened to be the most annoying people to deal with. They wanted things done now, because they demanded it, and then tried to find reasons to avoid payment.

When she asked the master why he didn't refuse some of them service, he'd shrugged, his white beard quivering as he said, "You don't say no to an Enclave family."

Meaning they had to accept that behavior. Those that protested and claimed all citizens should have equal rights? They paid a visit to the arena.

It proved simple to mix together the ingredients for the facial cream; after all she'd been doing this from a young age. She'd been apprenticed right out of the Creche but was now the only one left. The others the master trained were deemed lacking in talent and sent to the factories to help mass produce toiletries for the lower-ranked citizens.

Sofia knew better than to celebrate. She was still considered a step below her master, which meant she had to keep working hard.

"Why is this taking so long?" snapped Jezebelle, drumming her fingers unevenly, trying to disrupt Sofia's train of thought.

She knew how to tune the woman out and kept kneading. Once the mixture appeared smooth, she dug her fingers in it and whispered her intent into it.

Which sounded dumb. And yet, the master apothecary who taught her could always tell if she skipped the murmured command. She got a rap on her knuckles if she lied.

She closed her eyes and whispered, "Moisturize." That was it, along with strong thoughts of what that word meant. The *intent.*

Her hands heated as the ingredients reacted to each other, the spurt of warmth over as quickly as it began. She scooped the cream into a jar then turned to hand it over.

Citizen Jezebelle had her lips pulled down. "You did not make that correctly."

"I assure you, I did."

"Don't lie to me, apprentice. I saw you skimping from that jar with the green powder."

"The mint? That just gives it a refreshing feel."

"Did you just talk back?" Jezebelle recoiled, her rouged lips pulled into a rictus meant to feign shock. Yet it also hinted of jubilation. Jezebelle had found justification for her actions. "Insolent wretch.

I'll have you punished for this. Where is your master?"

"Attending more important people than you." There was horror and yet deep satisfaction in saying it.

The gaping expression on Jezebelle's face was worth the explosion. Quite literally. The citizen uttered a high-pierced shriek of rage, which rang in the shop. The waves of it sent Sofia to her knees, hands over her ears. Still the scream went on, shattering glass, shaking the very structure of the shop.

When it ended, Sofia lay huddled among glass and ingredients, her nose tickling at all the sharp scents. The waste of it incredible, especially since some of the items were very rare and valuable.

"You idiot. Look what you did," snapped Sofia. "You destroyed the master's shop."

"You provoked me."

"Don't blame me for the fact you can't control your temper." Sofia rose, shedding glass and powder.

"We'll see who's blamed."

"I'm not the one who just pulverized a shop."

"I was protecting myself," was Jezebelle's haughty reply.

"From what? This?" She held up the jar of cream that had remarkably stayed intact on the counter. "I can see the danger. Moisturized skin. Such a horrible thing to suffer. Totally justifies you having a tantrum." Once started, she couldn't seem to stop. The insults kept coming and coming. Given the shattered window, with citizens peering inside, she imagined it wouldn't be long before the city guards arrived.

Jezebelle must have realized it. She grabbed at some broken glass and lifted it over her arm.

Would she seriously...she did. She slashed herself a few times, shallow messy cuts.

"Everyone knows base citizens can be violent." She shot a triumphant smirk in Sofia's direction.

It was an utter lie. Yet, Sofia already knew they would believe Jezebelle.

Sofia would be placed in a cell. Execution would be the kindest thing if that happened. She knew what happened to those who were put on trial. She could end up being forced into labor on a farm or in a factory where people were literally worked to death. Pretty prisoners were often given to the soldiers as whores. There was banishment. Public humiliation. Death.

All horrible choices because of a rotten woman. An annoying, entitled, mean woman who delighted in attacking Sofia.

No more.

Before Jezebelle could put down the glass, Sofia

dove over the counter for her. If she was going to be punished, she wanted to have the satisfaction of hitting her at least once.

Not expecting the attack, Jezebelle staggered under Sofia's weight and hit the ground hard. Sofia grabbed the wrist with the hand holding the glass. She drew back her other hand and balled it into a fist.

Before she could hit that rouged mouth screaming for help, the door to the shop smashed open and guards poured in, yelling, "Halt, or we'll shoot."

She froze and released Jezebelle, raising her hands over her head. Before she could stand, Jezebelle slashed her across the cheek with the glass shard.

The hot blood heated skin as it dripped off her jaw. She gaped at the woman. "What is wrong with you?"

"Arrest her! She attacked me!" Jezebelle screeched.

"She started it." Sofia stuck to the truth.

Rough hands gripped her by the arms and dragged her away. The soldiers had no interest in listening to anything she had to say. She might be a citizen of the city, but she ranked low in the hierarchy.

The cell they tossed her into proved nicer than expected. A clean space of her own. An actual bed. Water to wash herself. Food three times a day. Blander than her usual fare, but better than nothing.

She only wished she'd had some access to herbs. Thread would have been nice. The wound on her cheek—the skin splayed open from the jagged glass—scabbed in a thick line. It would leave a mark if she couldn't treat it soon.

The day of her trial arrived, and the level of activity around the cells multiplied as the prisoners were prepared for their day in court. Less justice and more a spectacle, court took place once every seventeen days.

Given it was a show, she endured a scrubbing followed by a rinse in a room along with the other female prisoners. Through the water pouring steadily from the ceiling and sluicing down a huge drain, she counted thirteen.

When the deluge ended, they were blown dry quite literally by the large fans that sent blinding gusts, which whipped around hair and removed all moisture from the skin.

Those who had managed to retain their long hair were combed and plaited. Simple, shapeless, knee-length robes of coarse fabric were placed on them. Their feet were kept bare.

They were lined in a hall, more than fifty men and woman in total. Some arranged in small groups.

She was second to last. When it came to be her turn, she stood almost numb behind the door, knowing her fate was about to be decided.

Would she live, die, or be sent somewhere horrible, wishing she could die?

The door slid open. The guard by the opening, wearing the bright red armor that the queen insisted upon, gestured, and she stepped out slowly onto the large stone tiled floor.

The bright lights of the arena almost blinded, and there was a hum of noise. She managed a quick glance around and saw the walls ringing her broken only by a few doors. One being a rather large double metal portal with dents, as if something had punched it from the other side. That door was for the bigger monsters they sometimes brought to court.

No sign of blood, although the stones were still damp in some spots. They tended to be efficient when it came to cleaning up between court cases.

"Would the defendant take her position, or does she require aid?" an impersonal voice boomed, and the crowd tittered.

The creak of armor let her know the guard moved in her direction. Rather than be dragged, Sofia began to walk, noticing the etched circle in the stone, the one they'd told her to stand in. It made her an easy target, but what choice did she have?

She stood on the spot, staring down at her bare feet as a voice went through the theatrics of introducing her.

"Citizens, what we have here is an enigma. Let me introduce the usually well-behaved Citizen Sofia, assistant apothecary, avid reader of the biological sciences and a beautiful lady before the incident." The subtle jab at her scar almost made her raise her hand to it.

She remained still.

"Accusing her, we have the exemplary Citizen Jezebelle. Known for her voice talent, she's the daughter of Lady Jazinda."

Not one of the most powerful families in the Ruby City, but higher ranked than the majority of other citizens.

"Are you ready to hear the charges? See the evidence? And aid with the verdict?"

The applause proved energetic. That drew her glance, and Sofia noticed the hierarchy of seating. Where a person sat in the arena showed off their position.

Closest to the action were the Enclave members themselves, and their close family by extension.

Above them, friends to the Enclave, more family. Then there was everyone else.

Unlike most things in the city, the events that occurred during court were open to the public. Other businesses closed that day. Just about everyone went to the arena to see their government and justice system at work.

Sofia used to be one of them. One of those watching, cheering, and jeering. It was different being on the receiving end. She didn't like it one bit.

The charges were recited and received with boos aimed at Sofia. They already believed her to be some kind of violent offender.

"Citizen Jezebelle, state your case."

With grand theatrics, Jezebelle began telling her elaborate story, the truth of it lost in the exaggerations and utter fabrication. By the end of Jezebelle's rendition, even Sofia hated herself.

The crowd hissed in Sofia's direction.

The announcer returned. "That was a vigorous retelling. Now for the accused. How do you reply?"

"Jezebelle attacked me." A weak rebuttal.

"Can you provide proof?" the announcer asked in a deep rumble.

The crowd held its breath, hoping for an exciting twist.

She shrugged. “I can’t.” It was her word against a higher-ranked citizen’s.

But she’d forgotten that court, in the spirit of entertaining, sometimes liked to give the cases unexpected flair.

A giant hologram appeared overhead, suspended in the air over the area. A frozen image of the door to the apothecary shop appeared.

Sofia’s mouth rounded. A camera in the shop. She’d never even known. Only the city’s security force had access to cameras. Which meant they’d bugged the shop.

Why? Didn’t matter. The truth was about to come out, and she glanced in the stands to see Jezebelle fanning herself furiously.

“Citizens, it is our delight to announce we actually have video of the alleged incident. Would you like to see it?”

A resounding “Yes!” shook the air.

Which meant Sofia got to see and hear herself in action. Hear Jezebelle once more accuse her with no merit. Wince at her impertinence, cringe as the glass exploded. Then ache with pain in her cheek as she saw the moment she was wounded.

The video ended, and there was a second of hushed silence before a buzz of conversation clouded the air.

"Citizens!" The announcer spoke a little more loudly to catch their attention. "Citizens, the evidence is clear. The assistant started the altercation with her inability to do her job correctly. Then compounded her crime with her rudeness. Personally, I find citizen Jezebelle's actions justifiable. But what say the people?"

"Guilty!"

Sofia could only gape. How could she still be guilty? No. It wasn't fair. She turned around, looking for succor. All she found were walls surrounding her and a roar as people shouted, "Guilty. Guilty. Guilty."

"Justice has spoken. We need to pass sentence." The voice deepened. "There are three punishments applicable for this type of offense. Let us start with the most boring, sending the accused to the factories."

That received boos.

"A service position within the city on her feet or her knees. That's up to her new employer."

"She's too ugly with that face!" someone shouted, drawing attention to the imperfection she'd have to live with.

"How about my personal favorite?" the announcer purred. "Banishment to the Wasteland."

The reaction proved instant with cheering and whistles and calls to "Throw her out."

"Make her walk."

The crowd began chanting, "Banish. Banish."

A door at the far end of the arena opened. Sofia's breath left her. She wavered on her feet.

"Former citizen Sofia, you are hereby sentenced to banishment in the Wasteland. If you try and return to the city, you will be shot dead."

Thrusting her into the Wasteland would kill her, too. It might be gentler to get shot.

"Please. I didn't do anything wrong. I don't deserve this," she stupidly pleaded.

"Guards, escort the criminal to the door."

Panic had her breathing hard. A firm hand at her back shoved her forward, and she stumbled, tears clouding her vision, hearing the approving roar of the crowd.

They wanted to see her cast out. Approved of her death sentence. Just like she'd cheered in the past for others.

This was wrong. So wrong. But there was nothing she could do to stop it. The guards propelled her through the doorway into the tunnel. When it sealed, the sound of the audience was cut off.

She stood in the dark and waited. One by one,

lights lit, going down the hall in a long line. The floor underfoot began to move, shifting her along.

"Proceed to the exit," said a robotic voice.

She began to walk, her emotions numb. This couldn't be happening. She'd been a good and obedient citizen. Done everything she was asked. The unfairness burned.

Her steps slowed as she reached the far end of the long tunnel, hidden by a door. The moving walkway dragged her closer, and she knew she'd gone far enough to have passed the edge of the city wall.

The walkway stopped in front of the door. On the other side, the end of life as she knew it.

The portal slid open, and she looked out to see the windswept plain that bordered the top edge of the city. They didn't deposit her anywhere close to an actual road or some semblance of civility.

They banished her on the bad side, where even the air could kill her with its toxicity. If she lived long enough to breathe, that was.

"Exit the tunnel." The command came, and still she couldn't bring herself to step onto the dirt.

Taking that step was to accept her fate. To sentence herself to death.

Suddenly, rather than the robot voice, she could hear the announcer, "Uh-oh, citizens, it would appear the convicted former citizen is balking. What do we do to those who don't graciously accept their punishment?"

She didn't hear the crowd's reply but could imagine they were screaming for her death. The bloodier, the better. They wanted to see what came next. They loved the fierce desperation of it.

And once upon a time, so had she. She used to watch and cheer and gasp with the rest of them.

Now she was the one who oozed desperation. Who would struggle not to be a bloody smudge soaking into the dirt.

To survive, she needed to move, and quickly. Sofia ran those last few paces, bolting out of the door onto the arid edge of the Wasteland. She didn't dare look back. How many pitfalls could she remember? It was important she not get caught by any. The first was the easiest. In theory at least.

She ran for the ditch, wide and fairly deep, but she'd seen some of the banished cross it. She moved as fast as she could and leaped.

Missed the other side.

Her upper body and arms slammed into the edge. Her fingers scrabbled for purchase. Her toes dug in as well. She halted her slide. Panting, she heaved herself over the lip and rolled. She ended up facing behind her and got to watch the spiked ball exit the tunnel, chipping holes into the ground as it rolled and dropped into the ditch. It missed her.

But she wasn't out of danger yet.

She got to her feet. Five more traps to get through if she didn't want to die today.

There was a nest of roach-like insects with wings to her left. She'd seen a few exiles get flayed alive by their mandibles.

Too far right and she'd be close to the chasm, which spilled demons at night. At least that was how it looked from the footage the drones sent back to the city.

Straight ahead was pure desert, where people and drones went blind. All signals died at its border.

Who knew what happened once a person went in there? They probably died. Perhaps it would be less horrible than the death offered in the other directions.

Her bare feet scraping on dry ground, she ran for the desert, knowing if she took her time, the drones sent to document her banishment might hurry her along. She caught sight of one humming alongside her, capturing her every desperate expression.

Did it also capture the rude gesture she flung and the mouthed words of rebellion? Fuck the Enclave.

She'd been wanting to say that for a long time.

Fear gave her speed, and she flew. To her

surprise, there was a sense of exhilaration. She was in horrible, horrible danger, but she was free.

She laughed as she entered the desert. Kept laughing as the drones that followed crashed, their machine parts shut down. She almost joined them, feeling the strangeness in the air, the electrifying nature of it. She glanced ahead at the barren landscape and saw the smudge of a high mountain. A destination.

She just had to make it to those mountains. She trudged under a beating sun then shivered as it disappeared, leaving her in darkness. Suddenly where before there was quiet, she now heard the scrabble of life. The whisper of movements on the ground.

Every single horrifying story of monsters that devoured human flesh came to mind. Hugging herself didn't relieve the chill in her blood. Tightly wound, she gasped as a strong gust of wind wrapped around her, a cold, sharp breeze in contrast to the heat still radiating from the ground.

Slowing, she realized she could see a bit again, the stars above giving her a pale, pale light. Her bare feet were sunk in soft sand, a weird transition, given a moment before it was still hard. Now, in the starlight, the smoothness rippled. The expanses of land humped, the ground undulating.

As if alive.

Suddenly terrified, she finally looked behind her, expecting to see the lights of the dome, but instead she saw the haze of a storm approaching. A storm she couldn't hide from, its windy fingers already wrapped around her, sharply tugging. With no recourse, she trudged up the dune that formed in front of her, aiming still for the mountain. At the top she paused and groaned. A field of sandy humps stretched in front of her.

The wind grew nippier with each dune she crossed, and she wished for a scarf or something to cover her face. The sand scoured her skin. She lost count of how many hills she climbed. There was a never-ending amount of them, and they kept moving, shifting.

Then she crossed one and saw something dark against the ground. Something jutting from the sand, an edge that didn't belong. Excited, she ran for it, only to slow as it took shape.

It was the edge of a drone. The drone she'd been moving away from for hours. She'd been traveling in circles. She'd gone nowhere at all.

The wind lifted her hair and her filthy gown. She sank to her knees, exhausted and on the verge of crying, if she had any moisture left for tears. She gripped two fistfuls of sand as that wind circled around her, flaying at her exposed skin. She closed her eyes and wished hard to be safe, even knowing wishes never came true.

The gust turned into a tornado, and it sucked her into its whirling body, stealing her attempt to scream, making her lose consciousness.

When she next woke, she lay in a field nose to nose with something, staring into the big eyes of an animal, about to be eaten.

She screamed.

TWO

Snapping forward years later to Haven Dome, the new, if temporary, home for the Wastelanders led by Axel and his eminently capable and good-looking second, Gunner.

"We intersected another Enclave patrol sweeping a little too close," Gunner informed his boss.

Not that Axel liked the word boss. Axel would argue until he ran out of breath that he wasn't a leader, that he preferred to be alone, that people were a pain in his ass. He was also the first guy to literally give the shirt off his back, put his life on the line to help anyone he knew, and a bossy fucker who gave orders all the damned time.

Gunner hoped to one day be half the man Axel was. Only with better hair.

"I told you to stay out of their way."

"They literally ran into us. What did you expect us to do?" Ever since they'd stolen a dome, they'd been dealing with increased Enclave presence. A bad situation, given they were rebels.

The building they'd taken over as a command center? Formerly belonged to an earl. In their defense, the earl attacked first, and when they retaliated, they hadn't encountered much resistance. The men and women they'd found working at the dome proved to be docile to their rule. There were fewer of them than expected. The barracks for the employees surprisingly empty. Kind of like the tanks. A good thing. They worried about handling five babies. What would they have done if the full batch of two hundred were ripening?

"What happened with the soldiers?" Axel asked.

"We beat them, of course. No losses on our side," Gunner informed.

"Prisoners?"

Gunner shook his head. In the Wasteland, a person learned early on to always handle potential problems. That included loose lips.

"It's only a matter of time before those deploying

the soldiers realize that the patrols that aren't returning are all working in one area."

"Will they notice? We're assuming they keep track." Gunner had come across some serious arrogance when it came to the so-called citizens of the Enclave.

"They'll notice when patrols stop reporting in. Although it helps we're still accepting shipments from the other domes. Makes it look like business as usual."

"You're welcome." Gunner grinned.

It had been his idea to let the Enclave keep supplying the dome. It wasn't as if those who accompanied the trucks ever saw the earl who used to run the place before pissing off the boss. The earl didn't survive the change in ownership.

All they had to do to fool anyone who came visiting was pretend everything was normal. Axel put some of Haven's people in armor and had them act like guards, shooting the shit with the delivery truck drivers. They'd had no problems bringing in all kinds of goods, on the earl's account, of course.

Only problem was nothing was coming out. Especially not any of the babies.

The Incubaii Dome they'd taken over had an abundance of tanks, a few with tiny bodies in them. They were lucky. They'd just missed a batch being born, but they were coming up on another one due. No one knew what they'd do with the five babies that would suddenly birth. Just like they'd yet to settle on a plan for the Madres they discovered in varying stages of pregnancy.

The people who ran the domes were sick, using woman as nothing more than supplies of eggs and wombs for the rich. More astonishing, some of those pregnant women kept begging to be returned to the Enclave. Who wanted to be a slave?

Gunner couldn't handle it. He needed out of the dome. It was too much, a reminder of all the things he hated.

"I'm going to head back out in the morning," he announced.

"So soon?" Axel rubbed his chin. "Maybe you should take a few days off. Rest up."

"I'd rather be out there than in here." He gestured over his shoulder.

Axel grimaced. "Me too. But what can I do? Someone has to keep the peace. And apparently that someone has to be me. Living here has everyone on edge. I keep telling them it's temporary."

"But we need to find somewhere else to go." Gunner sighed. "I know."

Because when the Enclave did discover they'd taken over an Incubaii Dome, they'd probably send an army after them. At least they'd bought some time.

"Any word from the other camps?"

Haven wasn't the only band of Wastelanders out there.

"Nothing." Axel shook his head. "I kind of expected it. Forming an alliance is like declaring we're going to war."

"Cowards," Gunner growled. "We need a bigger ally. Someone with the numbers and infrastructure to help us."

"You're talking another city." Axel shook his head. "None will ever agree."

"Not an Enclave-controlled city. One is just as bad as another. I mean we need to find the Lost City of Eden."

Axel groaned. "Not this again. We talked about it. The lost city is a myth. A rumor."

"You said that about dragons, too, until we saw one last year," Gunner hotly retorted.

The beast was impressive, its wingspan big enough to cast a shadow when it crossed the Wasteland and headed toward the sun rising over the forest.

"The idea of a secret city is different," Axel said.

"How?"

"Because it's impossible. The Enclave rules for hundreds of miles around."

"Or so they'd like us to believe."

"Don't you think if there really was this magical kingdom, we'd have seen proof?"

"How many people talking about it does it take?"

Axel's lips pressed into a line. "Second-hand stories aren't a reason to uproot our people. We need more."

"Then I'll get you more."

"As in an actual location."

"I'll find us somewhere to go."

"And quickly. Oliander says those babies are coming in the next fourteen days. The next batch, forty-one days later."

"Making babies in a tank. I don't get it." He shook his head.

"It's to control their genetics," Axel growled. "If I had my way, I'd destroy this place."

"I'd like to kill a few people, myself."

The babies in the tanks were one thing. Gunner had a real problem with the babies being carried by the women kept prisoner in the Incubaii Domes. Women with desirable genes and magical gifts. Gifts others wanted to exploit. And so they bred those women with powerful men, believing those kinds of babies ended up stronger. More powerful.

All the better to rule.

As to what kind of power...To remain relevant in this new future, humanity had evolved. Necessity unlocked abilities. Some people, like Oliander, could do some light healing. Axel could talk to the Wolgar in the forest. His promised, Laura, could move things with just the power of her thought. Others could command minds.

Those were considered the desirable abilities. Extra limbs, fur, scales, or anything outwardly apparent was firmly rejected. When the Enclave detected an aberration in a fetus, they terminated early. If the mutant feature developed later, there were uses for them.

"Once the babies are born, we need to destroy those tanks."

"They'll just build more." Axel rubbed his face. "Don't forget, this isn't the only Incubaii Dome."

"I know. Just like I know the only reason there's not more tanks full of babies is because they had issues with fertilization." Some kind of contaminant had destroyed the ovum this dome had access to. "It's inhumane what they've done."

"To them, people are expendable." The very concept made the stomach roil. Axel rubbed his face in fatigue. "If the Enclave attacks in force, we'll have a problem."

"I thought the plan was evacuate, scatter in a few directions, and regroup at Chasm Falls since we don't have the numbers to hold the dome."

"It was mentioned to me we can't abandon the babies."

Gunner shifted. "I hadn't thought about them."

"Because we're used to moving pregnant women around, not a bunch of tanks. If we leave, the Enclave gets them back and we condemn those children."

"If we stay and die, we still condemn them."

Axel clenched his jaw. "Meaning, I'm fucked either way."

"If it's any consolation, we'll die heroes."

"I'd rather live a while longer."

There was a knock on the door, and Gunner opened it. Laura stood there, her slim figure silhouetted in the doorway, her honey-blonde hair tied back. She gestured. "Better get outside, there's some kind of a drone hanging out overhead."

"Fuck! Tell them to shoot it down!" Axel yelled.

Laura stepped aside as Axel bolted for the door. Gunner beat him to it and raced outside the command building. Dusk fell, and a hint of dust in the air brought his gaze overhead to see the gap in the dome. A drone had removed a panel and slipped in. The enemy had made its move.

His gun cleared his holster even as he made all the connections. His wasn't the only bullet to tear into the metal body. The drone hit the ground, and they stared at it.

"Sound the alarm," Axel ordered. "I'm going to assume the Enclave knows we're here, which means we need to start evacuating people."

"What about the baby tanks?" Gunner asked.

Axel swore.

Then swore again when Nikki came running. As a resident of Haven for a few years now, he'd gotten to know her steady nature. Not so steady now.

"Something's wrong!" she screamed. The panic on her face had them racing to meet her. "There's something wrong with the computers."

When wasn't there a problem with electronics? You'd think given the problems they had making them work properly and consistently that they would have abandoned them. But a place like the Incubaii Dome that relied on a small staff, computers, and automated systems could reduce the manual workload.

They could also be hacked.

"Gunner, you handle the problem with the machines. I'm going to get shit moving along," Axel said.

"Got it." Gunner jogged behind Nikki, who wasn't usually one to panic.

He re-entered the command building to hear Zara mumbling, "Lizard-humping, fucking steaming pile of—" Their resident tech expert could have a colorful repertoire of words. But no one corrected the sloe-eyed woman.

"What's happening?" Gunner demanded. Judging by the grim expressions, the tank problem had taken a critical turn.

"A remote signal managed to lock us out of the tank building's controls. And I mean locked out. The buildings with gestational units have been sealed."

"Any people inside?" he asked.

"Surprisingly no. But we can't get in. If we try to blow the doors, the whole place is programmed to flush."

"You're fucking kidding me." Now it was Gunner who rubbed his face. "What's the rest? I'm sure there's more shit news."

"There is a force coming our way. I don't know how we didn't see them. It's as if they popped out of nowhere and are only now being picked up on camera."

It didn't surprise him. Electronics were wonky at the best of times, and the Enclave had secret ways of protecting themselves. "Pack up and move out."

"What about the babies?"

"We can't help them. They'll be fine. We, on the other hand, won't be."

"Should I leave the office a mess?" Zara asked, standing with a glass half full of water.

"Let's not make it easy for them." He gave a nod and watched as she dumped it onto the electronic console, seeping into the cracks. It didn't have the same explosive result as the chair Nikki grabbed and smashed into the screens, but it did the trick.

Since they were handling shit, Gunner rejoined Axel, who barked orders to those who'd gathered. "Let's get the non-fighters on those vehicles. I want them out of here now." It didn't surprise Gunner when Axel said his name next. He had a sixth sense. "Gunner."

"Yeah, boss."

"Get the riders out on their bikes. See if you can lead some of the Enclave forces off to give the slower trucks a chance to get to the forest. I doubt they'll follow us in there."

"On it."

Gunner veered off, uttering a sharp piercing whistle. He did it all the way to the vehicle corral just outside the dome. People came at his call, the tough ones, wearing their leathers and the goggles that never left their necks. Neither did their scarves.

Always ready to move and fight at a moment's notice.

"Riders mount up. We're providing wing diversion. I want three of you ready to go in two minutes. The next wave, you leave three after that. Just like we practiced." Because they'd known this day was coming.

The riders in the first line ran for their bikes. They knew what to do, given he'd begun training them since their arrival at the dome. He had only eight riders in total, eight to buy time for the many to escape.

People poured out of the dome, mostly adults, but there were children too. They weren't whining or clinging, except to their things. Being a Wastelander meant being transient. It wasn't uncommon to pick up and move camp in the middle of the night. It wouldn't take long for them all to be loaded and moving out.

Gunner pulled down his goggles, and his scarf went up. He and Vera, a woman he'd paired with more than a few times when it came to Haven security, were in the final group.

Except Vera was cursing as she kicked at her bike. "It won't start."

"We don't have time to fix it. Throw it in a truck and grab a point spot."

"What about you?"

"Don't worry about me. I've got luck by my side." He winked and sped off, keeping to the timing they'd agreed on.

Each group moved out of the dome and arced off into different directions, spreading out in thin numbers to hopefully cast a wide net. With too many holes.

They were too few to mount a proper defense. If only they didn't have to run all the time. As he sped, he couldn't help but think of the Lost City. A city they'd never have to flee from. Axel could give up being boss if he wanted. Gunner could apply to the guard. People could stop looking over their shoulders and drawing daggers at every noise.

As a plume of dust rose behind him, he noticed the forest to his far left, a dark smudge that would provide sanctuary to those who reached it. Not safety mind, but the Enclave soldiers would be wary of entering.

He headed straight north. Hard to believe that used to mean pointing to some polar pole. According to the history he knew, the world no longer had stationary ice caps. Just a few massive moving continents of pure cold. Which he found hard to imagine. Stories spoke of water frozen into flakes or even into tiny icicles.

Pure nonsense. Straight north now meant toward the most barren strip of land that undulated with sandy dunes, which sucked at the tires and made fancy moves difficult. Not impossible.

He gunned the bike, rolling it up the hill as fast as it would go, peaking, and for a moment, he was airborne, the rumbling bike between his thighs, giving him a clear view. And in the dip between the dunes was a fucking tank. The cannon swiveled in his direction.

Gunner cursed. It felt as if he moved in slow motion as he leaned and wrenched on the bike, changing its angle of descent, still feeling the burn as the missile shot by. It hit the sand dune and exploded it. He hit the ground, front tire still too sideways. He spilled over and rolled a few times. Which hurt. Quite a bit.

He popped to his feet and sprinted, zigging and zagging, doing his best to draw the cannon fire, hoping his luck would hold. Another bike suddenly wheelied overhead. He waved his arms, knowing they wouldn't hear his yell.

The tank wouldn't be teased into following. They'd have to destroy it.

Changing direction, he ran for the massive metal weapon. He leaped for it, grabbing the edge so he could swing aboard. He headed for the top of the tank and raised his hands as the muzzle of a gun pointed at him.

Gunner grinned. "Hey, Casey."

Bang. The soldier pointing the cannon at him collapsed, and Casey glared at him from the other side of the nest. "Element of surprise. Stop ruining it."

"You got this?" He pointed to the tank.

She ignored him to pull out a saber torch. It lit, and she went to work on the hatch. He didn't take offense at her lack of loquaciousness. Casey tended to be very focused when it came to work. Mostly, he suspected to escape her overbearing brother, Cam.

"Where's your bike?" he asked. "Never mind. I see it."

He jumped to the ground and ran for the bike, gunning it. He wanted to see what lay on the other side of this dune. Hopefully not another tank, or something worse.

He crested the top and once more had to swerve, because it turned out the whining of bikes he'd been hearing? Not his riders.

The Enclave soldiers gunned their machines and aimed for him.

Gunner prayed to the god of luck and took off full throttle. In his mirror, he could see he'd drawn a good number of them. He just had to make sure he didn't lose them too quickly.

He hopped the next few dunes, happy to see no more hidden troops. In his mirror, he noticed the crowd behind him thinning.

He stopped atop the next pile of sand and stared back as they sped away. Why away? A gust of wind brought a silt of fine dust, making him wonder if they feared toxicity in the air.

He'd been born on these plains. Took his first breath choking on the poison. It made him stronger. But not immune to everything.

The wind picked up in strength, and he glanced the other way to see a worrisome sight. A funnel cloud was coming right for him. A dusty beast of howling winds and scouring sand.

"Fuck." He already wore goggles to protect his eyes, but his exposed skin was flayed. Thankfully the scarf covered most of his face, and his gloves protected the bulk of his hands. The lack of fingers had him tucking them into fists.

The wind kept pushing, and with the visibility gone, it was as if he didn't even move. He did the only thing he could, held on to his bike.

The storm proved stronger, lifting them both with its ferocity, and the terrible tearing forced him to let go and protect himself as it flung him around and around hard enough to strip away his goggles and scarf. Even with his eyes shut, the orbs burned as fine grit worked its way in. The wind stole his every cry. Sucked the breath right out of him before finally slamming him on the ground, half dead. Lost.

His next conscious memory was that of a feminine voice drawling, "Look what the cat dragged in."

THREE

WHAT POSSESSED HER DAMNED FELINE TO DRAG this man back to her place?

Sofia eyed the limp form, his clothes dusty and tattered. He lay on his back, eyes closed, showing off a face that was swollen and red. The exposed skin on his body hadn't fared well. Even with the fine layer of dirt covering him, she could see the many scratches and the darkening of flesh indicating contusions, but his limbs appeared unbroken.

Pity. A man with a broken leg or arm would have been easier to handle. Given his rugged appearance, she didn't expect much in the way of manners from him. Her last experience with a rough-looking guy didn't end well.

For him.

"What have I said about bringing home living

things?" She planted her hands on her hips and glared at her cat. By cat, most would picture something dainty and furry with long whiskers, pointed ears, and a whip-like tail.

But then multiply the size, more than a few times. Still cute, and thankfully Sofia's friend.

For her part, Kitty—the not very original name given to the cat she befriended—appeared innocent. Those big, beautiful jewel-like eyes glinted golden with a hint of green today. Kitty's big, furry head cocked, and she rolled her front haunches in a shrug, as if to say she didn't know how his body got in her mouth.

"If you want to play with your food, do it elsewhere," she teased the cat.

Kitty replied with a chuff. She didn't eat human, preferring fish from the river instead.

A fact Sofia was thankful for. What she didn't appreciate was the body she'd have to handle now. He was a big man. The kind that required sweating and cursing to try and move around. The problem with having a cat that outweighed her and seemed freakishly strong.

"You brought him here, you get to take him away." She pointed to the body and then off in the distance.

The cat stared.

Sofia shook her head. "We are not keeping him. Where did you find him?"

The cat looked off to the side, toward the section of forest farthest from the river. The area she currently lived in was bound by a few natural barriers, meaning it was very hard to reach and, once inside, impossible to get out. If the man lived, they'd have a neighbor.

Pity. She thumbed over the hilt of the knife tucked through the braided vine belt holding up her pants around her waist. She could handle the threat now before he woke.

The cat meowed.

"He's probably dangerous," Sofia said aloud. She realized full well she spoke to a cat. She was fine with it.

"Rowr." Kitty pawed the man's chest gently, her claws retracted.

"He'll probably wake up grouchy," she announced. Grouchy men were mean ones. They also expected her to serve them without delay. But did they do anything in return?

The cat turned those big eyes on Sofia.

Sofia said with a snort, "You want him, then you take care of him. Somewhere else." She tried to sound stern in the face of those expressive eyes.

Kitty sidled close and rubbed against her, almost knocking her over.

"Don't you use my love for you against me," she chided.

The funny sound Kitty made had her sighing. "I hate it when you do that. How about we start with a look." Might be best to see if he required disarming before he woke.

She crouched and observed him without touching. "He's a sorry-looking specimen."

If a big one. He probably had a few inches on her, and definitely outweighed her. The storm had done a number on him. His face was pretty scratched up. Nothing a bit of cleaning and a mud paste wouldn't fix. She had most of the ingredients in her pouch except for the mud. That would only take a minute to fetch, and she'd grab fresh water for rinsing his wounds first.

As she began mentally cataloguing everything to do, she frowned. She wasn't fixing him. She did, however, run her fingers over his jacket, feeling the pockets, pulling out a variety of small things. Mini torch that lit with a flick. A round disc cracked in half and barely holding together. A multi-function tool that went into her pocket. His gun holster was empty. Knife sheath too.

She sat on her haunches. Kitty meowed.

"I don't know what you want from me. He's a mess, but I don't think he's broken." Sofia ran her fingers down his arms and legs. Nothing felt out of place. She saw no signs of blood. Just a lot of scrapes and bruising.

No other sign of weapons either. Just like she had no idea who he was. He wasn't wearing a suit, the kind favored by dome guards and Enclave soldiers. If he lived in the city, then it was the poorest of sections, given his garb wasn't common. Not in civilized areas. Which meant he was probably one of the Wasteland Rats the Enclave complained about.

Despite never having seen one, there were always stories of their exploits. Brazen thefts. Attacks. Murders...

Those who lived outside the City were barely better than animals. Given how humans sometimes treated each other, she wondered which was really worse.

"I'm going to tie him up. He is much too disreputable looking to trust."

Despite not moving at all, he replied as if he'd heard her. "I swear, I clean up good."

"You're awake?" Her heart pounded, and her fingers wrapped around the hilt of her knife.

"I think I am. Or am I dead? Hard to tell." He groaned, stirring slightly.

"Don't move!" She pulled her knife. "I will slice you if you lay a hand on me."

"Sweetheart, I wish I had the strength to touch a woman and bring her pleasure." A raspy flirtation.

"Who are you?"

"Right now, I feel like a side of meat that's been pulverized by a truck." He pushed himself to a seated position, groaning at the effort. "Fuck, maybe I *was* hit by a truck." He palpated his body, slapping legs, arms, torso, getting a sense of his injuries, saving his face for last. He hesitated before he ran his fingers over the scraped skin. He only lightly touched his closed and very puffy eyes. "Well, those don't feel good."

"I wouldn't advise opening them." A begrudgingly given piece of advice.

"I wasn't planning on it. You have to tell me, though. How do I look?"

She pursed her lips. "That's really what you're worried about? How you look?"

"Must be bad since you're being so mean to me."

"I am not being mean."

"You wanted to tie me up."

"For protection."

"See what I mean? Most women would want to tie me up because I'm handsome and they'd like to worship my fine body. But not you. Meaning my face must be seriously messed up."

"It is."

"Way to crush my spirit."

She bit her lip, because the sarcasm came with a smile. How could he jest? Surely, he was in agony. "Who are you, and how did you get here?"

"Depends where here is. And as for who I am, maybe I should be asking, who are you? I've never heard an accent like yours before."

Accent? She frowned. If anyone spoke slightly different, it was him, with the way he rolled and drawled each sentence as if it formed a single fluid word. "I am the one asking questions. Who are you?"

"Gunner."

"That's not a name."

"I assure you it is. And you are?"

She couldn't see the harm in telling him. "Sofia."

"Hello, Sofia. I don't suppose you can tell me what happened to me?" He hadn't gotten to his feet yet, but he did gently palp around his eyes.

How much damage had they sustained?

"What do you remember?" she asked.

For a moment he didn't reply. "I was leading some Enclave soldiers away from H—" He paused. "I was being chased through some dunes, and then..." He trailed off. "I'm not sure what happened."

"Pretty sure I can guess what occurred next. You were caught in a funnel wind. Carried miles over the mountain range and dropped in a place where Kitty apparently found you."

"Kitty?" he repeated.

As if her name were invitation, the large feline shoved her head against the stranger's hands, drawing a startled gasp from him. "What the fuck?"

Sofia snickered. "Kitty is just saying hello."

"And what is Kitty?"

"A cat. When she found me, she was a lot smaller," was Sofia's reply. "A tiny furball I could pick up."

"Her head feels bigger than mine."

"She's a big cat."

He shook his head. "I know cats. And this might be feline, but it's not a regular pussy. More like an ancient Earth big cat. Maybe a lion. No wait, those had big fluffy heads of hair."

"She is sleek furred and lightly marked."

"I wish I could see her." The first real acknowledgement of his injuries. Yet he didn't ask her to tend him. Not yet. "Does the cat obey you?"

She rolled her shoulder then realized he couldn't see it. "Not really. You're a keen example of things she's not supposed to do. Can't exactly stop her though."

"You have a giant cat as a pet." He mused the words aloud. "Kind of jealous.

"Don't be, she can be a pest when she wants."

The cat rubbed her teeth on his hand, demanding a scratch, but the stranger didn't know that.

"Should I be worried Kitty will chew off my hand?"

"Depends on what that hand is doing. Touching my things will get you chomped. Touching me, a double chomp. And if you're eating something she likes...well...that's the risk you take."

"I see. And do you bite too?"

"Actually, if you do something I don't like, I'll gut you."

"Then I shall strive to be on my best behavior. Now, I don't suppose I could trouble you for a glass of something to drink. My mouth is so dry it's a wonder I can talk."

"And it starts," she snapped.

"What starts?"

"The giving of orders. Acting as if I'm your personal servant. I can tell by your clothes you're of no better ranking than me."

"I wasn't giving you an order. Just saying I'm thirsty, and I don't know where to get something to drink."

"And then after I fetch a drink, you'll demand food. It never ends." She wagged a finger at her cat. "This, this is why we don't bring strange men home. They are always difficult."

"I'm not difficult."

She whirled to glare at him, wasting the heat of it since he couldn't see it. "I say you are, and I don't want you anywhere close to me."

"I'm not keen on imposing either, but I'm kind of fucked right now. Would it kill you to show me a bit of compassion?" He'd dropped the flirting and showed signs of anger.

The last time she showed compassion, she was almost raped. "You mean nothing to me."

His lips pressed tight, and his nostrils flared. He said nothing; however, Kitty growled and drew Sofia's attention back to her feline, who seemed adamant they keep him.

"Don't you sass me," she exclaimed. "You remember what happened last time."

"What do you mean last time? Do you make a habit of kidnapping men?"

"No." The word blurted out of her. "But this place is small, so when a stranger arrives, it's inevitable we run into each other."

"And then they try to take advantage of you," he

murmured pensively. "I can assure you, I'm not that kind of man."

"Is of course what you'd say." She rolled her eyes. "I am well aware people lie to get what they want."

"What will it take to convince you I'm sincere?"

She shrugged, having forgotten his eyes again. "There's nothing you can do. I don't trust you."

"Fine, then I don't trust you. Using your giant pet to abduct men and bring them to you for a tongue-lashing, seems you're the villain in this scenario."

"Me?" She ogled him.

He faced serenely ahead, his eyes closed, his face... His poor face needed a good cleaning. She tucked her hands behind her back. Her behavior was out of the norm. She usually wouldn't be so mean, but what Braun did to her... She wouldn't let it happen again.

"Yes, you. I am the one disadvantaged here. You, the one in power. Why, I woke to you groping me, and in some pretty intimate places. I feel violated."

Her lips rounded. "I was not violating you."

"You didn't ask permission."

"I was checking you for injury."

"In my pockets?" he riposted.

"Fine, I was also checking you for weapons. But I won't apologize for making sure I'm safe."

"Then in the spirit of making you feel safe, I should let you know that you missed three throwing knives. One in my boot, and two in my coat.

If he spoke the truth, what should she do? Moving in close to remove them put her at his mercy and yet if she asked him to hand them over, he might try to use them instead.

"You can stop panicking," he said softly. "I'm not going to hurt you. Can you say the same?"

"No." Because she would act to protect herself.

His lips quirked. "Fair enough. I'll have to make sure I don't give you reason to defend yourself."

"That won't be a problem because you're leaving."

"You would toss a man who can't see out into the Wasteland?"

"We're not in the Wasteland."

"Not a dome either, I'd wager."

"How can you tell?" she asked.

"You don't forget the stale scent of a dome. This is much earthier. Cool. The space around me clean, not dusty."

"You cannot tell all that by just sniffing." She blinked at him as she tried to figure out how he'd guessed all that.

Perhaps he lied and could see? His eyes remained closed, though, and not just closed but glued shut. She wondered how he would look with his face healed instead of bruised and swollen.

"Not seeing doesn't mean I can't figure things out using other clues. But I'm having a hard time placing where we could be."

"You can try guessing all you'd like, and you'd still be wrong. This place doesn't exist on any map, I'll wager."

When the big wind had grabbed her after her banishment, she woke here in this place she called Exile. By her count, that was years ago now.

Years and he was only the fifth person she'd ever seen. Two died of their injuries almost upon arriving. The third tried to escape this impossible place. His bones decorated the spot he'd splatted upon when he fell. The last died by her hand and should count himself lucky she didn't carve him to pieces first.

The stranger didn't give up. "I've been around. Maybe I'll recognize our location. Describe it to me."

"I am not doing anything other than showing you the door so you can leave." She leaned down and grabbed a hold of his arm, meaning to heave him to his feet.

She'd forgotten the sheer bulk of him and didn't count on his strength. He didn't budge at all. He had the nerve to smirk.

"Get up," she growled, pulling with all her might.

"I am not getting up. From the feel of the floor, seems like your home is an actual structure. There are grooves indicating tile work. A bit worn, with some denting, but still proof there is something around us. Which means safety compared to outside. Given I need time to recover, I'm gonna have to ignore your wishes and stay."

"I said no."

"Thanks for your gracious hospitality."

She ground her teeth. "You can't ignore me. This is my house."

"And you're going to be an awesome host. Rest assured, I will do my best to help you out."

"You can't refuse to leave."

"I am staying." Said quite firmly.

"I will hurt you if you don't go," she said, hoping he didn't hear the quiver in her voice.

She could act, but it felt wrong to attack someone helpless like him. Although, given his firm statements, she had to wonder if he was really incapacitated.

"Please don't try. I will defend myself, and it won't end well for you," he said.

The cocky assurance had the desired effect. She released his arm and leaned back. Planting her hands back on her hips, an annoyed look crossed her face. Wasted on him since he couldn't open his eyes.

"I knew you couldn't be trusted. First chance you get, you threaten violence."

"I said I would only act if you attacked me first. You're being irrational."

"It's not irrational to not want to share my home with a stranger."

"Why can't we share?" he asked.

"Because there is only one bed. My bed."

"I'll take the floor."

"You'll be extra work. You'll eat my food." She gave the most obvious reasons.

"I'll help as much as I can and repay you once I'm healed."

"Repay me how?" she scoffed. "I don't need money."

"Maybe I can hunt down an animal for you. Get you some fresh meat."

The arrogance stunned her. "I can hunt my own meat." Now at least. In the beginning, Kitty did most of the hunting.

"I didn't mean to imply you couldn't. Just looking to make a deal. I'm sure we can find a way for me to repay you."

There was only one thing she wanted. And even that desire had faded the longer she lived here.

But seeing this man, this reminder of life outside this place...

She had an idea.

"You want to make a trade? Very well. I'll let you stay here, even give you a salve for your injuries."

"And what do you want in return?"

"A baby."

FOUR

GUNNER HAD SURELY MISUNDERSTOOD. "I'M sorry. What did you say?"

"I said, I'll help you until you can take care of yourself. In return, you'll impregnate me."

"And the request is still just as shocking the second time." He focused on her inane demand rather than the pain throbbing all over his body. He'd been fighting it since he woke, doing his best to take stock of the situation, which was admittedly dire. But now also entertaining. "Are we talking artificial insemination or actual intercourse?"

"You provide the ejaculate, and I will handle the rest."

The statement drew a chuckle. "Are you going to use a baster to put it up there?" He couldn't help the mockery. "I'm going to dangle out over a fissure and predict you don't exactly have a lab with the equipment for fertilization and gestation."

"Why would I need a lab? I'm not looking to make a factory or farm worker. I know what's needed. The seed of a man injected into a woman's flower, causing pollination and budding into new life."

The way she utterly ruined anything beautiful about sex floored him for a moment. "It's a little sweatier and more complex than that, sweetheart."

"Sweetheart is not my name."

"And what is it again?" He knew she'd given it to him, but with the pain blurring his mind, he had a hard time remembering.

"You don't need my name."

"Might be kind of nice to know, given you want to be the mother of my child."

"Mother." She mulled the word. "I'd not thought of using that title."

"Are you the type to have your child call you by your first name?" Personally, Gunner preferred the terms mum and dad.

"I hadn't thought of it. The Master allowed me to use sir when we were in private."

"You had a master?" he repeated.

"Didn't you?"

"I'm a free man." Said with pride.

"You're a Wastelander Rat." Her tone rolled with derision.

"And you're a brainwashed dome citizen. Guess which I'd rather be?" He tossed back the insult.

"I've changed my mind. I don't wish to negotiate with you after all."

Oops. He'd let pride and pain lead him to insult the one person he needed at the moment. "Now, sweetheart, don't be so hasty. I promise, any baby we make will be better than anything created in a test tube."

"You've had your genetics tested? You're not sterilized?"

He paused. "Um, no and no." He'd heard of the first being a big thing in the domes, but as to the latter...

"You are physically fit and attractive," she mulled aloud.

"I'll be even prettier once you get me cleaned up," he hinted.

"I doubt the word pretty applies to you."

"You're right. The terms rugged and handsome come to mind."

The soft snort she emitted brought a tug to the corner of his mouth. He couldn't see, not one bit, and he hurt, all fucking over, but there was something about this woman that intrigued.

"You should add conceited to that list," she said.

"It's not conceit if it's true. You'll see once my face heals up. So, do we have a deal?"

"You'll give me your seed to fertilize my flower?"

"Sweetheart, you help me out, and I will volunteer to give you my swimmers the old-fashioned way. Without the baster."

Her breath sucked in. "I am not a whore."

"Never said you were. Keep in mind, the easiest way for you to get pregnant is to do it the way we're supposed to. Naked, with my seed shooter slotted into your flower." He couldn't have said why he kept poking at her. Maybe because he wanted to see if he could get her to exclaim in embarrassment again. Maybe because all this fucking arguing wasn't making his face feel any better. He kept hoping the burning in his eyes would settle down. It didn't.

"Sex is not be indulged in."

"According to who?"

"It's what the Enclave teaches. And yet, most people don't listen. Why would they when the Enclave and their families break their own law?" She said it most indignantly.

"That's the Enclave for you. Is this why you want a baby? To snub those bastards?"

"My desire for a child has nothing to do with them."

"Then why do you want one?" When she didn't reply, he prodded. "To use as bait for your traps?"

"No."

"To eat? A nice plump baby roast."

"That's revolting."

"Then what do you need a child for?"

"Companionship." Said softly.

It made him wonder how long she'd been alone. "Wouldn't it be easier to move into a settlement or find a dome that will take you?"

"I would if I could, but there is nowhere to go."

"Maybe you just don't know how to get there. I'm pretty savvy when it comes to moving around the Wastelands. What are we close to? The Chasm Fields? The Ajatarai forest? The Ruins?"

"I don't know what places you're talking about. This forest is not anywhere near a dome is all I know."

Which was more than he knew a moment ago. He also now knew that she was more than passing familiar with the Enclave. Her beliefs gave her away, meaning she was probably a dome resident runaway.

"You said forest, as in trees?"

"It's not a forest without them," she retorted hotly.

He wondered just what she looked like. Was she young or old? "Are you here alone?"

"Kitty will be offended you forgot about her."

The giant cat rolled in his lap, and he absently stroked through her fur. She didn't purr, not like the smaller version of a feline. "Kitty and I are fine," he muttered. "And you didn't answer the question."

"No, I didn't." He heard the cool amusement in the words. "But then again, neither did you. Do we have an agreement?"

"Recovering in your company in exchange for a baby. That's a rather large demand." He'd thought about becoming a parent. One day. In the very distant future.

"So is having you stay here."

"Who will help you with the child after it comes?" Because he had no plans to remain longer than he had to. Axel and the others would be worried when he didn't meet up with them.

"I don't need help."

He heard the defiance in her words. He wished he could see. See if that husky honeyed voice had a face to match. What of her shape?

"Everyone needs a hand once in a while. What if you get sick? Or have an accident and die? Then who will care for the baby?"

"I am not alone."

"Kitty doesn't count. The cat can't help you birth and care for a human child."

"We'll have to agree to disagree then. And why do you care? You won't even be around."

"What if I wanted to visit the child? Maybe take some time off from my regular duties in Haven and visit."

"What's haven?" she asked.

He realized he'd slipped. Rather than lie, he explained. "Haven is my community. My family." None of them by blood, unless that spilled fighting for their lives counted.

"You think you're going to return."

"I have to. But I want to make visitation part of the deal." Because it occurred to him that a child of his deserved to at least know his or her father.

"If you insist, then yes, you may visit the child if you manage to leave and return," she begrudgingly agreed.

"I'm hard to kill, sweetheart. Now since we've got a deal, didn't you say something about a cream to fix me?" Because he was done talking.

"I do. First, we must rinse your face and other injuries. The dirt needs to come out of the wounds. Follow me."

He sat there in the dark and listened as she moved away.

Waited and waited before she said, "Are you coming or not?"

"You know I can't see you. You'll have to guide me."

"Stupid, useless man," she huffed before stomping close enough to snare his hand.

He rose and realized that long strides weren't the way to travel when he stubbed his toe. "Ow. Fuck. Shit. Damn."

The words spilled out of him, and she uttered a... giggle. A sound both startled and sweet.

"This isn't funny," he said through gritted teeth, his toe throbbing.

"I haven't heard anyone swear like that, well, ever." She chuckled.

"Let me hit my toe again and I'll expand your knowledge of bad words. I didn't realize the deal didn't include keeping me safe from further injury."

"You are being difficult. When I landed here, I didn't have anyone taking care of me."

"Are you implying you're tougher?" he asked incredulously.

"I thought I was stating."

"And were your eyes sealed shut?"

"No. Because I remembered to cover them in the storm."

"Are you going to be long at this whole berating thing? Going blind here."

"Such drama. I'll guide you. Stay close to me and I'll keep you safe from the furniture."

She placed his hand on her waist, a solid waist, not skinny or fat, but pleasantly indented, indicating flaring hips. Out of curiosity, he placed his other hand on the other side. He couldn't quite span it but came close.

She tensed. "If you try anything, I will hurt you."

It shouldn't have surprised him she thought he might. Just like some men were all about honor, others weren't. "I don't force women."

"Good. Because it would be a shame if you accidentally fell off a ledge."

"Would you really push me?"

"Yes."

He liked how she said it firmly and unapologetically. Behind her back, where she couldn't see, he smiled.

She led him outside. The sudden contrast in the air stopped him short. He inhaled, trying to make sense of all the scents. He wasn't like Axel, who had an affinity with the wolgar and some of their heightened ability to smell.

Gunner mused aloud, "The smell, the air, it reminds me of the Ajatarai Forest. And doesn't at the same time." Most forests were musty and dry places. Yet here, the moisture hung thickly in the air, mugging the skin, dampening the clothes. It made him wonder how she kept the inside of the house cool. "Do the trees move around at night?" The Seimor Woods had that particular characteristic.

"The trees change locations?" she scoffed. "Of course not. They are planted in the ground, but still pose dangers. There are some you cannot touch, or you'll burn your skin. And never trust a vine."

He chuckled. "That's right up there with don't smell the flowers."

"Or eat the yellow ones. They make you quite sick."

"Sounds like you've had to learn a lot," he said. A subtle dig for info.

As she led him, her steps slow enough to keep him from stumbling, she replied, "I went from a dome with meals, a roof over my head, and safety to a place out of an ancient story."

"Good place or bad?" he asked, not exactly liking being in the open unable to see and lacking his gun. He still had a few of his smaller knives in their sheaths, though.

"A bit of both."

"You going to expand on that?" he prodded.

"You're being demanding again," she grumbled.

"Just trying to get a sense of where we are."

"Lost," she muttered. Then louder, "Watch your step."

The terrain sloped downward, and he heard the rush of water.

"Have you lived in this area long?" he asked.

"Ever since my own storm dumped me here."

Those words caused him to stumble. "Hold on. You mean a giant wind brought you, too?"

"I told you I handled it better than you. Happens a few times a year. It doesn't always bring back presents, though."

"So you were dumped here and liked the place so much you decided to stay?"

She dashed his hope. "There's no way out that I know of. I'm sure once you're healed, you'll find a way even if no one else ever did." She patted his hand.

"Meaning?"

"Others have tried. You can see the skeletons lying where they failed."

He tried to not let the news panic him. Just because this woman didn't know a way out didn't mean one didn't exist. His luck would guide him. Hopefully better than it had when he got swept into the storm.

"We're at the stream. Kneel."

He heard the murmur of water over rock. "Is it safe?"

"One would assume since I'm still alive."

Good enough for him. He hit the ground on his knees a bit harder than he meant to, but the spongy nature of it softened the blow even as it also soaked his pants. He leaned forward until he felt water, cupped some, and brought it to his mouth.

The cold, crisp taste did a lot to revive him. He gulped a few more mouthfuls then began splashing his face, feeling the stickiness of blood and dust sluicing away. It ignited all the little scratches, making them scream in irritation. It was probably vain to be worried that they might not all heal properly.

"That is some good fucking water," he exclaimed, leaning back on his haunches.

"It is."

"How far does the river go?" he asked.

"I don't know."

"Have you followed it to the end?"

"Only to the hole in the mountain where it drains."

A hole meant a way out.

As if reading his mind, she said, "There are many jagged rocks in that area, and it flows quickly."

"Is it deep?"

"In some areas."

Getting her to give him full answers was proving a challenge. He kept questioning. "What about right here?" He flicked the water. "How deep?"

"Not very," she replied. "About thigh high on me, but—"

Rather than keep listening, he splashed forward, stumbling and falling face-first in the water. His feet touched bottom easily, as did his knees. Thigh high for her wasn't as deep for him.

She squeaked at him, pulling at his arm. "You idiot. Are you trying to drown?"

He knelt, flung his head back, and chuckled. "It's not deep enough to drown. It feels damned good, though." Amazing how a brisk bath could revive. "Anything alive in the river? Anything that bites?"

"Not currently. We had a problem a while back with some kind of scaly creature. Nasty bite on it. But Kitty and I handled it."

Meaning she wasn't aware of anything, but it could be in there. Keeping that in mind, he moved cautiously. Shuffling on his knees, he noticed the incline as the shore sloped into the river channel. He had to stand to keep his face and upper body above water.

Away from the shore, the current tugged at him. It moved to his left. Bending only his upper body, he placed his face in the current, letting it stream past his face, cooling and cleaning the now looser debris in his cuts. When he finally flicked back his head, his face felt refreshed, which only made the throbbing of his orbs more pronounced.

He still couldn't open them. Which caused a mild panic. But he couldn't allow that emotion to control him. First rule of living in the Wasteland, don't freak out. His mother used to chant that at him every time his fear rose.

Giant ten-legged arachnid with pincers as long as his hand? Don't panic. Spear it and bring it to mum for dinner.

Lightning all around and the choice was a single tree or a pitted landscape of past strikes? Play a game of pit hop, because they said lightning never hit the same spot twice.

Possible blindness...sucked, but if it happened, not the end of the world. He could get some freaky-ass stone orbs like that seer out by the Chasm. Learn to use his mind to see and kick ass like that fellow who'd spent the night in the camp with him and his parents when he was a kid. A blind man with a cool etched staff. A man who royally trounced Father when he tried to steal the staff. And less than a year later, he had a sister who looked nothing like his father.

At times he wondered what had happened to his sister. When his parents died, she was already off living with those travelling women. The Nuns Templar.

"You going to stand there all day?" she grumbled, the water sloshing as she returned to shore.

"Maybe. The water is nice."

"Then maybe you should stay here then," she said dryly.

"And miss the pleasure of your company? Never, future carrier womb of my child," he teased as he turned and slowly made his way to shore.

"You're mocking me."

"It's called flirtatious conversation. The concept will come back to you, I'm sure."

"I don't flirt."

The sad part was he rather believed her. "But you obviously love, or you wouldn't have that giant furball as a pet. Speaking of, where is Kitty?"

"She's not crazy about water."

"Water is life." Another Wasteland mantra.

"You have water where you come from?"

"Depends on where Haven is. When we were living inside a hill, we worked our asses off getting a pipe to the shelter and, at the same time, keeping it hidden from Enclave patrols. But we lost the Hill, and as far as I know, the Enclave took back the dome."

"You stole a dome?"

His lips curved. "Fuck yeah, we did. An Incubaii one with a right prick running it. He kidnapped the boss's promised and beat the hell out of her. But in the end, we fucked him up good and took over the dome."

"Since when do the Wasteland Rats want to live in a dome?"

"Since we've always wanted a home." It was the one thing they all craved. Freedom was all well and good, but no one wanted to constantly have to fight to stay alive. Some days, it would be nice to lie in bed and not worry everything would go to shit.

He stood, dripping. "I need a place to hang this to dry." He stripped off his coat.

"I can hang it, but I don't have dry clothes for you." She tugged the coat from his hands.

"What about a towel?"

"Not down here."

"Be forewarned, I am not walking back in cold, wet garments. If you're shy, don't look." Because he had no shame, he removed his shirt and wrung it out, wondering if she liked what she saw.

It wasn't conceit that told him he had a good body. It was the number of people, men and woman, who watched him when he trained. Gunner never lacked for offers. But like Axel used to do, he was smart and kept his encounters to strangers and not those living in Haven where if things went wrong, he'd have to see them every day.

"Hand me your shirt. I have a place to dry them."

"Is there room for my pants?" His hands went to the buckle.

"There's room to hang you and your enormous ego. So go ahead and remove whatever you like, although you might want to keep your boots on for the walk back. There's bugs that like to burrow if you're not paying attention."

"Maybe I'll keep the rest of my stuff on." Boot and pants given he wasn't convinced she wouldn't shrivel him with the right word.

"Good idea." Her words hinted of mockery. "Your upper body appears mostly undamaged with the exception of your hands."

He held them out. "Fingerless gloves." They fit like skin and didn't retain any moisture from the river.

"Why no fingers? What's the point? I thought gloves kept hands warm."

"These are for gripping." He made a fist. "Good when I'm riding a bike or need to use a weapon."

"You fight a lot?"

"I'm fond of surviving, so yes."

The tips of her fingers danced over his knuckles, and he froze, even as his skin heated. "These should heal easily. The wounds are superficial. A bit of lotion to soothe and in a day or so you'll be fine."

"What about my face?" He didn't mention his eyes.

"Well…" she said slowly. "The good news is you still have a face."

"What's the bad?"

"There's still some grit in some of your wounds. If you want to heal properly, I'll need to clean it out."

"Do it." He braced himself.

"You're too tall. I need you to sit. There's a rock behind you, about two paces," she offered.

Gunner shuffled his hands out and hit the stone easily enough. He planted his ass on it, hands on his knees, able to move quickly if needed.

"This will probably hurt," she warned.

"Always does," he grumbled. "At least you have a nicer voice than Oliander."

"Who is Oliander?"

"The guy who usually patches me up."

"Do you require patching often?"

"Have you already forgotten the part where I said I had to fight to survive?"

"Doesn't sound like this Haven is a great place," she remarked.

He fought not to not flinch when a wet cloth stroked over his raw skin. "Haven is the best thing to ever happen to me." Once his parents died. "The only thing that would make it better would be to find a place we could call our own that the Enclave isn't trying to destroy."

"I never understood why they cared."

"Because the freedom we represent is a danger to their tight-fisted rule."

"I never thought of it that way." The cloth lightly brushed his eyes. "We are taught that you are dangerous, carriers of horrid disease, and always sowing violence."

"And yet the truth is nothing close."

"So you claim."

She scrubbed harder in some spots, but he bore it. In the Wasteland you learned to never neglect any open wound. Infections could be deadly.

"I am curious as to how a citizen got caught in a wind storm. I didn't think you ever went outside the dome." The Enclave population was taught from birth that the very air outside the dome was toxic because of the dust particles in it.

"It was my first time. Give me your hands," she snapped.

He held them out, and she scrubbed in between the fingers and along the nails.

"I'm impressed by your attention to detail."

"I've had grit heal under the skin. Removing it isn't pleasant."

"Thank you." He said it softly and could have sworn the fingers touching his hand warmed. Did she blush to the tips of her extremities?

"Just keeping up my end of the bargain." She released him abruptly, and he heard the rustle as she stepped back. "I think we're done here. I'll grab a bucket of water, just in case, and then we'll head back to the house."

Without being bidden, he stood. He already knew he'd top her by at least a hand, maybe more. He couldn't have said her age though. Her voice sounded young, but her words were that of someone mature.

"Would you like me to carry it?"

"If you insist."

It took only a moment before she nudged his hand, passing over her burden. The bucket handle was made of a strange braided material, the weight more than he would have expected.

His free hand went to her waist, and this time she didn't tense as badly. He felt much more alert now. The throbbing in his eyes was uncomfortable, but the water had some restorative properties, because he felt ten times better already.

"You don't have running water to the house?" he remarked.

"No. But it's not far from my home, and before you ask, I didn't build it. I found it abandoned, most of the rooms caved in. What remains makes a great shelter."

"Someone used to live here." He hummed aloud. "That's promising."

"I feel like I should mention I did find skeletons in one of the rooms."

"Could be they died of old age."

"Your optimism is astonishing."

He grinned at her sarcasm. "You appear to have a doom-and-gloom view of life. I think it's too short, so I prefer to think happy thoughts."

"And how is that working for you?"

"Pretty well if you ask me. After all, I was rescued and am now being ministered to by a beautiful woman."

She snorted. "Far from beautiful, I assure you."

Did she think herself unattractive? He found that hard to believe. She had such a honeyed voice. A firm manner that bespoke confidence.

"Everyone is beautiful in their own way, sweetheart."

"My name is Sofia."

He wouldn't forget it this time. "And I'm—"

"Gunner. You already said. Such a violent name," she remarked. "Step up, we're almost there."

"My parents named me. Said it would make me tough."

"They might have overdone it. You're rather large."

His lips quirked. "My mum liked to make sure I was well fed. Then there's the fact I was raised in the Wastelands. When I was born, my first breath was toxic air. It changes a man." To survive required strength.

"There isn't any dust here, and yet, I am stronger than before," she admitted. "Which means you'd better not stick around too long, or you might become a giant."

"Think that's what happened to Kitty?" Speaking of which, he'd not felt or heard the giant feline since their visit to the river.

"I think," she said, pulling him past a threshold onto a solid flat floor, "that is very possible given her size when I found her. Hard to believe she used to fit on my lap."

"And she carried me to your house?" Surely, he'd misunderstood that part, waking as he had with his mind jumbled.

"Kitty likes to collect treasures."

"I'm a man."

"And your point is? Sit down." She pushed him onto something hard.

Feeling with his fingers, there was a flat, smooth rock under his ass and, beneath it, a chunk of wood forming a makeshift stool. Simple furniture, but at least it showed her innovative nature. She might have begun life in a dome, but she'd adapted.

"Is there anything else out here that is larger than normal?"

"What's normal?" she asked.

"I guess that is subjective." He heard the crinkle as of dried foliage being crushed. "What are you doing?"

"Mixing up a paste to ease your injuries."

"You know how?" he asked.

Oliander was always complaining they needed to find themselves an alchemist. He claimed it would make his healing treatments more effective. The only one they knew lived in Emerald City and sold illegally—and very carefully—via a roving vendor who moved between the Wasteland camps. Meaning they paid a pretty penny for some of his wares.

"I was trained to make all kinds of remedies. Although the ingredients here are different. I had to devise new mixtures."

"Smart."

"Necessary," was her brisk retort. "I'm going to put the paste on now."

"And how do I know it's not some poison or acid meant to kill me?"

"Can't give me a baby if you're dead," she declared.

"You could be a little more reassuring."

"I wouldn't have thought a big tough Wastelander like yourself would need to be coddled."

His lips twitched. "If I do die, can you at least promise to not eat me? I really don't want to end up digested by somebody. Or something."

She chuckled. "You don't have enough fat to tempt me."

He might have retorted but instead gasped as the cream went onto his skin. It felt cold and wet when she smeared it on his face. Smelled kind of earthy, too. It didn't hurt. Didn't burn.

"Don't move. I'm going to put some over your eyes." She covered his entire face before declaring, "Done. How do you feel?"

He shrugged. "Gooey."

"Is it hot or cold?"

"Warming up a little now."

"Don't move." The heels of her hands suddenly dug against his sockets and she whispered,

"Soothe." The cream heated, hot enough he almost yelped.

The discomfort began to ease, and he sighed instead. "That feels better. I didn't know you were a healer."

"All apothecaries can ease symptoms. It's in the combination of the ingredients."

He frowned. "That's not what happened. You used magic."

She snorted. "Magic isn't real."

It was, but he let it go for now. "Thank you. I am feeling a hundred times better than when I first woke."

"Hmmph." She made a noise. "We should bind your eyes so you don't accidentally open them and do more damage. Let me see if I can find a cloth to spare."

He heard ripping, and then some fabric wrapped around his head, bringing her close to him. Her scent was floral and fresh.

It seemed normal to put his hands on her waist. She stepped out of reach and moved behind him, holding the bandeau over his eyes taut.

"You speak a lot about fighting. Are you a soldier for this Haven?"

"Yes and no."

"Meaning?"

"I fight for what's right. To help my friends. Resisting whenever I can."

She finished his bandage before saying. "Resisting what?"

"The Enclave of course. I am against their tyrannical ruling of the people in the domes."

"Why? You're not a citizen."

"And I thank the Wasteland every day that I was born and bred outside a dome. No offense."

"You really prefer living outside, don't you?" she said musingly.

"Me and everyone I know like our freedom."

"There are many Rats?" she asked, pulling the knot tight.

"Rats." His lips twisted. "That's the name the Enclave gives us, trying to make us into bad guys. In reality we're no different than any other citizen of the domes."

"Aren't you, though? You said it yourself that living outside has exposed you to the perils of the Wastelands."

"What doesn't kill me makes me stronger."

"Or it festers within until it explodes out of you and takes a few lives before it can be torched into ash."

"That was a little too specific. Care to explain?"

"No." She moved away from him.

"How is it that you ended up living here?"

"I told you, a wind stole me."

"But how? The domes protect, which means you went outside. Are you a soldier?"

"No," she scoffed. "I am an assistant apothecary."

Which he'd expected from what she said before. "Were you outside collecting ingredients when the storm hit? Or did you just decide to run away?" A few of the people who ended up in Haven had chosen to leave. Freedom had a way of luring folks.

"I was banished actually," she said tersely.

"For what?"

"According to the Court, attacking a citizen." Her words emerged clipped and tight.

So he asked the most obvious thing. "Did she deserve it?"

A pause. Then, "Yes. And more. But I never even landed a single blow, not that it mattered at my trial. Because she was related to someone serving the Enclave, they declared her innocent and condemned me to exile."

"Then you got off lucky." His words were grim because he knew all too well what sometimes happened to those who'd earned punishment. More than a few people he knew had scars on their bodies to show how they'd been taught a lesson.

"Lucky?" She uttered a soft snort as she helped

him to his feet. "They sent me out into the Wasteland unarmed, with no food or water. I should have died a hundred times over."

"But you didn't. Because you're smart." The compliment emerged with ease and no guile, yet she growled as if he'd called her something rude.

"Smart. Ha."

"You had to be," he insisted. "You say you were banished and then got kidnapped by some wind and dropped in a strange place. A dangerous place."

"Who said it was dangerous?"

"New Earth isn't gentle." The closest they got was less dangerous. "You never did say how long you've been here."

"What year is it for you?

"Three hundred and seventy-two since the Fall." The fall being the meteor shower that helped reshape old Earth into new.

"That long?" She sighed. "It will be almost five years then."

He whistled without meaning to. "Shit, that's gotta be lonely."

The pity wasn't welcome given she barked, "You mean peaceful. No one to order me around. No lashings for being slow or impertinent."

"I'm sorry." He apologized even as he understood her request now for his seed. She wanted a child to keep her company. But what if he could offer her something better?

"You know, there are places, not the domes," he hastened to add, "that would welcome someone with your skills. You don't have to live here by yourself."

"I'm not by myself. I have—"

"Kitty," he sighed. "Yes, so you keep telling me. But what about someone to talk to?"

"I'm talking to you, and I have to say, it's not the most pleasant thing I've done today."

The insult made him bark with laughter. "You know how to put a guy in his place."

"And you don't take offense at anything," she murmured.

"Thick skin, sweetheart."

"Sofia."

"A sweet name, for a lovely woman."

"And you're back to the flirting." She sounded amused. "Since I'm done with you, I have work to do."

"Work? What kind?"

"The kind that will feed us later. You should rest. You're probably tired."

"Just point me to a spot on the floor."

For some reason that made her sigh. "Come with me." She tugged him by the hand.

He followed, using his other senses to avoid

disorientation. After a short distance, the smell changed, from the wildness of growing things to that of something dusty and dry, yet hinting of her floral fragrance. They'd entered a different space.

She placed his hand on a spongy surface. "You can sleep here."

"I thought you only had one bed."

"I do. But since I won't need it until later, you can borrow it."

With those words, she left, a door closing behind her, which surprised him. He'd expected her to possess a simple shelter. Something that resembled a lean-to. Or a cave. After all, she claimed a wind had brought her to some kind of valley and trapped her. That would mean no tools, no ability to purchase goods.

Yet, she had a bed. How curious. He ran his hand over the mattress, noting the fabric that slid when tugged. A blanket with many seams, as if many pieces of cloth had been stitched together. A firm press of the mattress made a crinkling sound, and running his fingers over top of it, he recognized leather and more stitching. She'd made her own mattress.

Not bad for a dome citizen. But while she'd created the bedding, she didn't build the house, he'd wager. This wasn't some small shelter of hacked together branches and vine. It had presence, shape. It had been built.

He dropped to his haunches and ran his fingers over the strange bed frame, which emerged from the floor as if carved from it. The floor was tile, the ridges even, the surface pitted less severely than the flooring in the other room.

"What are you doing?" Her sudden arrival sent him off balance, and he landed hard on his ass.

"You should knock. What if I was busy getting you that seed you demanded?"

"Were you?"

"No. But now that you're here, would you like to milk me yourself?"

"Absolutely not!" He heard the hot embarrassment. "I came back to ask for your pants."

"I will gladly remove them. I take it this means you changed your mind about how we'll make the baby?" He intentionally goaded her because it amused him and annoyed her.

"No!" she huffed. "I was going to hang them with your shirt to dry."

Feeling for the bed, he rose and sat on the edge. The mattress sank, and the stuff inside crunched. He nudged off his boots before putting his hands on the waistband of his pants. "What is this place?"

"Shelter."

"Obviously. I know you told me you found it. Long abandoned. The fact there's anything here is—"

"Astonishing, I know. It has been here a while, judging by the decay. Partially made of rock and partially of cement with metal bars inside it. It must have been grand once, with many rooms. Now there's only a few that are safe."

"So it's some kind of ancient ruin." The very idea piqued his interest. "Is it the only one? What can you tell me about it? How big is the structure? Do—"

"You talk too much, and I don't have time for it. Sleep." A powder entered his mouth.

The next time he woke was because something was licking his face. Probably readying him for dinner.

FIVE

Sofia managed to shove Gunner the right way when the sleeping powder took effect. He fell over onto the bed, his face slack, his eyes wrapped with a strip from her skirt, his jaw showing stubble.

Even in repose he appeared wide and intimidating. His body was firm with muscle. His jaw square and strong like him. He'd make her a pretty baby.

Her gaze strayed lower. He'd kept on his undergarment, form-fitting shorts with a prominent bulge in the front. The rod that would spew the seed she needed. He'd even offered to give it to her from the source.

Perhaps she should accept his offer. She ran a finger down his fine torso. His skin shivering at her touch.

Shocked at her actions, she looked away. It

wasn't proper. While technically forbidden by law, sex happened in the city. Not with her. She'd never been with a man, although she'd dabbled with a woman a few times. Someone who stayed at the shop with her when the Master had to leave for a period of time.

She'd found it pleasant but not worth losing her life over. Yet she knew others went to dangerous lengths to indulge. Babies had been created by accident during trysts. Lives lost over sex with the wrong person.

Surely that indicated there was something about it she'd yet to grasp that made it desirable. Perhaps it required the right man. She wondered if it was her extreme isolation that saw him as different because being near him did bring a flutter.

Her cat, finally making a reappearance, nosed into the room and prowled close to the bed. The frame—made of an unfamiliar-shaped material that was smoother than concrete—didn't move. A good thing, as Kitty jumped up and flopped beside the man, almost crushing him.

"And where did you go?" she asked, shaking her finger at her cat. "What if he'd tried to murder me at the river?"

The feline's nose twitched.

"Fine. He didn't. But he could have. I hope you

were doing something constructive. Like fetching us some dinner."

"Meowr."

"No, I did not catch a fish while I was at the river." She was too busy handling their guest. "Guess I'll check the traps when I go out. You need to watch him. Don't let him touch my stuff."

Kitty yawned and lay her head on her paws, closing her eyes, feigning sleep.

While her lazy cat sleep-guarded, she was going to see if the storm had brought anything other than a talkative man. The odd and ends she'd scavenged during her time here had arrived via wind, the dark cloud rising over the mountains, dropping some of its stolen treasure into the bowl formed by the peaks.

A goodly amount of it proved useless. The sand and dust it carried absorbed by the loamy ground. The furniture it sometimes managed to steal smashing to bits. A shame because she would have dearly enjoyed a real chair. At least she had a few books. A city perk that she'd missed until the first soggy one she found. It eventually dried out, and most of it remained readable. The bucket was scavenged at the same time she found the single fork.

She had clothing, an eclectic mishmash, mostly made from found scraps and animal skin. Not that her appearance mattered out here. Kitty didn't care how she looked.

And neither would Gunner. He couldn't see, and she actually didn't hold out much hope he would. Perhaps had she been in the shop with the highly skilled Master aiding her, they might have managed a concoction strong enough, but it was just her along with whatever herbs and other ingredients she scavenged. But she would do her best, and he would keep his end of the bargain and give her a baby.

Someone for her to care for like she'd done with Kitty. A reason to live rather than give up.

She owed Kitty her life. Sofia well remembered finding the small cat, and not that long after she'd arrived, too.

After the wind grabbed her in the Wasteland, she'd woken to find something nudging her. Opening her eyes, she saw a creature looking back at her and shrieked, sending it scampering.

It took a moment to take in the fact she lay face-down on something fragrant and moist. She'd lain still for a moment, taking stock of her body, noticing all the aches but no stabbing pains of broken bones. The skin on her face and hands, even her legs, burned, rousing a memory of those flaying winds as they tossed her around and around while all she could do was clench her fists and wish with all her might she didn't die.

Someone listened. She lived and quickly realized she wasn't in the Wasteland anymore. The moistness against her face and the texture, so strange. She turned her head to the side and opened her eyes to see a wall of grass. Long grass, never trimmed, with stalks bending in the light breeze, the flowered heads swaying hypnotically.

Flowers? Outside the palace gardens? She'd only ever seen them in pictures or the videos they showed the populace. Flowers were for the wealthy. The closest she got was the crushed petals of a few types useful for healing.

Had the wind dropped her in the palace garden? Impossible. The dome would have prevented it. Its entire purpose was to keep the city safe from peril.

So where was she then? Sitting up, she took a long look at where she found herself. Then glanced again because it made no sense. The grass extended into a field—a knoll really—dusted with sand. No sign of the creature that nudged her, just one confused Sofia.

She stood, and more of the grit shook free, sprinkling the grass she'd crushed when she landed. As expected, the sight of her legs showed them scraped and bleeding in spots, but not as bad as feared.

Hugging herself, she turned around in a full circle. It only served to perplex her further. Nothing she perceived made sense.

She stood on a hill. The top was flat and several paces across before rolling away. On one side it dropped sharply into a river. An actual river with flowing water.

Directly on the other side of the river a sheared chunk of rock rose high enough she had to crane her neck and then wondered how high it reached given the crown was covered by clouds.

The wall extended left and right as far as she could see. Whereas behind her, down the gentlest part of the hill's slope, a dense line of trees moved upward.

"Where am I?" She'd asked the question then, and years later, still had no answer. It wasn't a dome. Or the Wasteland she knew about. It was a lush example of what she imagined old Earth used to be.

She wouldn't call it paradise, not at first. It was much too frightening for one thing.

All around her, things grew. Thick trunked trees that towered high above her, the leaves fatter than she was, the boles too wide to hug. The blades of grass were wider than her fingers, the flowers, the size of a fist.

Everything in this place felt larger than normal,

and things that were different could be frightening at first. Especially when some of it proved dangerous.

She remembered the first time she felt a slithery tickle and turned to notice a vine trying to twine itself around her. Since she couldn't tear it in half, she'd panicked, wound the vine around her fist, and then yanked, pulling it loose. In severing it, she saved her own life.

She fought off fat bugs that enjoyed feeding on flesh. Almost drowned in the river because of the fat fish that teased her. As if to taunt, they would flip out of the water, showing off their meaty bellies before flopping with a splash. Tastier than anything she'd ever eaten in the dome, especially once she discovered how to cook them. But she didn't catch her first fish. Kitty was the one who gave it to her.

The night they met started with a plaintive meow that woke her. She slept sitting on a branch, leaning against the trunk of the tree, the vine she'd killed wrapped around her to keep her from falling. She learned her lesson the first time she nodded off and pitched to the ground. Right after the lesson on not sleeping on the grass. Like the vines, it tried to grab hold of her. Only at night, though. The daytime sun made the grass lethargic and safe for her.

She untied the knot and crouched, listening.

"Mee-uuu." A sharp, sad sound, the first since

her arrival that wasn't a buzz. She knew there was life out there. She remembered those eyes when she first woke. Could hear it rustling in the underbrush. She kept a stick with her just in case. A whacking stick. She only hoped she could whack when her life depended on it.

The sound was familiar. A cat. Maybe the same one she'd seen before but had been too frightened at the time to comprehend.

Cats were considered nuisance animals in the dome. Yet, for all the attempts to rid themselves of the felines, the city always failed. Their ability to disappear into the sewers kept them from complete extinction.

If a feline found itself here in this place, it must be scared. She understood the feeling.

"Hold on, kitty. I'm coming," she muttered as she climbed down the tree in the dark, trying not to miss a foot- or handhold.

She made it to the ground and held her huffing breath to listen. *Buzz. Rustle.* The regular noises then a snuffling meow.

She moved toward it, the stick waving out in front. Not the most elegant method, probably why her foot caught on a root and she tripped. Fell flat on her face, bouncing off her healing cheek, scraping it anew.

She yelled, “Seriously!” Was she fated to have ill luck forever? She’d sighed into the loamy ground and the grit of the protruding root.

Realized the meowing had stopped, but she knew what it meant. She wasn’t alone. She’d not realize until that moment how terrified she’d been of being the only living thing around.

The next day, when she went to splash herself with river water, she found a fish lying on shore. She eyed it. Was it edible? She poked it with a finger and found it still damp and cold. Fresh.

Belly rumbling, she couldn’t wait to eat. Having no knife, she used her teeth, biting through the scaly skin, tearing its flesh into chunks she could chew. And chew.

And gag.

Good thing she had little to bring up. The first raw piece emerged, as did the second, but the third stayed down, and her belly stopped protesting. She found herself unwilling to eat more than a few mouthfuls.

The sun beat on her, hot enough to bake. Her eyes popped open as she wondered...*Can I cook it?*

She dug her fingers into the flesh and laid some thin strips on a flat rock by the river, using the heating rocks to cook the fish.

As it went from raw to possibly edible, the

meowing started again. This time, more surefooted in the daylight, she followed the sound. It appeared to come from close to the edge of the woods.

"Where are you, kitty?"

"Meow." The sound came from overhead.

Sofia tilted her head to look. The scraggly little feline sat on a branch, its green eyes huge, whiskers trembling. Its fur was a tawny brown and spotted.

Since it looked so cute and small, she stupidly reached for it. The bloody scratches across the back of her hand were the proof it wasn't defenseless.

She sucked the torn skin and glared at the cat as it climbed higher. "Idiot. I was trying to help."

"Meow."

"Whatever. Save yourself," she grumbled.

Returning to her camp, she was pleased to see her fish had changed color. Tearing at a piece, it flaked. Tasted better, too, if a bit dry. She let it cook a bit and went back to the woods, for the first time truly paying attention to the foliage. Just because she didn't recognize any of the plants didn't mean they weren't useful.

She collected them, being careful to not grab the strange plants with her bare skin, not until she'd observed them more. Something grown in the wild could have toxins she wouldn't expect. Seeing a bird plucking at berries was the only reason she dared try any.

The tartness shocked. Made her eyes water and her mouth gasp. But the flavor... In a flat rock with a hint of a depression for a bowl, she crushed them into a paste, added some water then an herb she actually recognized, a kind of mint.

She let it cook too, hiding in the vee of the trees and watching over it during the hottest part of the day. The humidity made her filthy gown cling to her.

When the sun finally dipped past the edge of the mountains and the heat died, she returned to the river and her evening meal. Her mouth actually watered but, first, a bath.

She found the shallowest part of the shore, only knee high. She'd seen too many things floating in the deep parts to trust going any farther.

Kneeling, she bathed herself as best she could, even her gown. She emerged, shivering, and walked quickly to the warm rocks and her dinner. A dinner being stolen by a cat!

"Drop that!" she yelled, running across the pebbles, feeling the sharp sting as they cut her feet.

The cat bolted for the trees, and she grumbled, but not for long, seeing it had taken only one strip. The rest of the fish and the berry mush she'd made more than filled her belly. She slept deeply that night, tied in her tree, knees tucked to her chest, and only woke when something with a bit of weight was dropped on them, meaning fur tickled her nose.

She opened her eyes to see a carcass.

With a scream, she shoved it from her and scrambled to untie herself. She almost fell out of the tree but finally managed to make it to the ground where the dead thing had fallen.

There was a mocking," Meowr?" to her left.

Sofia saw the kitten sitting nice as you please, head cocked. It eyed the dead creature then her.

"Did you bring that for me, kitty?"

To this day she would have sworn the cat nodded.

"Would you like some?"

Apparently, that was a yes. She tore at the creature and discovered it wasn't like a fish. It was messy and hairy. The cat liked a few of the organs, hissed at others. Those she tossed away. Rinsing her rock first, she then lined it with some fragrant moss she'd found, and placed the raw meat on it. It cooked all that day, along with the new batch of berries she harvested.

She and Kitty dined like rich Enclave citizens that night.

When night fell, the cat left, and she tied herself to her tree branch and wondered if the cat would return in the morning. She hoped it did. It was nice to not be alone.

She awoke that night to hear hissing. Startled, she opened her eyes and, through the scant starlight filtering through leaves, saw the cat on the branch with her, standing sideways, its back arched and fur bristled. Kitty made a strange noise. Growling and hissing.

She saw the glint of amber eyes in the dark. She wrapped her hands around the stick she always kept handy and swung. A few times.

Then breathed hard for a moment longer before swallowing and saying, "Dinner's on me today."

That night, kitty curled herself around her neck as she slept.

They'd been inseparable since. Until Gunner appeared. Now her traitor cat was sleeping with him.

Which was fine. She didn't need Kitty to help her scavenge. She knew these woods. Knew them to the sheer edge of the mountain and every pace of the embankment along the river.

She'd had time to mentally map every part of it. Which meant she could guess where Kitty found Gunner. Given they both arrived dry, she hadn't forged where the river split the land, meaning the wind had dumped Gunner somewhere on this side of the river.

Eyeing the area outside her house, she then took note of drag marks coming from the right. From the outside, the building appeared as seamless stone, melted and shaped from the rock it rested on. She wondered how it was created. Who created it?

By the time she'd stumbled onto it, not much remained inside other than the bed frame that didn't move and part of a table, its pedestal rising from the floor, almost half of the flat top sheared away. She'd found the other sections in pieces in a far room.

The house proved the best thing she'd found, after Kitty. It meant she didn't have to wake cramped from sleeping in a tree.

Knife in hand, the blade pitted with age, Sofia strode through the woods. It gave her a sense of security, especially because it felt familiar. She used it for everything, cutting, killing. She hoped to find another one before it snapped in half.

She used it now to whack a trail through the underbrush. It seemed thicker of late, maybe because the moisture in the air had gotten so heavy, more humid than she ever recalled. Even the river flower wider and faster than before, yet there hadn't been a single rain to account for the change. Sunny days and windstorms, that was all she ever got.

As she moved farther away, she saw signs of a recent wind drop—dust lingering on the leaves, some of them twisted and bent. Her toe nudged something that moved, and she bent to find a pair of goggles, the lenses intact. She put them around her neck.

Moving on, she found a wheel, twisted and unusable. Then a gun, the barrel cracked. She still removed the cartridge with bullets and kept both parts. The knife embedded in the tree—the metal hilt caught her eye—proved to be a nice surprise. After a lot of cursing and groaning, she heaved it out and tucked it into the sash at her waist, keeping the weapon she knew in hand.

She doubted anyone else was out here. Five years, over a hundred storms, and only five other people had ever been dumped. Six now with Gunner.

The appearance of a bike, the kind with an engine and not pedal power, took her by surprise, especially given it looked intact. Did it belong to him?

She dropped to her haunches and ran her fingers over the compartments on its sides. She undid clips and opened them to find a treasure. A map that did her no good. A canteen, which would prove useful. Rations, dried meat of some sort, and something wrapped in an oiled cloth that looked soft. She tucked it into her pouch with everything else.

Having emptied the storage bag, she struggled to pull the bike upright to get to the other side.

She found more items that excited, and she'd just finished emptying it when she heard a noise. She pretended as if she didn't, standing and acting nonchalant even as her nape prickled. While these woods were home to many creatures, very few of them were dangerous. Unless the wind brought something new.

Surely if there was danger, Kitty would have warned her. Another rustle, straight ahead. She crept forward, the fingers holding her knife sweating.

Rustle.

She whirled suddenly, brandishing her blade, and noticed nothing behind her. Which seemed strange. She could have sworn she sensed something.

Thunk.

The sharp blow to her head sent Sofia to her knees. She remained conscious, if stunned. But not too stunned to act.

Snarling, she slashed with her knife and scraped over metal.

A robotic chuckle sounded. "You ain't cutting through my suit with that."

The words brought fear, fast and quick. The sight of the green armor made her heart pound. Not the red she was used to seeing but still the right equipment indicating an Enclave soldier.

Danger!

She shoved at him, and he didn't budge even as she whirled to escape.

"You can't outrun me." The robotic claim brought a wheezing cry to her lips.

She ran through the woods, away from her house because the soldier was in her path. She angled, cutting around, hearing only her panting breath, the pulse of pain in her head where he'd struck her.

Rushing always brought out the clumsy in her. Or the forest conspired. Whatever the case, she snared her foot and dove forward, hands and knees digging into the forest floor, scraping and scratching.

The panicked breath rushed out of her, especially as she expected to roll over and see him coming for her.

There was no one there. Perhaps she'd outrun him in his metal suit? Getting to her feet, she ran again until she emerged onto the shore of the river, its surface higher than this morning, the ground getting softer as it rose. She raced across the strip of shore, not sure what reaching her house would accomplish. An Enclave soldier in full armor wouldn't be beaten by a stick.

Unless...

The gun in her bag? Could it be used?

A quick glance behind her showed no one following, and she slowed and ducked her head to rummage in her bag, pulling out the gun and then the clip. She slammed the pair together just as he stepped out from the woods.

The green robot mocked, “Is that for me?”

“Don’t come any closer, or I’ll shoot.”

“I wouldn’t. Split barrel like that you’re more likely to lose your face. Which would be a shame. It’s a pretty face.”

“You’re lying.”

It was odd to see the big metal armor shrug. She’d only ever seen them as emotionless monsters before. They didn’t talk much, only ever showed up to arrest those the Enclave deemed guilty.

“Lying is for those who don’t hold all the power.” The soldier took a step.

She waved the gun. “Stop.”

“Make me!”

The soldier dove, and those mechanical hands gripped her, ignoring her struggles. When she tried to scream, he tore her shirt, ripped it clean from her body, and stuffed it into her mouth.

Because who else but a he would then fondle her breast and say, “This day is finally getting better.”

Shoved to the ground, she rubbed her wrists and

glared.

He removed his helmet and showed off a handsome visage made ugly by its leer. Blond hair cut short, bright blue eyes, full sneering lips. "You and I are going to have some fun, right after you tell me who else is here."

"No one. It's just you and me," she lied.

He must have suspected, because his gaze narrowed. "You can't be living here by yourself."

"Why not?"

"Because no one lives alone outside the domes. Not even the Wasteland Rats. Where are the others? Tell me. How many are you?" He reached and twined his fingers in her hair, tugging sharply, drawing a cry of pain.

"None. Leave me alone, damn you." Clawing at his arm did nothing.

"You yelling to try and warn them?" He slapped her, hard enough to split her lip and cause a deep throbbing in her face. "Stay quiet, or I'll rip your tongue out."

She didn't doubt he would. She lay on the ground as he shoved his helmet back on, making himself impermeable to most harm. The surface of it was dented and scratched. Dusty, too.

Obviously he'd arrived on the same storm as the man already in her house. "Are you a friend of

Gunner's?"—asked in the off chance it might make a difference.

"Is that who I have to kill?" The soldier kept his grip in her hair as he hauled her to her feet. "Let's go see who else is here."

Sofia expected him to demand she show the way. Yet, the soldier easily followed the trail she'd created going back and forth from the water's edge, which was clear to see.

As the house came into view, with its left side leaning lopsidedly and the layered patches of fat leaves she'd made on the roof showing someone cared for it, she opened her mouth to shout. Kitty would already have sensed the danger, but she should give Gunner some kind of warning. Maybe he could offer some help, even if only in the form of distraction.

The soldier backhanded her before she could make a sound. Dark spots danced in her vision, and she wavered on her feet. The hand in her hair began dragging again, and she clung to his wrist, trying to ease the painful pressure.

The soldier's robotic voice called out before they reached the entrance. "Come out, come out wherever you are! I have something of yours. Now you may scream." He shook her, the yanking of her hair painful.

A cry ripped out of her. There was no answering snarl.

"Who is inside? Are they armed?" he asked, dragging her higher.

"No. It's just my cat and a blind man," she sobbed.

"I knew you were lying."

The robot soldier strode to the entrance and kicked open the door that only hung precariously. It went toppling off its fabricated hinges, the vines snapping. It clattered to the floor and still no Kitty pouncing with a snarl.

The soldier thrust her into the room, and she reeled before hitting the edge of the broken table with her hip. She gasped. Another bruise. She cast a glance at the bedroom door, which remained closed.

The soldier took in the room quickly. He dismissed everything, even the passages leading off into the damaged areas in favor of the one room sealed from him.

The true chill came as she noted the weapon in his suit rising from the arm, the muzzle deadly and ready.

Kitty couldn't fight bullets. Despite knowing she might die for the warning, Sofia screamed, "Run, Kitty. Get out."

The bedroom had a window that had long since

lost its glass. She'd covered it with leaves and wood to close it from the outside. But it wouldn't stop a determined feline.

"Shut up!" The blow sent her to the floor with her ears ringing. As her eyes blinked at the dust, it occurred to her she really should sweep it more often.

Thump. The bedroom door was kicked open, and she listened through the buzzing of her ears for the snarl of her cat. Even a word from Gunner.

Instead the soldier stomped back out. "Where is this Kitty? Is it another woman? A child? Answer."

He leaned down to shove his helmet in her face, inhuman, just like his actions. A hand on her throat cut off air. He was so intent on her, he never heard Gunner behind him.

Wham.

The rock that formed the seat for her stool slammed off the helmet, and the soldier fell sideways with a clang. Gunner followed, swinging again. His eyes were still bound, and yet the stone landed with a crunch. Again, and again, until the soldier went still.

And though she throbbed with pain, she couldn't help but sob in relief.

SIX

Sofia whimpered, the sound broken and terrified.

Gunner's voice ended up gruffer than expected. "Are you okay? Did that asshole hurt you?" The strong woman he'd met, who bullied him, wouldn't cry over nothing.

"I'm fine." She sounded embarrassed by her tears. "Just...relieved, I guess. Which is horrible. A man died."

"No, that was a fuckwad who doesn't deserve any sympathy," Gunner grumbled. "Not surprising given he was an Enclave soldier."

"How did you know to hide and help me?"

"Luck."

It had only been chance that woke him from a drugged sleep. Chance and a giant cat licking his face. The raspy wet tongue went after his cheeks, surely ruining all the progress he'd made with the cream he'd bargained for.

When he grumbled and tried to roll away, a paw pinned him and flexed its claws, pricking skin. He froze and mumbled, "Nice, Kitty."

The cat butted him with a large head. "Meowr." The feline jumped from the bed, landing with a soft thud, and he heard a scratching.

He expected the woman to let it out.

The feline scratched again and uttered a low, rumbling growl.

"Guess that's my cue to get my ass out of bed."

Perhaps it had to piss. Better outside than somewhere he would step in it. And who knew, if Kitty got impatient, she might decide to sharpen her claws on him next.

His limbs still sluggish, Gunner levered his legs out of bed. The tile floor proved solid, and he pushed to his feet, swayed and swallowed. He felt disconnected from his body.

"Your mistress drugged me." It made the most sense, even as it didn't. She'd not fed him anything. Just blown powder in his face.

A pretty potent powder. Must be some alchemist thing.

Scratch. Scratch.

"I'm coming." He steadied himself before taking a shuffling step. It was then he heard it, from far off, a cry. One of pain.

"Shit." He moved forward, arms outstretched, shuffling lest he slam into something.

The cat moved close and brushed his leg. He reached down and dug his fingers into the fur. With the cat as his guide, he made it to the door, feeling along it for a handle or a latch. He pulled it open, exited, and closed it behind him.

He paused, listening, and heard it, the clomping of metal boots. The Enclave soldiers were well protected in their armor but never quiet.

When the soldier yelled his demand, the cat pulled him in another direction.

"I hope you know what you're doing," he muttered.

With his eyes bound, he was dependent on others and chance.

Luck, don't fail me now.

He heard a door being kicked open, the soldier too cocky to wonder if he walked into danger. Gunner bit the inside of his lip when he heard Sofia cry out, and while the cat bristled at his side, she remained quiet.

A good hunter never let the prey hear it coming.

Another door was kicked open. The bedroom.

And then there was yelling and fear in her screams, meaning he had to act.

Gunner couldn't see but that didn't stop him from moving out of the alcove, counting his steps, his bare feet silent, his movements sure as his trailing fingers snared the stone for the stool. He followed the choking sounds and the creak of metal joints. The whimper brought his lips back in a snarl. The scent of her fear filled him with anger.

The soldier deserved each blow of the rock. Deserved his death. Gunner just wished he could have done it before Sofia got hurt.

"Luck?" She snorted, bringing him back to the present. "I wouldn't call it luck that an Enclave soldier ended up here."

"He must have been grabbed when I was. The Enclave soldiers were chasing me just before the windstorm started."

"They as in more than one?" she asked.

Casting back his recollection, he replied, "I think there was something like eight or nine of them."

She sighed. "Which means there could be more of them out there."

Which wasn't a good thing obviously. "I'm sorry."

"What for?" She sounded startled. "You didn't cause the wind that brought you here."

"True, but you seemed to have everything under control before my arrival."

"I did. And I'll get things there again."

"You're going to exterminate Enclave soldiers on your own?" He couldn't help a hint of amusement in his reply.

"If there are more, yes. Although, I'll admit, it seems unlikely. I've never had two people arrive in a single storm before, let alone three."

"But those weren't soldiers. The armor might protect them better."

"Maybe we got lucky and they landed in the river."

"And if they didn't?"

"Pushing them in and letting the water handle it might be easiest," she mused aloud.

"Are you stupid?" The words hung between them, and he could sense more than see her simmering anger.

"Would someone stupid have survived five years on her own?"

"Depends, how many people have died trying to save you?"

"Jerk!" She huffed the words, but she didn't touch him.

Casey would have decked him. Actually, Nikki, Vera, and probably Zara would have, too.

But Sofia sounded insulted. Hurt. He also still sensed fear.

"I won't apologize. Not when you're about to do something foolish."

"What else can I do? This place isn't huge. If there are more soldiers, they'll find the house eventually."

She had a point. "I don't like the idea of you confronting anyone on your own."

"What else would you suggest?" she asked.

"Bring me with you."

She scoffed. "Because an injured blind man is more useful than I am."

"That's not what—"

"It is exactly what you're implying," she huffed angrily. "Yet this useless woman is the one who is taking care of you. No more. I should have tossed you out the first moment we met. You know what, it's not too late. Get out."

"Now, sweetheart. Don't be like that," he soothed.

"I said get out. And take the dead soldier with you."

"To do what with him? You said it yourself, I can't see."

"You saw well enough to wield my stool. I'm sure you'll be fine."

How was he supposed to explain luck guided his aim? "If you kick me out, then how am I supposed to accomplish my end of the deal? We haven't made a baby yet."

"Deal's off. Get out."

"Be reasonable."

She made a noise full of frustration. "You know what, you stay, I'll leave."

"To go where?" he asked as he heard her steps moving away.

"Somewhere safe. Coming, Kitty?"

The feline sat down beside him, and he knew Sofia was hurt at the abandonment by her pet.

"Traitor," she said bitterly before stomping away.

Leaving him alone. With no vision. And a dead body. Maybe even more soldiers in the woods.

He sighed, and the feline chuffed with him. "Guess it's me and you, Kitty. I don't suppose you know how to use a shovel." Hell, did Sofia even own a shovel?

In the end, he dragged the body outside and kept dragging uphill until the cat butted him.

"This better be the cliff I asked for," he grumbled, giving the body a heave. It was a long while before he heard a splash. Kind of disconcerting to realize he was on a cliff that high.

At least he wouldn't die of dehydration. Or boredom. Between Kitty and Sofia, he had company and entertainment galore.

Not that he'd be staying. The moment his eyes healed he'd be looking for a way out, leaving behind a possibly pregnant woman—if he held up his side of the bargain.

Then again, what were the chances any sample he gave her would actually impregnate her? Birth rates were low in the Wastelands for a reason. It wasn't that easy.

Even the Incubaii domes were having difficulties. Unviable fetuses were happning more and more often. Humanity had gotten stale.

Or so Oliander claimed when he'd had a few too many fermented brews to drink. The doctor claimed a healthy society required intermingling. With the domes being so contained, fraternization frowned upon, and only a small number of women chosen to donate their eggs, genetic variety was lacking. Which, according to Oliander, would lead to lower birth rates, even more defects, and a population less capable of adapting. The only solution was one the Enclave would never agree to, a return to the Old Earth way of increasing the population by letting people procreate as they pleased with whom they pleased.

That would never happen, not with the Enclave in power.

Returning down the slope, his hand only lightly touching Kitty, he found himself relying on his other senses. Listening for sounds that might indicate motion or the creak of armor. Smelling even as he recognized little of what he scented. It sure beat the dry dust of the Wastelands.

He didn't hear Sofia, and yet he sensed her nearby. Watching over him perhaps? Using him as bait if there were other soldiers? A smart thing to do. Would she try and smash them with a rock now that she saw it was possible, or did she have a better weapon?

He forgot to ask.

Given he might not see for a while—if ever—he spent some time learning the space inside the house. Eight strides from the main door to the bedroom, three more to the bed. Almost ten to the alcove he'd hidden in. When he was certain of all the pacing, he went outside and began learning the area around the house. He knew it was one hundred and forty-five steps up the hill to the cliff. Less than twenty to go past the house and hit the edge of the woods.

The entire time he walked and counted, his nape prickled. He was well aware of the eyes watching, which meant he didn't act surprised when she drawled, "You should walk five more paces to your left."

"It's farther than that to the cliff."

"I know. I was hoping you'd fall in the slither hole."

"The what?"

"I don't know what it's called, but there's this thing that slithers out of a hole in the ground. It has no legs or paws, nothing. It wiggles to get places and, like the vines, squeezes its prey to death after it bites it and renders it immobile."

His lips pursed. "It's called a snake and, knowing it's out here, why have you let it live?"

"It's harmless to bigger animals, and its venom is useful for numbing wounds."

"And how does one find out it numbs?" he asked. "Is there a test you can perform?"

"Yeah. It's called getting bitten."

The reply, delivered so dryly, surprised a chuckle out of him. "I guess that would be a good way of testing. You're lucky it wasn't more poisonous."

"I'm aware. It hasn't been easy trying to separate friendly foliage from rip-your-stomach-to-shreds-and-make-you- think-you'll-die. Which reminds me, are you hungry?"

"Depends, are you going to feed me something that will make me wish I'd died quickly?"

"Maybe." She laughed, a husky sound he enjoyed way too much. "Perhaps as a rite of passage, you should suffer the way I did until I learned my way around."

"Now that's just mean."

"I guess." She didn't sound sorry at all. "Do you know it was almost a year before I got my hands on an igniter?"

"You couldn't make fire?"

"Nope. I cooked my meat on some black rocks by the river that heat up in the sun. When I got my first igniter, I was so excited and ignorant I almost burned down the forest. I never realized fire could be so hungry and spread so fast. I was close to the river at least and had a bucket to put it out. I was more careful after that."

The fact she'd had to learn on her own impressed him. "You've had to learn a lot."

"It was learn, or die."

"You sound like a Wastelander."

She snorted. "I'm not a rat."

"Neither are we."

That quieted her.

To his surprise, she apologized. "I'm sorry."

He changed the subject. "What happened to hunting down more possible soldiers?"

"Night is coming. I don't go in the woods at night."

"I thought you said the trees don't move."

"They don't. But there are other things out there. It's just safer to be indoors."

"I don't suppose indoors has that food you mentioned?" he asked rather hopefully. The water he'd drunk earlier had long since left. His stomach gurgled with hunger.

"I don't have any fresh meat. I was too busy with other things today. But I do have some dried strips, along with some leftover berries."

To his surprise, she moved close enough to grab his hand.

He felt compelled to say, "I'm sorry I called you an idiot." He still thought her plan to wander the woods looking for soldiers was a bad one, but she was right. If there were more of them out there, then they should be located and taken care of.

"I'm sorry I broke our bargain and asked you to leave."

"Shall we kiss and make up?" he asked.

"No, we will not," said with soft surprise.

"Let me know if you change your mind." He still had no idea how she looked and quite frankly didn't care. She intrigued him, this woman with so much bravery and intelligence. A true survivor. A child of theirs would be strong.

She tugged him into the house. There was noise as she shifted the door. Sighed. "It won't stay in place even with the branch across it. That stupid soldier busted the vines I had holding it."

He didn't mention the fact that short of reinforcing it with metal and concrete it wouldn't stop the next one that decided to kick it in. "For tonight, we might want to try sleeping in one of the less accessible rooms. Just in case."

"The mattress I stuffed won't fit," she said almost mournfully.

"You can use me as a pillow," he offered.

To which she snorted. "You're too hard to be comfortable."

He couldn't resist and teased her. "But you want it to be hard if it's to be pleasurable."

Her audible gasp had him grinning.

"I told you we would not be fornicating to make the child."

"And I'm telling you that it's the most reliable way to ensure it gets done."

"I am not having sex with you."

"Fine. But will you at least feed me? I am starving. A man needs his energy if he's to provide strong seed."

That brought a wry, "I'll feed you, but only because you'll stop talking if your mouth is full."

The food proved tastier than expected, the dried meat flavorful and easy to chew. The berries had been baked inside some leaves along with nuts, and the water they shared out of a cup had a minty taste to it.

"That was delicious."

He could hear the pleasure in her voice as she said, "It took a while to perfect some of the techniques. I never had to cook before coming here. I never realized it was like the creams and medicines I make, where proportion and certain blends create the most incredible textures or flavors."

"It seems being an apothecary has its uses."

"Some."

"Does it extend to poisons?"

"I didn't poison your food," she exclaimed.

"I never said you did. I am asking because a poison would be another way to defend yourself against soldiers."

"Except I can't inject them while they wear a suit."

"No, but you can feed them if they take the helmet off. Or smear it on their skin if they get close."

Her voice went low. "I'd rather they stay away in the first place."

"Which reminds me, we should find that spot to hunker down until morning." Maybe by then he'd have some use of his eyes and not feel so fucking useless.

"I know where we can go, but you'll have to squeeze through a tight spot," she said.

"Meaning it will be very hard for them to follow. That's good. We should make this place look abandoned. Toss some dirt around, spread some leaves."

"If they've seen me, it won't matter."

"Let's assume they haven't." Because he doubted they'd wait to attack if they had. "If they think this place abandoned, they won't look as hard."

"Leaving the door opens makes it easier for things to come in, you do realize that?"

"If any come close, then that will mean fresh meat for breakfast."

The remark made her laugh. "If it doesn't eat you first."

"I've got tough skin. Let's set the scene."

It didn't take long with her doing most of the work quickly, hiding anything that might appear as if someone still lived here, while he stole the blankets from the bed then bundled the fur covering the foliage mattress. Taking handfuls of the mattress, he did his best to throw it around.

Sofia grumbled, "You're making a huge mess."

"Better a bit of tidying later than not waking up at all."

He wished he knew if there were more soldiers out here. He'd smashed the headset of the one he'd disposed of, meaning he couldn't check if he'd had a comm system active. For all he knew, the guy relayed the fact they weren't alone to others.

But surely if he had, they'd have attacked by now.

"I don't think there's anything more we can do to wreck the place," she said.

"Both doors are wide open?"

"Front door is leaning partially on the floor. Looks like someone used to live here but nature is slowly taking over."

"Perfect. You have a weapon?"

"A knife."

"Gun?"

"A broken one in my bag."

"Which is useless." A rule learned young was never use a damaged firearm. It tended to fuck up the person pulling the trigger.

"Well excuse me. I found it today and grabbed it."

"Lead me to this hiding spot you were talking about."

"It's through the collapsed hall to the right of the table."

He knew the hole she meant. He'd groped it earlier. It would be tight. "Have you used it often for hiding?"

"In the beginning, I slept there every night. It's only got a small hole in the ceiling, meaning fresh air to breathe, but only one way in."

Which meant one way out. He didn't quite like it, but then again, defending one entrance would be simpler than two. He had to hope it didn't come to them fighting anyone off.

Kitty had left as they prepped, and Sofia didn't seem concerned. Given the size of the feline, it seemed doubtful much would bother it. He just hoped Kitty knew to stay clear of any soldiers. Bullets would easily penetrate the soft fur.

"Ready?" she asked.

"Yeah."

She placed his hand on the rubble forming the hole. "It's tight only for the first few crawls, and then it gets wider."

Not the most reassuring thing, but then again, he couldn't see, which meant he just had to pretend there were big open spaces around him. He heard her scooting, her arms full of fabric. He had his own bundle, and he tucked it to his chest as he crouched.

The slanted slab that formed the triangular entrance required him going in at an angle then doing a weird side shuffle until the slant tilted, making it easier to waddle. They kept quiet as they moved, only the brush of feet marring the silence. He did his best to pretend the ruins weren't closing in. Fought to not think of what might happen if the rubble suddenly shifted. Seismic vibrations still happened from time to time. What if a tremor hit while they were trapped in here?

She whispered softly, "We've reached the room."

"Can I stand?" he asked.

"Yes."

Still clutching the blankets, he rose, feeling some of his tension ease as he felt the space around him expand. He trailed his fingers over the wall and counted in his head, trying to get a sense of size for the space. Larger than expected. Taller, too, enough he couldn't touch a ceiling.

"It's big," he said softly, the sound louder than he liked in the echoey space.

"It is. I'm not sure what it used to be. I do know it was used before by someone else."

"How can you tell?"

"It was clean. Emptied of debris."

"Why did you stop sleeping in here?" he asked.

"Well, having a large cat as your companion

helps, but mostly because at one point I realized I didn't want to be hiding all the time. And what if an earthquake brought the place down."

He grumbled, "Not the most reassuring thing."

She laughed but quickly stifled it. "Shhh."

A good point. Their hiding place wouldn't be worth anything if someone heard them and decided to collapse it.

"Let's get some sleep so we can start our hunt early in the morning," he whispered.

"We?" she scoffed.

The reminder set his lips. He wasn't used to be seen as useless. He didn't feel useless. Losing his sight hadn't affected his ability to fight. He could still wield his knives with deadly accuracy. He'd spend time tomorrow practicing throwing blind. If he was going to be relying on sound to be his guide, then he'd better hone that skill.

"You are not hunting soldiers alone," he stated firmly.

"Do you really think there are more?" she asked softly.

"Doubtful." A lie. With those suits, they would have fared better than he did in that storm.

But they could do nothing at night, and they needed to rest. He lay on the ground with the bundle of furs under his head.

He could hear her shifting not far from him.

"It's not as comfortable as your bed," he remarked.

She didn't reply.

Undaunted, he made her an offer. "You can use me as a mattress if you'd like."

"The last man I shared my house with assaulted me," she said matter-of-factly.

"What? I—" Saying he was sorry seemed trite. But what else could he say? "I am sorry you were hurt. But I assure you not all men are assholes."

"I know. The only reason I'm telling you is because I will protect myself if you try and hurt me."

"Please do, because I would never do a thing like that." In his mind, rapists deserved a slow, torturous death.

"Oddly enough, for all your flirting, I don't think you would. Braun was aggressive from the moment we met. I should have been firmer with him from the start about his behavior, but I was curious and alone. However, he proved to be quite brutish with no understanding of the word no. He attacked me."

"And Kitty killed him."

"No, but she did help distract him. When he shot her, I stabbed him."

It took him a moment before he could say in a

low voice, "You should have poisoned him before that ever happened."

She chuckled. "I know that now, but the attack took me by surprise. Naïve, I know. I guess I assumed a soldier would abide by the Enclave laws and have some honor."

He uttered a disparaging sound. "That really was naïve. Most of them are power-hungry asses. I swear, something about the suit turns them into brutal thugs. I'm glad you managed to kill him."

"At times I can still feel his hot breath and hear the rip of fabric. Hear the report from his gun and the scream Kitty made." She went silent, and he wondered what she was thinking. Wished he could see her expression.

"A wise woman once told me that the hardest thing about survival wasn't the things we must do in order to live but the haunting memories," he said

"She was right."

He wished he could reach out and...what? Console her? She probably wouldn't welcome an overture given her experience.

"Given what's happened before, I can see why you're leery about men." He kept talking to her softly, the fact he couldn't see her adding to the intimacy forming between them. When was the last time he'd talked this openly with anyone? "In Haven, that kind of thing isn't allowed. Axel, the guy in charge of shit, would string any man up by his balls if he even suggested it. And I'd be right there helping him."

"Are there many people in this Haven place?"

"Too many according to the boss." How many times had he heard Axel complain? "But annoying and hard as it can be at times, we're family. We take care of each other."

She sighed. "When I lived in the city, all I did was take care of others. The moment I left the Creche at the age of four, they had me apprenticed to a master of apothecary craft. I was one of three apprentices tasked with doing all the work in the shop. Cleaning, errands, crushing of herbs, sorting, and labeling. Then, as I got older, I began working shifts in the shop."

"Sounds boring." His nose wrinkled.

"Yes and no. I did enjoy the work. I just didn't like serving the Enclave."

"Because they're entitled assholes who take everything and don't give shit back."

The soft chuckle made him smile. "According to them, they should be accorded every advantage because they protect the citizens."

"From what?" he asked. "Seriously, all those rules and what do citizens get? Because it's not a choice. My understanding is you get told what you will do and how you will do it. If you don't, punishment."

"Your understanding is correct," she said. "And for a long time, I thought there was no choice."

"I'll be honest, I can't imagine what it's like to grow up so restricted. I grew up in the Wastelands where we always made our own decisions. Which isn't to say it was a better or easier life," he hastened to add. "My parents were always moving around. Never staying for long anywhere."

"Why?"

"Because of the danger. The lack of food. The patrols that never left us alone." He went silent as he recalled those times he'd been woken in the middle of the night. Running, always running.

"You said your parents. You actually knew the people who birthed you?"

"I called them mom and dad," he teased. "They had me the old-fashioned way. The way babies used to be made and raised."

"It seems so strange to me to think that in ancient times there was no Creche for babies and young ones, no academies for sorting. Or even apprenticeships of the children considered worthy enough."

"The Creche and all that hierarchy bullshit is an Enclave creation," he muttered. "In the Wasteland, we are born from a woman, not a tank, and raised by our family. We choose our path in life."

"Is that such a good thing, though? You said it yourself. Your existence as a child was fraught with uncertainty and danger."

"I'll take that any day, given it also means freedom."

"Look at what happened to the ancients, though. They had all the freedom in the world, and humanity was almost wiped out."

"It wasn't completely their fault. The meteor fall did most of the damage."

"Now who's making excuses?" She laughed, the low sound pleasing.

She was pleasing.

"Just saying that the Enclave curtailing the rights of its citizens isn't necessarily in the best interest of those citizens."

"The Enclave might be corrupt now, but in the early days of rebuilding, their method proved most effective at maintaining and expanding the population."

"Wastelanders have been effectively procreating, too, sweetheart. The Enclave has been obsolete for a while now."

"Is this your revolution speech?" she mocked.

"Trying to convert citizens to your side to overthrow the evil empire?"

He smiled even if he knew she didn't see it. "Maybe. Care to join the Deviant side of the battle?"

"Technically I became a rebel the day they banished me." She said it almost musingly.

"Once you have my baby, you'll be a seasoned criminal." The words spilled out of him, and he could have choked. Since when had he come around to the idea of spreading his genetics?

"You sound sure your seed will take root. Do you already have children?" she asked.

"No. Not yet." He'd been waiting. He just couldn't have said for what. The right time? The right woman?

"Are there many children in Haven?"

"More than a few. My friend Sally, who already has a daughter, just had another kid. And I hear that two more women are pregnant."

"So it's easy to have a baby?" she asked.

He debated for a second what to say then stuck to the truth. Both sides of it. "It's not. It's hard, and sometimes things go wrong during the pregnancy or birth. Even having a doctor isn't a surety."

"You seem to be implying I shouldn't have a baby."

"No, that's not what I said. As difficult and

fraught with danger as it can be, the birth of a child is miraculous." And how much greater would it be if that child was actually his? "If you want a kid, then by all means have one, but I would recommend you not have it in isolation. You shouldn't go through that experience alone."

"It's not as if I have a choice. I told you, there's no escape."

Then he said the most unexpected thing. "Then I guess that means I'll be around to give you a hand."

SEVEN

Sofia's mouth snapped shut. Gunner had implied he might stay. With her. To raise their child.

A child they'd not yet created, but would.

The very idea had her heart racing. Especially given he'd offered to impregnate her the ancient way. By touching her and...

She knew all about sex. She'd provided lubricants that stimulated for Enclave members who didn't try very hard to hide the fact they indulged. She'd experimented a bit but never understood the allure.

Braun had tried to give her a violent version of sex. She still remembered the fear of being pinned under him, his breath hot on her face, his hands rough as he tore at her clothes. The scalding spray of his blood when Kitty slammed into him with her claws. When Braun shot Kitty, Sofia recovered her wits enough to deliver the killing blow. He didn't look so big and scary bleeding out on the floor.

Yet her experience with Braun hadn't tainted her. She knew most people weren't abusive jerks.

Like Gunner, for example. She'd not known him long, but he showed his character in a few ways. His positive attitude really stuck out for her.

He'd arrived injured, blind, and lost. How frightening. She knew that first-hand. Yet he took it all in stride, handling his new reality with good humor. Even flirting.

Holes in the ceiling offered enough starlight that she could see his dark shape on the floor close enough that she could reach out and touch him. She had a feeling he'd let her. But after Braun, she found herself leery of the idea of being close to a man. Getting intimate meant putting trust in someone.

Could Gunner change her mind about sex? Could it be her lack of interest was because she'd not been with the right person?

She felt different about Gunner for many reasons. He was at times a strange man who spouted the most interesting statements about the Enclave. He disapproved of them and had valid reasons. He said the things she'd thought but never dared say aloud.

His sharp mind engaged hers, and she loved it. Loved also checking out his body. His shape pleased, and his face, while battered, possessed good lines.

But aside from his looks and intellect, the best part of Gunner was he didn't frighten her. Although he did make her pulse race.

She hadn't said anything in reply to his offer to stay and raise their imaginary child, but she heard the scrape as he shifted on the floor. His hands went to his head. She imagined him toying with the bandage over his eyes.

"Don't play with that."

"I'll play with it if I want to," he growled.

"Are your injuries bothering you?" she asked.

"The orbs are doing a weird stabby thing, and the skin on my face itches something fierce."

"That would be the cream at work," she stated. "And probably a sign you need another layer." She rummaged in her bag for the fat leaves she'd wrapped around some leftover paste then shuffled to his side. "I'm going to take off your bandage." She gently tugged it free, but couldn't see in the gloom if the swelling had gone down or not. "This will be wet."

He remained still while she smoothed the mixture over his skin, brushing it lightly over his lids. Then because she'd made it hours ago, she lightly pressed his face, making contact with the cream, and muttered the intent. "*Heal.*" A spark ignited inside her. Her hands heated, and he gasped. His fingers wrapped around her wrists lightly, but even when she removed her hands from his face, he held on.

"That feels better. Thank you." A sincere expression.

It flustered. She pulled free her wrists. "I should wrap your eyes again."

"Let me sit up to help with the task."

Because he was taller, she had to kneel and move closer to manipulate the bandage around his head. She became very much aware of how near he was.

Apparently, he noticed the proximity, too "How is it you smell so good?"

"I bathe every day using a soap I made." It had taken her a while to create something pleasant. It made her happier than it should have to hear him compliment it.

"It's a good thing I can't see," he grumbled.

"Why?" she asked. Did he know of the scar on her cheek? The mark that took her once pretty features and turned them ugly.

"Because then I'd be able to actually picture you bathing. Right now, you're just this sexy and mysterious voice in the dark."

The admission should have startled. Yet, for all

he might lust, he didn't touch. Even though she had her breast right in front of his face, close enough that the air crackled between them. He could have touched her, yet he didn't even try to stroke. His hands remained in his lap.

Gunner was nothing like Braun. He was like no man she'd ever met.

She finished tying the bandage and settled on her haunches to bring her face more in line with his. "You wouldn't want me if you saw me." Braun had told her he did her a favor. That no one would ever desire her. As if she wanted desire. She knew the word of one want-to-be rapist shouldn't be enough to convince her, and yet, she stroked that scar daily. A reminder of her stupidity.

"I don't think you can tell me what I want or don't want. Because I will tell you right now, I want to kiss you."

"Kiss me?" The memory of fetid breath and sloppy smears had her cringing.

"You just thought of that asshole, didn't you?" He sounded angry. "Don't ever flinch from me, sweetheart. I would never do anything you didn't want."

"I don't see the appeal," she admitted honestly.

"Because you haven't kissed me."

"You think you're that special?" For some reason,

he made it easy to flirt. It helped she kept her hand on the hilt of her knife.

"I'd like to be. Would you let me kiss you?"

"I don't know." A soft admission of the truth. She wanted him to and didn't.

"Would it help if you controlled what happens?"

"Meaning?"

He purred softly. "You kiss me."

"Me?" The very idea flummoxed and teased. "I don't know how." The admission of her naivety made her cheeks burn.

"You are killing me here," he groaned. "Tell you what. You do what you want. I'll sit on my hands so you feel safe. I won't touch you." He shifted and placed them under his rump.

Except, she kind of wanted him to touch her. She stared at him. He leaned toward her.

She almost met him. Instead, she turned aside. "I am not going to kiss you. Nor do I want to." A lie because she wondered how his mouth would feel. It was the one area that didn't have any cream on it.

"Then don't kiss me." He shrugged. "The choice is yours."

Choice. There he was again with that titillating word. Before she could think twice about it, she pressed her mouth quickly to his and pulled away. He didn't move.

"I did it." She'd kissed him. And it wasn't unpleasant at all. It wasn't much of anything, but her heart still pounded.

Gunner chuckled. "That was barely a kiss, sweetheart. You're supposed to move your lips over mine."

She heard the taunt. "I don't see why. Mouths are for talking and eating."

"They can also feel good if touched the right way."

"Are you claiming I did it wrong?" she retorted.

"You kissed me like a grandmother pecks a child. A real kiss involves the sensual slide of lips and tongues."

"I don't see the difference."

"Try it and see," he cajoled.

"You're bossy." But lucky for him, she was curious.

She moved back in and slanted her mouth against his, sliding her flesh along his, feeling a strange warm shiver between her legs. Then a spurt of heat when his mouth tugged her bottom lip.

"I thought you weren't moving," she whispered into his mouth.

"Only my hands, sweetheart. Mouth is fair game."

With that, he showed her a real kiss. Showed

her how it could feel to sensually engage in a lip dance of soft strokes, sucks, nibbles, and mingled breath. The first touch of his tongue against hers had her straddling his lap, fingers gripping his shoulders, deepening the embrace. Moaning into his mouth.

She ground herself against him, lost in the kiss, feeling an exquisite pressure pulsing between her legs.

Demanding something.

Hungering.

Needing.

Hiss.

She froze at the sound. In a heartbeat, she'd pulled her knife. Before she could stab in the darkness, he rolled out from under her. She heard another hiss, a grumble, then a grunt, followed by an end to the hissing.

"It's dead," he softly announced.

The statement brought Sofia to her senses.

What was she doing? Indulging in distraction when they might be in serious trouble.

How dare she enjoy herself?

She could almost hear the Enclave in that thought. A low-level citizen like herself wasn't allowed much time or opportunity to do something just for the pleasure of it

He returned to her, his hands reaching, but she slipped out of his grasp. No more distractions.

"Good job killing the slither," she stated.

He sighed. "I take it the kiss is over?"

"It was nice," she felt compelled to reply.

"Nice?"

She smiled at the disgruntled tone. No point in telling him he was right. A proper kiss did feel good. "We should take turns sleeping. I'll take first watch."

"I—"

"Sleep." She blew the sleeping dust at him and caught his upper body as he slumped. She lay him gently on the floor but, rather than move away, snuggled against his body. He'd never know given his unconscious state, but she was very aware. The spot between her legs throbbed. Her lips tingled.

Maybe, just maybe, she should accept his offer to make a baby via actual intercourse. She found him a lot more appealing than anyone else she'd ever met.

It would be a shame if he forced her to kill him.

She must have fallen asleep listening for danger, because when she woke, it was to find herself splayed atop him, his arms loosely circling her, and sunlight peeking through the hole.

When she stirred, he rumbled, "Morning, sweetheart."

His body felt hard and hot and perfect. It almost

gave her enough reason to start another kiss. Instead, she moved away. "We should see if we had any soldiers visit last night."

"Good thing none did considering you drugged me."

"You were being difficult."

"What if we'd been attacked?" he countered.

"I'd have handled it."

He snorted. "Handled it how? With a knife against armor? How well do you think that would go?"

"I don't know but keep shouting because if they're here they've already heard us," she hissed.

"You're being this way because of the kiss last night."

"That kiss meant nothing to me." But it did draw her gaze to his mouth. The skin on his face looked much improved this morning. All of him looked—

"You are such a liar." He huffed the word.

"And you're conceited if you're going to imply it meant something."

"It did." Said in a low tone.

How did he know? Or was he just guessing? "We don't have time for this."

"You will make time to discuss that kiss. Better yet, maybe you should finish it." The soft burr of the words managed to bring a shiver.

“What do you mean, finish it?” She couldn’t stop herself from saying it.

His reply brushed hotly over her mouth. “There’s only one way to end a kiss properly.”

“With a baby in my belly.”

EIGHT

SHE WENT FROM EMBARRASSED TO WINNING THE battle between them. The mention of a baby shriveled his ardor. Gunner wasn't sure he was ready for that. And she knew it. Somehow, she'd grasped his reluctance.

Bravo. He admired how she'd flipped that around because, a moment ago, he could have almost grabbed hold of her embarrassment it was so thick. Better than grabbing her throat to wring it.

Once more, she'd put him to sleep. One word, a bit of dust, and poof. He passed out hard. If they'd been attacked, he'd have never known. It angered and frightened all at once.

Gunner would, however, admit to enjoying waking up underneath Sofia. She'd chosen to snuggle him, and while not one to share his resting spots, the feel of her against him pleased.

It also made him hornier than fuck. His cock throbbed, all too easily remembering the kiss and grind of the night before.

He couldn't have said if it was the fact he could only rely on some of his senses, but that kiss rocked him. Shook him. Made him want this woman more than anything he'd ever desired.

Pity she didn't appear to feel the same way. He couldn't blame her. She might have glossed over the abuse of the man she'd killed, but he wasn't stupid. He was well aware of the depravity some people indulged in. It killed him to know she'd been sorely hurt.

But he'd say the kiss they shared might have helped her realize not all men were the same. Or not.

She snapped her fingers. "Are you coming or waiting for me to check things out first?"

"I'm coming." Just not in a way that would make his dick soften.

His face felt much better this morning, the insane itching gone, the bruising on his body less intense. A quick pass of fingers over his features showed the swelling gone, but he didn't dare tug at the fabric over his eyes. Not yet. The orbs still throbbed.

She paused, and he bumped into the back of her. She whispered, "It doesn't look like anyone came by."

She shuffled forward before he could reply, and he quickly followed, a knife already in hand, just in case. But he emerged to hear her crooning to her cat.

"There you are, and you brought us breakfast. Good Kitty."

A kitty who wanted all the attention, as she slammed into him next, hard enough he stumbled into a wall. Two big paws landed on his shoulders, and a raspy tongue licked at his face.

"I'm going to guess this is her way of saying good morning," he said, letting the cat lick him. It seemed safer than fighting her off.

"She also likes the purple herb in the lotion on your face."

"Nice to know I'm wearing her favorite seasoning," he grumbled. Before he had a chance to escape, the cat shifted away from him and made a sound.

"Meowr."

"What's that mean?"

Sofia snorted. "As if I know. But if I had to guess, given she just pawed the fish she brought, I think she's hungry."

So was he. Sofia headed outside, and he followed, inhaling the damp morning air, only to wrinkle his nose a moment later at the acrid stench of smoke. She'd started a fire.

"Is it wise to announce our presence?" he asked.

"One, we have no idea if there are more soldiers. Two, I am not eating raw fish. So stand guard while I cook."

He almost chuckled at the command, but he also took it seriously. He practiced his pacing, keeping count in his head as he did a small perimeter check, Kitty close by his side. In a playful mood, apparently, given she kept rubbing into his thighs and making odd noises.

When the feline abandoned him, he headed back for Sofia in time for her to chide the cat. "Don't eat it yet. It's still too hot."

"It smells delicious." His taste buds watered at the fragrant aroma of cooked meat.

"Come here and I'll give you some." Funny how he didn't exactly need her voice to be tuned in to her location.

He moved toward her and only stopped when her hand hit his chest. "Any further and you'll be sizzling on the fire. Sit." She gently shoved him sideways, and when his legs hit a rock, he sat down hard.

"Hold out your hand."

"You're bossy," he stated.

Sofia was back to her brusque self as if their intimacy in the night never happened.

"Because I'm hungry, but I can't eat until I've fed you."

"I can feed myself, thanks." The leaf in his palm heated with the food she'd put on it.

As they ate, he began to think of their next step. "We need to find out if there are any more soldiers."

"How about I leave you out here as bait?" she teased.

"Not a bad plan, but that means sitting around and waiting for them to come find us. Not to mention, we have the same weapon problem as yesterday. We need something better than a knife and a broken gun."

"You think I don't know that? I am well aware my knife won't even scratch their armor."

"The plated parts are too tough," he agreed. "You have to go after the joints. The flexible material is softer there."

"That's actually good to know, even if it requires me getting too close. Once was enough, thank you."

He cringed. "I am sorry it took me so long to act."

"It's not your fault but mine for being so complacent. I'll know to be more careful from here on out."

"I don't suppose you've scavenged any round

discs? Usually dark gray in color, about this big." He held out his fingers.

"I found one, but it was broken. What is it?"

"EMP pulse disk. They're ideal for incapacitating and stripping soldiers out of the suits."

"I've only ever fought one soldier before, and he didn't have the armor. The other men who came here by accident previously were citizens who'd escaped."

"I'm all too familiar with soldiers," he said with a grimace. "I wish I didn't have to fight them, but they've been after me and those I call family my entire life."

"Why? Why do they chase you?" she asked, her voice closer.

"Because they're Enclave."

"How is that an answer?"

He wished he could see her face because he couldn't tell if she was being sarcastic or not. "Given our discussions, you obviously know of them. And if I remember correctly, you're from a city."

"Why does it matter?"

"It matters because, depending on your class, you're kept more ignorant than others. Some of the most sheltered Enclave citizens are the sawrs. They actually think sex is against the law."

"It's not encouraged in the cities, either," she noted.

"No, but according to you, it still happens, and do people get punished for it?"

She shook her head.

"Creche sawrs are not allowed physical intimacy of any kind. Not even hugs. They believe all children are born in gestational tanks."

"Surely they can't actually be that ignorant," she exclaimed.

"They are according to one I met recently. Laura's been learning a lot about what the Enclave claims and what the truth is."

"The truth is they're liars," she remarked, the words bitten off and terse.

"At least you're aware. How did they lie to you?"

"Shall I list the ways? Starting with the fact the air outside the dome is not poisonous as they claimed. Not that I knew it when they banished me to the Wasteland wearing nothing but a gown. I didn't even have any shoes."

"You said before that a citizen lied about you attacking. Did you not have a chance to refute the claim?"

"At my trial, Jezebel spun a story of being a victim. A ridiculous fabrication that was believed even though there was video proof of her starting the altercation that showed I acted in self-defense, but no one cared."

"That's not a trial," he stated.

"No, it wasn't. They'd already decided to convict me for the entertainment of the crowd," she said softly, and he felt her sit beside him on the rock. "The thing that galls most is I used to be one of those spectators who cheered when they banished the guilty."

"At least you survived."

"Against all odds. Up until that point, I'd spent my entire life inside a dome. I went from a Creche right into the home of my master."

"Who was a pharmacist."

"Apothecary."

"What's the difference?"

"We make all of our remedies by hand specific to the client."

He couldn't help but remember the heat both times she applied the lotion to his face. "Then you infuse your stuff with magic to make it more potent."

"Magic? Don't be ridiculous," she said too quickly.

Could he be mistaken? "Is it normal to feel heat when you apply it?"

"It's a component reaction."

"It was already mixed and didn't heat until after being on my skin."

"Your skin is the last ingredient." The reply was weak, and it was clear she knew it.

"You've heard of magic." He changed the direction of the conversation.

"Who hasn't? People see magic in the simple things. Even sleight of hand can seem like magic if you believe."

"You're skeptical."

"Aren't you?" she replied. "Don't we know by now that things that seem like magic end up based in fact? The histories show—"

"What histories?" he asked with curiosity. "What do you know of our past?"

"I've come across many works that form a pretty clear picture of our past, before the Meteor Fall."

"Before? You saw these? With your own eyes?" The domes had a few advantages, one of them being knowledge of their past to draw on. Transient Wastelanders tended to start over often enough that they didn't really put down roots or accumulate things like books. Although his friend Titan—who'd gone missing—had made a point of searching out stories, especially the older ones.

She spoke of these books as if they were an ordinary everyday thing. "I've seen pictures of the past and been able to compare them to now. I've read books, old and new. The lifestyle described is vastly different from today."

"Where did you get the books?"

"The Library of course."

"You really are from a city," he said softly. "I've never met anyone who left the city before."

"You forget, I didn't leave voluntarily," she said with a snort.

"Do you miss it?

"Yes!" she exclaimed. "I miss the safety of it some days when I get lonely and something scares me. But..." Her voice softened. "There is something to be said about being answerable only to myself."

"Which is the very definition of freedom."

"How would you know? You're not free. You said you lived in some place called Haven. Which means you follow someone else's rules."

"I do. But gladly. Axel is a good man. Hates being in charge but he's damned good at it. I know he's ready to hand it off. He keeps hoping we'll find a place we can call our own."

"A hard task. The domes don't take people in."

"I know," he drawled. "They like to know the lineage of all their citizens. Although I'm sure they make exceptions for people with the right kind of magic."

"There is no such thing as magic."

"You keep saying it, sweetheart, but we both know you've got something happening with your hands."

"I don't."

"Really? Let's test that, shall we?" On a hunch, he reached out, his fingers brushing her leg, startling her.

Her fingers clasped his, and he laced them together.

"How does the healing work?" he asked. "Touch is the most obvious aspect since the heating only occurred when you placed your fingers on me. Do you need to picture the injury? Think about how you're going to fix it to activate your power?"

She snorted. "It's not power, just science. I use a blend of ingredients. Herbs mostly, blended with fatty agents when we want to make it more cream-like."

"The cream might help with the healing, act as building blocks so to speak, but the magic is what pulls it together."

She yanked her hand free. "There is no magic. It is a matter of promoting the right kind of microcellular repair with a careful measurement of ingredients. Which then react to provide an intense therapy."

If he could have blinked at the bullshit answer, he would have. "If that was the case, anyone could be a druggist."

"It takes skill."

"You said it yourself, it's about measurements and ingredients. Anyone could do it." He intentionally baited her, and she took it.

"No, not just anyone can!"

"Because not everyone has your kind of magic."

She huffed. "Magic isn't real."

"Really? Then explain why the Enclave can do things other people can't." He wondered if she'd deny it. Not everyone was aware they wielded power.

"What the Enclave can do isn't magic." She laughed.

"Then what is it?"

"Psionics."

That was a new word. "What is psionics?"

"How do you not know what psionics is?"

"Because I'm not Enclave, and I've never lived in a dome."

"Hmm. How to explain it?" she mused aloud.

"Try a basic definition first."

"Psionics are those who have developed psychic abilities that allow them to manipulate certain types of energy on a non-physical level."

"Meaning?"

"Meaning they use their minds to accomplish tasks. Some are incredible thinkers, able to process logic from complex math to reciting an exact passage from a book. Some can use the power of their mind to subdue that of another. It is said they can read everything that's in there and even plant commands."

"Mind control is a bad thing," he said softly.

"On that we can both agree. Thankfully it appears rather rare. The more common kind manipulates the elements. Ignite fires, control the flow of water, launch lightning bolts."

"I know people who can do those things, but they're not Enclave."

"Impossible."

"Denial in the face of evidence is stupid."

"What evidence?" she scoffed. "It's just you insisting."

"I am telling you, these powers you speak of, these psionic abilities, are not as special as the Enclave would like you to think, or as rare."

"Perhaps there are some with very minor traces."

He snorted. "Laura can toss people around without breaking a sweat or touching them. Axel talks to the Wolgar. I can assure you, both are far from being Enclave."

"That you know of. Could be they were never recognized."

"Meaning?"

She sighed. "I keep forgetting you're a Wastelander who doesn't understand how the domes work. When a child is born, they are sent to a Creche to see if they manifest psionic ability. If they do, then they are assigned to the Enclave. If they don't, they're either matched with a mentor or sent to the academy for further testing and dome assignment."

"You said you were sent to a Master."

"I was. Master Murray has been teaching me since my fourth year since birth."

"That's young."

"We are not the only ones who begin at that age. The culinary assistants, seamstress, cobblers, and more are apprenticed young, too."

"That is seriously messed up." He shook his head. "What I don't get is you said the Enclave has family. How come they get to keep their babies?" He'd only ever heard dribs and drabs of how the city worked over the years. City life might prove easier in some respects, but not everyone wanted that kind of confined existence.

"Yes and no. Usually a child presents its powers from birth and they remain with the Enclave, placed in special nurseries. If they don't, then—"

"The child goes to a Creche for a few years of observation to see if anything manifests." The very idea they were sorting people based on their powers was...fiendish yet brilliant. They were trying to encourage the proliferation of the Deviant gene. "You do realize they're segregating the population based on some strange principles."

"Never said I agreed with it. You asked how the Enclave members were chosen. I'm telling you."

"Does it ever happen that a regular citizen manifests this psionic power?"

"No." Said too quickly.

He prodded. "You're lying. You have heard of it happening." Heck, Laura, Axel's promised, was a late bloomer at almost thirty.

"I guess I don't need to pretend anymore." He could hear a frown in her tone. "It does happen. Not often, but enough you hear of it. A rumor that seems unbelievable until it happens to someone you kind of know and they exhibit psionic ability just like the Enclave."

"What happens when they're seen to have magic?"

"Psionic ability," she corrected.

"Whatever. What happens to them?"

"That person disappears. They don't join the Enclave that we're aware of. They're just gone."

"Did you never wonder what happened?"

"People who question also disappear." He could almost hear the shrug in her words.

"Given what happens, anyone exhibiting power might be cautious about letting it show," he mused aloud.

"I know what you're implying."

"And?" he prodded.

"And what? I don't have a psionic ability."

"So you say. Yet my face hardly hurts at all."

"The cream—"

"It's not the cream. It's you." He couldn't have said why the certainty. "Put your hands on my face."

"No."

"Then on my arm or hand. Find an injury."

"You have nothing fresh. Just some bruising and scabbed scratches."

"Proving my point. I shouldn't be that healed already."

"I make good remedies."

"Because you infuse them with magic!" he declared. "But I'll bet you don't need any fancy mixes at all. You can heal. Try it without the cream and see." He held out his arm.

She gripped his wrist. "This is dumb."

"Do it."

"Heal oh injured arm," she mocked.

"Say it like you mean it," he growled.

"You sound just like Master Murray. It must have intent," she said in a deep voice. "*Heal.*"

This time there was a burst of heat, nothing intense. She removed her hand.

"How does my arm look?"

He felt more than heard her shrug. "It's still bruised."

"I felt something."

"Because you wanted to. I'm not a psionic healer."

At her exclamation, Kitty returned, butting her head in his lap. He stroked the silky fur and veered the subject. "Given you don't have experience with children, why do you want to be a mother?"

"Why not?" she huffed. "And speaking of children, when are you going to start giving me samples so I can try to make a baby?"

"Any time you want a sample, just sit on my lap, sweetheart."

"Looks like that spot is taken."

Indeed, the cat wasn't budging from her sprawl across his thighs. "I'm sure we can find some privacy."

"You mean *you* can find some privacy. I'm sure you don't need my help collecting a sample."

He cringed. "Can you not call it a sample?"

"Then what should I term it? The fluid of possible progeny?"

He groaned. "Stop making it sound worse."

"Or what?"

"Or I won't be able to give you what you want."

Her tone was quite wicked as she said, "Don't worry. I have a cure for erectile dysfunction."

"There is nothing wrong with my cock."

"But you just said it couldn't perform."

"Forget it. I'm fine." Except he wasn't fine. He was blind, horny, and with a woman now convinced he couldn't get it up.

And then she made it worse. "Do you need a lotion to help make it bigger?"

NINE

"I don't need help with my size." He sounded rather choked. At least he fell quiet.

Sofia, a smile lurking around her lips, took a moment to study him. It wasn't as if he'd know. His eyes remained bound, and despite his belief she could perform psionic healing, the ravages of his injuries still showed. The scabs were almost ready to fall off. The skin under those that had, pink. He would be free of scars in another week so long as he kept putting on the cream. As for his eyes? Those would depend on the damage to the retinas.

She'd hurt herself pretty badly a few times while learning to survive. Luckily the oasis she'd fallen into possessed mud and herbs with excellent restorative properties. Or was she a latent psionic as he suggested?

Magic his people called it, even as there was nothing magic about it at all. Scientists in the city had measured and documented and written papers about psionic abilities. They had confirmed only Enclave members inherited it.

And she'd believed it. She stared at her hands. Surely it wasn't possible...

"Shouldn't we be going on the hunt for more soldiers?" he said.

"Not before you give me a sample. Just in case we find some and you don't survive."

"Your faith in me warms my heart," was his sarcastic drawl.

"Just being realistic. Once you've produced some seed, we'll go."

"How am I supposed to pass on my, um, donation to you?" he asked in a choked voice.

Was he ill? Perhaps she should wait. She didn't want a defective batch.

"We'll need a container. Will a cup be large enough, or should I gather the bucket?" She wasn't quite sure how much seed to expect, given Braun never managed to rape her. And a good thing, too, because he would have never impregnated her. He'd been proud of the fact he'd been sterilized.

He shouldn't have been so smug. It was the Enclave's way of ensuring he didn't accidentally procreate. They could be very particular when it came to the mixing of genetics.

Gunner coughed hard as he said, "No need for a bucket. A cup will be fine."

Would it still be warm when she got it? Or cold? Should she lie upside down and just pour it in? All she had was whispered stories of how to make it work outside a lab without having to actually copulate.

"I have a cup in the house you can use."

"Um, you're not going to watch, are you?"

The suggestion had her sucking in a breath. It sounded shocking, mostly because she wasn't sure what to expect. Did he require aid in expelling his seed?

"Do you need me to watch?" she asked on a high note.

"No," he growled.

"Good. Stay here and I'll get a cup."

"I am not doing it outside," he yelled, getting to his feet.

Kitty flowed under his fingers. Sofia could only stare as the man avoided a hole in the ground, lifted his foot over a rock, and weaved to avoid the corner of the house, yet she would swear he couldn't see.

And because she wanted to be sure, she called

his name, "Gunner?" Her fingers went to the hem of her shirt.

He paused. His head angled as he said, "What?"

She lost her nerve. "Nothing. The cup is in the bedroom. Left hand of the door. There is a hollow log against the wall." It contained items she'd scavenged.

He grunted before he went into the house, leaving her to pace as she mulled over the fact he was about to give her his seed. She'd then need to insert it. The very idea made her sick and giddy at the same time. It felt wrong. She just couldn't explain why. But the urge to have a baby overrode it. Having a child, an apprentice to teach, would rid her of the loneliness.

Then again, so would having a partner.

She glanced at the house. Was he done? Had he started? How long would it take?

Sofia moved toward the door and walked inside to find the main room empty. The bedroom door remained open. Surely that indicated invitation because he'd finished.

As she entered the bedroom, she noticed Kitty splayed on the bed while he sat with a pile of her things spread around him.

"I found your log and the stuff inside. Is this all you have?" he asked.

"Yup," she lied. She didn't keep the things she really valued in the open now, not since Braun. He'd taught her the reality of a woman on her own with no recourse.

Gunner appeared so different from him. Not prone to fits of violence. His language calmer and less insulting.

"You found a broken plate." He held up the half that remained. "A dented cup. A hunk of metal." He shook his head. "There's nothing useful in there I can use to fight with."

"You have a knife."

He laughed. "Which won't go far if we find another soldier."

"Even if I did have a better weapon, you can't really expect me to arm you." Braun came with a gun. In the end, it didn't save him, and she wasn't as stupid anymore. She wouldn't let anyone harm her.

"Not going to hurt you, sweetheart. I wish you believed me."

"I'll believe you when you keep your end of the bargain. Where's my sample?"

He choked again. Was he getting sick? "It's, um, too early in the day. I need some exercise if this is going to work."

She got the impression he didn't tell the truth, but then again, who was she to know? She sighed as she sat on the edge of the stripped bed. Kitty rolled and poked her legs in the air like she did when a kitten. On a grown feline, it was ridiculous. And cute.

"Silly Kitty." She rubbed the fur on her belly.

"She's another wind victim, isn't she?"

"More than likely, given I've never seen another." She rolled her shoulders.

"I always wanted a pet. Kylie, a little girl I know, has got a cat of her own, not as big as Kitty. Whereas, Axel, my boss, is part of a Wolgar pack."

"What's a Wolgar?" she asked.

"Big ferocious creature. A cross between the old wolves from the ancient days and felines. Some have long tails, kind of like Kitty. But their faces are mostly canine. Their coloring varies from white to black with gray and spotted in between."

"Kind of like humanity. Everyone has their own unique appearance."

"They also have distinct personalities according to Axel. They speak to him and even somehow understand him."

She frowned. "Kitty doesn't talk to me."

"But you understand her."

She shrugged. "Yes, but not because of any actual words. Just years of learning from each other."

"I'm glad you weren't alone." For some reason,

the soft admission brought a tremble to her lips and a moistening of her eyes.

He rattled among her things. "So where's your real stash of treasures?"

"I don't know what you mean."

"Come on. This is junk. You can't tell me you've never found anything better than this."

"Why would I show you?" Or in this case, let him grope. "I worked hard to comb these woods to find things before they were rendered useless."

"I am not going to steal anything. Maybe borrow, but only so I can protect us if indeed there are more people in the woods."

"You think there are?" She'd gotten relaxed again, given the lack of danger. Kitty didn't seem worried, and usually she took her cue from the cat.

"I don't know. And I can't see anything to track. Not yet, at least." He didn't say not ever, but it hung in the air.

How frightened he must be. Unable to see. She moved closer. He didn't react. She stared down at him.

"A gun won't be any use to a blind man," she remarked.

"You'd be surprised. Or have you forgotten the way I nailed that creature last night?"

"Luck."

He snorted. "Very possible. But I'll need more than luck if all I have is a puny knife to defend us."

"I don't know what you want me to tell you. There is nothing else. The winds giveth what they find."

"The winds should have given you a sword."

Her lips parted at the word. "Actually, I know where there is a sword. But I couldn't pull it free. It's embedded too deep in stone."

"Can you bring me to it?"

She hesitated. Should she arm him with a proper weapon? "Will you promise not to use it on me?"

"Don't be ridiculous. Of course, I won't use it on you or Kitty." He sounded insulted she even suggested it.

"Will you give me your seed after we fetch it?"

"Yes, dammit. Can we go?"

Sofia whistled. "Kitty, let's take Gunner to see the sword in the rock."

Bounding off the bed, the feline immediately placed herself by Gunner's side, and his fingers twined into her fur.

Sofia led the way, only occasionally glancing back at Gunner being led by her cat. He was surer footed than he had a right to be. She had both her eyes working and still managed to stumble more than once.

Getting to the rock required following the shoreline, which was why she noticed the river flowing even higher than before. "The water is rising."

"How high does it usually go?" he asked.

"That's just it. I don't know. Five years I've been here, and I've never seen it rise above the banks before."

"And you said it never rains."

She shook her head, caught herself, and said, "No."

"But this place is so damp," he mused aloud.

"Meaning?"

"I don't know. It's just odd. Speaking of damp, do you see any footprints in the ground? The heavy suits usually leave an impression."

She shook her head before replying. "Nothing. We're probably worrying about nothing."

A feeling that grew as they actually did come across some strewn debris. Parts of them the remains of Centurion suits, the torn and bloody marks on them leaving no doubt as to the fate of their owner.

The trip to the mouth of the river took the rest of that morning. It was a full day's trek moving from one end of the valley to the other.

"We're here," she shouted as the water emerging from the mountainside gurgled loudly.

"Tell me about the sword."

"I told you, it's sticking out of the rock." The winds must have whipped it into the stone because it simply appeared one day a few weeks ago. She eyed the handle, the dull metal thick, leading to a thin blade with the tip embedded in the stone. A frown creased her brow as she noticed water dripping from the sword, a steady stream that appeared to be fed by the crack around it. A pocket of moisture in the rock obviously leaking.

"Can you put my hand on it? I'd like to touch it." For some reason, he smiled.

"You'll have to lean and try not to fall in."

"I won't fall if you don't push."

Interestingly enough, the thought hadn't occurred to her until he mentioned it. "I'll do my best to resist."

She took his hand and tugged him closer to the river's edge, the rigid stone unlikely to sluice off into the water. She leaned across his body and placed their linked hands on the pommel. His other arm curled around her waist and held her.

"Can you feel it?" she asked, a tad breathlessly.

"Yes." A single low syllable.

She straightened, and yet he didn't release her; he held her closer. She should demand he unhand her. Instead Sofia started at the squareness of his rugged jaw. She'd seen handsome men in the city.

Everyone was attractive in their fashion. However, Gunner had an extra element to his features. They appeared vivid and real. A man who'd lived. A man who felt. A man she desired...

"I've been thinking about our kiss," he said.

The comment took her by surprise. "You have?"

"Can you blame me? That kiss was hot, and I wouldn't mind a repeat."

The very thought baffled her. She touched her cheek, feeling the rigid scar. It wouldn't go away no matter how many remedies she applied. It remained a reminder of her banishment. He'd never kiss her if he saw it.

But he couldn't see it.

She also remembered the heat of the kiss. Was it just the intimacy and fear of the dark that made it seem so wonderful?

"You may kiss me."

"Thank fuck." He growled the soft words against her mouth, and this time, in broad daylight, she kept her eyes open.

She stared at the fabric wrapped around his eyes. He couldn't see her. It seemed only fair she not see him. She closed her eyes and held her breath as his mouth touched hers.

Gently. Teasingly.

It drew halting breaths from her as he slid his lips back and forth.

As with the last kiss, she tingled all over, and the ache between her legs returned. He kissed her harder, sucking on her lower lip, parting and claiming her mouth in a way that had her panting, heaving for breath, clutching at him, her body trembling and pressing against his.

He groaned her name, "Sofia," and pressed her against the rock wall only a pace from the edge that fell into the river. Yet she didn't ask to move. Not with his frame hard against hers. His mouth hot. His hands roamed her body, igniting her in a way she'd never imagined. Teasing a response that had her aching. Her past experiences never prepared her for this. This was what they meant by passion.

He slid a hand past the waistband of her trousers and cupped her. Her legs buckled, and she would have slid to the ground if he'd not caught her.

He held her, and a single finger began to stroke. The intimacy of it shocking. Titillating. Not the pain she expected. No fear to make her tense.

She panted against his mouth. Small cries escaped her.

He penetrated her with a finger, his kiss deep, his tongue joining and making her sob with pleasure.

Her hips quivered, and she felt tight inside. Tight and desperate and...

Something happened. A strange force possessed her, and she arched, screaming as her body pulsed. So good. It felt so damned good. She radiated with heat and lethargy. She didn't realize she clung tight to him until he gasped.

"Fuck me. Oh. Fuck," he murmured against her mouth as his finger rested inside her pulsing body. His hips were pressed against her, pinning his hand between them.

He leaned his forehead against hers and breathed hotly. "That was incredible."

It was. And a good thing he had a mask, because she doubted she could have hidden how much it shook her. Because she now finally got it. And wanted it again.

TEN

Sofia pushed at Gunner, and he moved away. His hand came out of her pants and brought the scent of her with it.

He might have gotten hard if he hadn't heard her gasp. "Why are the front of your pants wet?"

Gunner wanted to sink into the ground. Throw himself in the river. Anything to remove himself from the embarrassment.

When she'd come, a wave of something slammed out of her. The best word he could say was pleasure. She hit him with her pleasure, and his body immediately orgasmed.

"Remember the part where I said it was incredible?"

"But I never even touched you. Don't you require...I don't know, some kind of manipulation?"

His shame grew, and he stammered, "Usually, uh, yeah, um." He cleared his throat. "I'm sorry. But the feel of you made me lose control."

"Me?" She sounded so surprised.

"Yes, you. This doesn't usually happen," he grumbled.

To which she giggled. "Is this the wrong time to remark we should have brought that cup?"

He groaned. "This isn't funny."

"Depends on who's embarrassed, and judging by the expression on your face, that would be you." Her laughter rang out, and he couldn't help but smile.

"I promise I'll do better next time."

"Who says there'll be a next time?" she sassed.

There would be a next time if he had anything to say about it.

"So did you want to try and yank on the sword now?" she asked.

"I might need a few minutes to recover before we start yanking on it."

It took her a moment. But she finally gasped. "I didn't mean that sword."

"Probably best you don't touch me yet, or we'll never get anything done."

"You need to be serious." She sounded flustered. "Give me your hand, and I'll place it on the shaft."

His mind went to a dirty place, but he remained

quiet. Mostly because he didn't want to tease her too much. The very fact she'd trusted him enough to kiss and fondle her was amazing. He'd still have to be careful. Her upbringing and experiences made her skittish.

Her fingers tugged at his. Gunner leaned to the side, anchoring her close with an arm.

She made a satisfying sound that had a tiny moan in it.

"Do you have it?" she asked, wrapping his hand around the hilt.

"I've got it." And he didn't just mean the sword. "Step away just in case it comes too fast. I don't want to knock you out by accident."

"What if you lose your balance?"

"I can swim."

He felt the loss of her body the moment she slipped to the side. His fingers tested the grip of the sword, feeling the ridges. The thickness just right. He gave it a slight wiggle. Up and down, side to side.

Not much give.

He tried a tug. It didn't budge a bit.

"Told you it was stuck."

"I'll get it out." Mostly just because it felt like a challenge. He began wobbling it again, up and down, a little side to side, felt it loosen.

Quiet up until now, Kitty growled, a distinct rumble over that of water rushing past.

"What's wrong?" Sofia asked.

"Take cover," he advised.

"I'm not taking cover. Someone has to check out whatever is agitating her, meaning me. I'll go, while you work on the sword."

"What if it's another soldier?"

"I'll aim for the joints," she riposted.

But he didn't find the situation amusing at all. What if another enemy roamed the woods? What if Sofia needed him?

In that case, he'd need a weapon.

He wiggled the sword. It had a little give to it now. It wouldn't be long surely before it came free and he had a few feet of steel to swing around.

Over the rushing of water, he heard the crunch of gravel. Doubted it was the cat. Kitty had a way of walking silent, and his instincts told him it wasn't Sofia.

"Well, well," said a voice without the benefit of the comm speaker in a helm. "Looks like we're not alone here after all."

The use of "we" was worrisome. Where had Sofia gone?

His fingers tightened on the hilt. It didn't budge.

The soldier chuckled. "Thanks for making this easy."

Acting on instinct, Gunner released the sword and ducked to the ground while, at the same time, sweeping a foot. That only managed to bruise him given the robot armor added weight and stability.

"Fucker." He didn't entirely miss the fist that came swinging, the edge of metal knuckles snapping his head sideways.

Gunner shook it off and popped to his feet, arms up in defense. But he couldn't stop the staggering blows. The soldier might have lost his helmet by the sounds of it, but he'd kept on the rest of the suit.

His body was bruised with each hammer punch, but Gunner grunted and rolled with the pain, using all his other senses to try to keep up a defense. Hoping to get a chance. Until the blow that knocked him to the ground.

His ears rang. His head spun. His body refused to get up.

Through the rushing in his ears, he heard Sofia yell, "Leave him alone."

"Or what? Better be nice to me or I'll kill your friend. Get on your knees. Hands behind your head."

"You heard Opie. On your knees, woman." The second voice brought a chill.

Two soldiers.

A roar showed Kitty had joined the party. The *rat-tat-tat* and the shriek of pain followed by Sofia's scream made his blood run cold.

"Kitty," Sofia sobbed.

Please let the furball only be injured. He'd gotten attached in the short time and would hate it if Kitty died.

"Strip her and turn her over. I don't want to see her face when I'm inside her." The crudeness came from the one who'd felled Gunner, the one called Opie.

Opie's friend wasn't happy about the plan. "How come you get to go first again?"

"Because I'm higher ranked than you."

"Like fuck."

While the soldiers argued, Sofia sobbed, a wrenching sound that tore at him. He had to help her. He pushed to his knees, his fingers sliding over the rock and off the edge of it. It helped orient him.

Feeling with his other hand showed the location of the wall, the very same one he'd just had Sofia pressed against while he made her come. It burned that someone threatened her while he lay useless on the ground.

If there was ever a time he needed good luck, it was now. He rose to his feet and leaned, reaching for the sword, grasping it and heaving it free with a mighty groan.

Screech.

Apparently, there was a sound when a sword freed itself from stone. A jarring noise that drew attention.

"Looks like the blind bastard wants another beating. Tell you what, you go first and warm the slut up for me. I'll take my turn right after I kill her friend." The soldier spoke his last words while giving Gunner a direction.

"Aren't you a big man, attacking a defenseless woman and a blind man," he taunted.

Clomp. Clomp. The noise of the soldier gave his position away. Gunner feinted the blade toward the man, knowing he'd raise an arm to deflect it. Standard defense tactics. Only Gunner didn't follow through but instead dropped and slid the blade between the man's legs before ramming up at a soft part of the armor.

The scream proved strident and short as he finished the job and tipped the soldier in the direction of the river.

Then he listened. Heard nothing but grunts.

He was too late. "Sofia!" he yelled, striding toward the sounds, only to hear her scream, "Don't swing; it's me!"

He froze, sword raised. "Sofia? Are you okay? Where's the other soldier?"

"Dead."

She didn't say how as she threw herself at him and sniffled against his chest. "He never thought to check me for a knife."

"Are you hurt?"

"No. But that jerk shot Kitty."

"We'll find Kitty and fix her. Are you sure you're okay?" He wanted to say so many things, starting with an apology. He'd been so intent on pleasuring her that he'd let his guard down. This was his fault.

"Just bruised. I attacked the soldier while he was in the midst of taking off his armor. I stabbed him in the neck."

"Good." He stroked her back. "Did you spot signs of more?"

She shook her head against him. "Not living ones. I did see some robot suit pieces in the woods, though. They still had body parts in them."

"Here's to hoping the rest are all dead."

"If not, you have a sword."

"I do." Despite not being able to see it, he lifted it.

"I think you broke the rock it was in. It's got all kind of cracks now, and they're weeping water even worse than before," she noted before yelling, "I see Kitty!"

She moved from him, and he heard her fussing over her pet, which was enough to bring him slowly toward her.

"Do I need to carry Kitty to the house?" he asked.

Sofia snorted. "Do you want her to bite off your head? Her wound must not be too bad. She's moving on her own."

"And you're sure you're okay to walk?" he asked.

"I told you, I'm fine. It's—"

The rumble wasn't just a sound but also a sensation that evolved into a loud cracking and many splashes. When it was done, the river noise had increased ten times.

"What happened?" he yelled, getting the sense this wasn't good.

"The rock the sword was in broke, and now there's a torrent of water coming in. It's making the river rise."

"Let's get to higher ground. It will probably taper off once whatever reservoir was behind it empties," he suggested, extending his hand.

She gripped his fingers, and while she tugged him, he also got the sense she peered back often. He wished he could peek, too. The river roared as it rushed past.

"Can you tell if the flow is abating?" Assuming she could still see the start of it.

"No. The hole has gotten bigger, and the shoreline is almost gone. We need to hurry." She broke into a run, and he did his best to follow, but she didn't have a smooth gait like the cat.

He released her. "Go ahead and pack a bag. Two if you have enough supplies."

"Why?"

"Because if the water keeps rising, then we'll want to be on the highest ground."

"Oh. But you said it would stop."

"I don't know if it will. We should be prepared." He heard her steps scrambling from him, and the cat took her place, the sleek fur under his palm familiar and welcome. He felt the hitch in her stride. "Hold on, Kitty. Once we get to safety, we'll get Sofia to try some of her healing on it." If they survived the next few hours.

He had a bad feeling about the situation.

ELEVEN

Something bad was about to happen, and she had no one to blame but herself as she ran in a state of panic for her house. She was the one who'd led Gunner to the sword in the stone. If he'd left it wedged, the river wouldn't be rising so rapidly. Then again, if he'd not grabbed that sword, they'd probably both be dead.

The reminder pressed her lips into a tight line. She was getting mighty tired of being treated as if her wishes didn't matter. Gunner was the only one who never treated her that way. He might tease her, but he didn't command her. He did, however, please her.

She made it to her house and went around the side looking for the sliver of shadow that marked the spot. Inside a tiny little passage hid her real treasure store, containing one makeshift bag filled with emergency items. Dried food, herbs, clothes. She quickly fabricated a second sack using a sheet to tuck in spare shoes that didn't fit well, more clothes, and an empty flask that would need filling.

As she emerged with her two bags, Kitty came into view, guiding Gunner.

"The water is still rising," he announced as if he knew she stood there.

"How can you tell?"

"Because there were four fewer steps coming up. Now please tell me we can go higher than the cliff I tossed that body off of."

"You think the water will flood the house?"

"I think it's a distinct possibility. Depending on how much of it needs to exit to equalize, that water could rise much further."

"We can move to a higher elevation than the cliff, but it will require climbing." Which wasn't the easiest thing for someone raised in a city to learn. She'd torn her hands open and scraped herself quite a bit teaching herself how to survive.

"Do you have any rope?"

"I've got some vines."

"Good enough. Give me what you grabbed while you fetch them."

She handed him only one of the sacks. She didn't need him to carry hers. When she returned with two bundles of vine, he'd somehow managed to sling the sheet sack so it hung over his shoulder. He took a bundle of rope and wound it around his waist. She followed suit.

Was it her, or did the water sound louder? She glanced down the path to the river and could have sworn she saw a glint. Surely it hadn't crept to this level this quickly?

"Ready?" he asked.

"Not really," she grumbled.

He bumped into her before snaring her hand. "We'll be fine. The water will probably taper before it even reaches the house. This is just a precaution."

The words were meant to sound soothing, and yet she got the impression that, underneath, he did worry.

"What will we do if the water doesn't stop rising?" They were trapped inside a veritable bowl.

"Let's handle that problem if we get to it. One thing at a time. Since you know where the highest point is, you lead. Kitty and I will follow."

Giving her a task actually helped to focus her. It wasn't as if she'd not climbed the location before.

She moved for the rock ruins behind the house.

The collapse from the mountain wall had crushed the back end of the home and any yard it might have possessed. A shame she'd thought upon discovering it, but now, needing to get onto elevated ground, it provided a slope that took them well above the roofline of the house. Unfortunately, their elevation didn't quite reach the top of the mountain.

By the time they panted their way to the peak of the debris, she realized it wouldn't be enough. The sun had begun sinking in the sky, but she could still see the dilemma creeping toward them.

"The water is still rising," was her grim announcement.

"I was afraid it might. I'm just surprised it didn't happen before now. The pressure that must have been behind that rock..."

The scarier thing was it could have happened at any time. She now understood that the leaking she'd seen coming from the sword was a warning. She should have heeded the change in the river. Lucky for her, at least she was able to stay ahead of the rising waters. She didn't want to imagine what she would have done if the house flooded while she slept.

"What are we going to do if it reaches us?" Because it showed no signs of stopping.

"Can you swim?"

"No. And what good will that do? We can't swim forever. How will we eat? Sleep?"

His lips pressed into a line. "I wish I could see."

"How would seeing change the situation? We're going to drown." She couldn't help the morose statement.

"We are not giving up yet. How tall is the mountain still?"

"At least another four or five of you."

"Which is longer than our ropes," he mused aloud. "Anything else around? A ledge? A hole?"

"Nothing we can reach." She saw an actual cave far to their left. A dark maw that reminded her of the one the river entered and exited via, now submerged.

"Time to use those vines. We need to tether ourselves, so we don't lose each other."

"What about Kitty?"

"Kitty is a survivor. She'll be fine. I'm more worried about you. Stay close to the wall. As the water lifts us, try and use any hand- and toeholds you can find it to keep your face above it."

His hands worked quickly, taking her vine and looping it around them both, staying balanced despite the slim lip of rock they stood on.

The last slice of sunlight began to slip past the far edge of the mountain, and her pulse raced in panic. "I'm scared, Gunner."

"Don't be, sweetheart. You're tough. You'll survive this."

"How can you be sure?"

He reached for her and held her hands. "Because I didn't just find you to lose you."

She knew he said it only to soothe her, but she still enjoyed it. "I'm glad I met you." Glad she met a man who brought her pleasure, not fear. Who didn't mind how tightly she gripped him when the sun dipped past the mountains and they plunged into darkness.

"Breathe, sweetheart."

Instead she squeaked as she felt the first lap of water against her toes. Cold water. It rose past her ankles.

Kitty let out a very unhappy meow.

"If we survive—"

"Not if. We are going to live to see the dawn." He squeezed her hand.

"How can you be sure?"

"Because I refuse to die until you and I have done our best to put a baby in your belly."

For some reason, she blurted out, "I forgot to bring a cup."

Which made him laugh. A boisterous sound with no fear at all. "Screw your cup and a sample. We're going to make a child the ancient way."

"Oh." In the darkness, her cheeks heated.

He drew her to his chest and did his best to keep her tucked as long as he could. The water crept higher, past her knees, and moved up her thighs. The amount of liquid was staggering. The rapidity of the rise even more astonishing. Soon they were gripping the rocky wall to stay afloat. The water kept rising, and her feet lost purchase.

She squeaked, and Kitty let out a mournful yowl.

It was Gunner who murmured, "Hold on. It can't keep flowing higher forever."

Maybe it would. Maybe it would lift to the top of the mountains and then carry them over to be dashed over the other side.

"Do you feel that?" he asked suddenly, his face a lighter shadow in the scant starlight.

"Feel what?" Cold. Wet. Miserable. She didn't want to complain, given they weren't actually dead.

"The water's starting to tug."

She opened her mouth to refute his claim then felt the slight current. "What does it mean?"

"A way out."

Her eyes widened. "The cave! I thought I saw one. But we couldn't reach it before."

"Let's see if we can reach it before it's flooded."

"How are we supposed to find it in the dark?" she asked.

"Follow the current."

The good news was the hole the water found not only gave them a direction it also slowed the water. The closer they drew to the cave, the stronger the current.

"Hold on to the rope," he advised. "I think we're about to go on a ride."

Before she could ask what he meant, the current sucked them all in, much to Kitty's yowling displeasure. Sofia went from seeing stars to pure darkness. The echo and roar of water being tunneled through the mountain surrounded her, moving faster and faster before sloping down. She screamed, the sound lost in the rush as the water flung her, bouncing her off rocky walls, dunking her head under, and trying to drown her with mouthfuls of water. The only thing that kept her sane was the tug of the rope around her waist. Knowing he was near.

After forever, the water shot free and dragged her along with it. She screamed as she felt herself go airborne.

She jolted as the tether on her waist held. It didn't stop her from swinging and slamming into a rocky face.

"Ouch," she whimpered against the rock.

Amidst the constant roar of water, she heard Gunner yell, "Hold on. I'll pull you up to the ledge."

A glance through wet lashes and enough starlight meant she saw him silhouetted against a rocky wall, his hands gripping the vine. Doing his best to pull her up.

Which was when the vine snapped and she plummeted.

TWELVE

Horror filled Gunner as the moment the vine tore and Sofia plummeted.

The jolt almost dragged off him the ledge. He moved quickly to pull up the rope; he just wasn't fast enough. Kitty, who'd managed to somehow claw her way to safety on the other side of the hole, roared when the makeshift rope snapped.

He almost yelled too because he knew Sofia couldn't swim. If she didn't die in the fall, she'd drown. He didn't even think twice.

"I'm going after her. See you at the bottom, Kitty." Gunner dove off the edge.

The chance was strong he'd die, especially if the water was shallow. If he didn't die pulverized by rocks, then he could still drown, especially if he lost his way under the water.

He could get eaten. Monsters lived everywhere, and all of them had a taste for human flesh.

Or he might finally get a decent break and find Sofia before she sank and get them both to shore.

Luck, don't fail me now.

He hit the surface of the water and dropped like a rock, far enough that he wondered if there was a bottom. He hit it with enough momentum he was able to bend his legs and push. He kicked to the surface and emerged, yelling, "Sofia!"

If she answered, he didn't hear it over the roar of the waterfall.

"Sofia!" He floated on top of the water, not hearing anything above the sound of falling water.

He kicked, moving outwards, following the slight current. Something bumped him from underneath, and he froze, making his body as still as possible. He was nudged again, and suddenly, finding shore seemed a very good idea.

He swam for it, muttering, "Fuck me. I will not be eaten by a fish."

"Don't fight it! It's not dangerous."

The shout had him freezing again, because it sounded like Sofia. "Sweetheart? Is that you?"

"Gunner!"

"Holy fuck. I'm coming. Keep talking." He

aimed for her voice. Whatever bumped him along was bringing him closer.

Anything that didn't eat him was good. His feet hit bottom, and he realized he could stand. He sloshed forward, barely keeping his balance as Sofia threw herself at him.

"You're here! How did you get down so quickly?" she exclaimed.

"I jumped."

"To save me?" she squeaked.

"Of course." Then, because he was ridiculously happy to realize she was alive, he cupped her face and drew her close for a kiss. A long kiss. "I told you we couldn't die."

She laughed. "I can't believe we're alive. Where's Kitty?"

"Up top most likely. I'm hoping she can find a way down."

"I'm sure she will. She's clever that way."

"What was that in the water? Did you see it?" he asked, amazed there existed something in this world that wasn't trying to kill him.

"Some kind of strange creature. Like a slither, but bigger, with a fin on its back. It was hard to see. It only popped out of the water for a second."

"I'm glad you didn't drown." He kissed her again,

passion simmering, but he was too tired, wet, and cold to do anything about it.

He pulled away reluctantly and took stock of their situation. They had almost nothing left. They'd lost their packs during the wild ride, and while he'd been lucky enough to keep the sword strapped by his side, and Sofia a knife, they had nothing else, not even a flint, which meant huddling on a rock, her body spooned against his, shivering in their damp clothes, waiting for the dawn. It didn't prove to be a restful slumber.

The dawn, when it appeared, prickled his lids hotly, making him realize he'd lost the bandage sometime during his swim.

The morning glare glowed orange, and holding his breath, he tried to open his eyes, only to cringe as they burned. "Fuck."

"What's wrong?" She obviously either slept lightly or not at all.

"My eyes still hurt." They also watered fiercely.

"You lost your bandage," she chided.

"A bandage isn't going to make a difference. You need to try and heal me again."

"I can't. I don't have anything to put on your eyes."

"You don't need any creams or potions. Use your

magic. Or psionic power. Whatever you want to call it."

"I don't have powers. Let me see if I can find something that might soothe," she grumbled.

"Don't go far. We don't know what kind of dangers might lurk."

"Is this a good time to mention we appear to be in a dead forest? The land is dry and cracked, the trees twisted and stunted."

"What of the water?"

"Good thing we slept on high ground. Looks like the lake we landed in rose overnight."

"Are we in danger? Do we need to move?"

"I think we're okay. The higher waterfall has stopped pouring."

"What higher waterfall?"

"The one I think we came out of. There's still another one much lower. I bet it's the one by the house that exits the mountain." Her voice came from his left.

"Any sign of Kitty?"

"Not yet. Don't move and keep your eyes shut." Something cold and slimy was smeared on his face.

"That better be mud."

"What else would it be?"

"Poop." He said it bluntly.

Sofia giggled. "That would mean touching it, so no. Ew."

Her mirth did something to him. Wrenched him inside. "You should laugh more often."

"Hasn't been much to laugh about," she remarked, spreading the mud.

"Maybe that will change."

"Given we left a place that could feed and house us and are now in a dead forest, I doubt it."

"Where there's water, there is life," he said.

"No spare clothes or supplies. Not even shoes. I lost mine in the lake."

"We'll find you some new ones. One day at a time, sweetheart. We escaped. Next, we survive."

She sighed and leaned into him, her comfort around him a thing he took pleasure in.

"And then what?" she asked. "Feels like all I've been doing is surviving. When does it become less work?"

For once he had an answer. "When you share that burden with someone else."

"Is this an endorsement to join your Wasteland gang?"

"And if it is?

"How can they help me? I thought they were looking for a home."

"Once we find one..." He shrugged.

"Then what?"

What indeed. It was probably cocky, but he said it anyway. "We make a baby. Maybe even more than one."

She snorted. "Who says I'd want you to make a second?"

He tugged her close. "Because you can't get any more awesome than me."

"Conceited much?" she teased, but she didn't pull away.

"Admit it, I'm growing on you."

"I admit nothing." She pressed her fingers to his muddy lids and whispered, "Heal." Then more deeply. "*Heal.*"

The heat hit, igniting his lids, and he couldn't help but place his hands on her waist, drawing her close, his face nuzzling her damp top. The heat from her fingers stuttered then increased as the digits slid away and only her thumbs pressed. The change in her grip meant he could press even closer and feel the rapid flutter of her heart.

If he touched her between the legs, would he find her as damp as before? She'd been so wet and ready for him. Responsive to his touch.

He kissed her through the fabric of her shirt and

rubbed his mouth sideways to skim the curve of her breast, loving how her breath hitched.

When the heat finally stopped, they both panted. Rather than kneel by him, she straddled him, her core pressing against him, his erection ready to redeem itself. He cupped her cheeks and drew her in for a kiss.

Her sweet, soft lips parted and welcomed it.

"Good morning," he whispered softly and opened his eyes. The mud and sunlight stabbed them, and he shut them again, feeling them tear and burn.

She chuckled. "You might want to wash the mud off first."

What he wanted was to take off his pants and sink into her. Have her ride him until she came so hard again she literally exploded.

But his eyes burned as if they had soap in them. The water was nearby, and he spent a moment rinsing his face. When he was done, he blinked and got a blurry mash of colors. He shut them and used the hem of his shirt to wipe at his face. Then opened them again before he yelled in relief, "I can see!"

He whirled and looked for the woman he'd been spending the last few days with. More beautiful than he could have imagined. Her hair long and dark.

Disheveled, but he'd felt the silken sheen of it when washed and brushed. Her figure was trim yet curvy, which he knew by feel. Her head ducked, giving him only the barest curve of her cheek.

"Sofia," he teased. "Look at me. You healed me."

"No, I didn't." She wouldn't lift her head. "The mud here must be potent."

"You're potent," he grumbled and swept her into his arms. "You're the one who saved my eyes." Who'd saved him.

The woman who melted at his touch but now acted as if she couldn't bear to look at him.

"What's wrong?" he asked as she kept her chin down and her hair fell in her face, covering it.

"Nothing."

"Then why won't you look at me?"

A heavy breath heaved out of her. "Fine." Her chin angled, and she looked him square in the face. Her eyes vivid, the lashes thick. Her lips a sensual bow he wanted to taste again.

"There you are," he said with a crooked smile. He went to drop a light kiss on her mouth, but she pulled away.

"You don't have to pretend."

"Pretend what?"

"That you still want me."

He blinked. "I am not pretending."

"Please. I know you can see the scar. It's hideous." Her hand lifted to her cheek.

The slash went across it in a silvery line that he barely noticed. But apparently it bothered her. "If you don't like it, then heal it."

Her lips turned down. "I tried. They must have done something so it wouldn't heal. Nothing I've applied to it has worked."

"Then don't worry about it. It's a scar. So what." He shrugged. "Everyone has some."

"You don't."

"What are you talking about? I've got plenty. See..." His voice trailed off as he lifted his hands to show her. He frowned. "What happened to my scars?" His hands remained calloused, but the slash across the back of the left one, recently a jagged strip, showed only a light line, as if he'd tanned wrong.

"I don't know what kind of doctor you have, but with the right remedy, scars can be removed."

"Ain't no cream can fix that. It's your magic."

"If I had that kind of magic, don't you think I would have fixed this?" She angled her cheek at him. Angry. And so wrong about the look of it.

As if he cared. He shook his head at her. They'd really done a mental wash on her. What would it take for her to grasp that what she did was special?

"You're beautiful to me." When she would have

turned away, he cupped her face and made her look at him. He rather liked her eyes with their hazel centers flecked with gold. "I think you're beautiful."

"And I think I'm going to puke," drawled a deep voice. "Grab 'em!"

THIRTEEN

Sofia could have borrowed some of Gunner's curse words at the interruption. The intensity of Gunner's gaze, knowing of the pleasure that might follow the kissing...

Gunner murmured, "Stick close while I handle our company."

After what she'd had to do lately, she was more than happy to let him deal with it.

He used his body to partially shield her from the two men in front of them. Burly fellows wearing strange half-pants made of a dark, coarse fabric that ended loosely at the knees. Leathery vests covered their bare chests and did little to cover the piercings. From the nose on the freckled one with spiked reddish hair to rings dangling from the nipples on the dark-skinned man.

More worrisome, they each held a weapon. A gun for Freckles and a curved dagger for Rings.

"Keep your hands where I can see them." Freckles had a guttural way of speaking.

Gunner still had his sword, but he held his hands out to his sides, as if trying to appear benign. Would these men show strangers any mercy? She'd always heard of the Wasteland Rats being murderous people. Braun certainly was, yet Gunner proved far from it. There was obviously more than one type.

And these ones looked particularly rough. The animal hanging from the belt on Freckles especially chilled because she'd not seen any signs yet of her cat. She worried something fierce about Kitty. In the morning light, she'd searched every visible inch of the mountain face from the opening where water had stopped running, all the way down, hoping to see her nimble feline. Nothing. The rising dawn showed the tops of lush trees submerged by the enlarged lake that coasted from the waterfall. A new shoreline had been created, muddy already and showing signs of growth. Farther from it, where they'd spent the night, stunted trees, dry and brittle, the reason why they'd not seen the two men sneaking up on them.

"Morning," Gunner said, still pretending he wasn't worried.

Rings snorted. "Not so good for you now that we've interrupted your tryst." He leered, and she tucked closer to Gunner.

"Your timing could have been better," Gunner admitted wryly. "But I'm glad to see you. I don't suppose you can tell me where we are. I don't recognize this area. What part of Emerald is this?"

"Emerald?" Freckles guffawed and spat. "This ain't that Enclave queen's land. You're in the Marshlands now, and the king will reward us richly for bringing him foreign spies."

"We're not spies," Sofia exclaimed. "We came here by accident."

"Sure ya did," Rings drawled. "Except for the fact there ain't no approved road in this direction, meaning you skipped the checkpoint and the mountain pass tolls."

"We were caught in a storm and lost our way," Gunner interjected smoothly. "We would be more than happy to be shown the correct path."

"We'll show you all right," Freckles snickered. "Even give you a ride."

"That's nice of you, but we prefer to walk. My woman likes to collect plants."

"And yet she doesn't have a bag, or even shoes." An astute observation.

"The storm." Gunner shrugged. "We lost just

about everything when it viciously shoved us into the lake."

"A likely story from spies. Hand over your weapons."

Freckles aimed the gun at Gunner, and she felt him tense. Still, he pulled the sword free from the straps holding it and knelt to place it on the ground.

It was Rings who said, "The knives too."

Gunner pulled his other blade but not the one hidden in his boot. No one even looked at her, and she kept her hands by her sides lest they try and disarm her as well.

"Hands on your head," Freckles ordered. "Tie 'em up."

"With what?" Rings snorted. "The rope's in the truck."

The mention caught Gunner's attention, not that he said anything. He laced his hands over his head as ordered.

"You, woman, hands on your head, too."

While she wondered at Gunner's plan, she obeyed, quickly placing her hands on her crown. She hoped the hilt of her knife wouldn't peek from her waist, where it remained tucked under the vine belt, hidden by the loose folds of her shirt and pants.

Something cracked in the forest, drawing Freckles' attention, but not Rings'. He sidled close to

Gunner and whispered, "Move the wrong way, and I will gut you."

"Did you see that?" Freckles asked, frowning off in the distance.

"See what? There ain't nothing in those woods."

"I don't know. I thought I seen something." Freckles glanced to the lake. "King is going to want to know about the water getting so high." He pointed. "Maybe they weren't lying and there was a storm."

"Either way, they're coming with us." Rings shoved Gunner. "Get walking."

She wondered if she should be insulted the men didn't pay her any attention and just expected her to follow. Given she didn't want to remain here alone, or get murdered, she did.

Gunner had yet to act, meaning he probably had a plan. Or so she hoped. This new man, with his beautiful blue eyes, wasn't the same one she'd gotten to know. He walked with a casual swagger. Appeared so unconcerned he managed to look over his shoulder at her and offer a wink.

A wink, as if they were on a merry stroll.

Yet she had to admit his ease helped with the fear that kept her muscles taut with tension.

As they walked, Freckles and Rings discussed the new lake.

"Water hasn't been this high since my father was a lad," Freckles announced.

"Fucking lake buried my patch of weed."

Rings snorted. "Shit stank."

"Because it was potent," Freckles insisted. "Now what am I supposed to trade?"

"Grow a new one. It's not like it takes long to sprout."

"I guess." Freckles glanced in the direction of the water that she saw occasionally through the trees.

The scraggly bushes thickened, the dry branches tugging at skin and clothes. When she cried out as a sharp stick snarled in her hair, Gunner whirled, his expression creased in concern.

"You okay, sweetheart?"

"She's fucking fine." Freckles shoved him and waved his gun. "Keep your ass moving."

"Don't worry about your sweetheart. I'll take good care of her," Rings said with a low chuckle. He wrapped his fingers around her arm and forced her through the roughest scrub.

By the time they emerged from the forest, she was covered in scratches, surely had bruises from the fingers gripping her, and had closed her ears to the vile things Rings kept whispering he'd do to her. She knew Gunner heard them, too, from the way his spine stiffened.

Parked in front of them was a vehicle with the back open. It had an enclosed cab and a huge hood.

That drew a whistle from Gunner. "Is that a combustion engine?"

"It's a steam engine, meaning it uses water, the cheapest fuel around." Rings was the one to sing the praises of his truck. He shoved her at the passenger door. "Get in and sit in the middle. Don't touch anything."

She glanced at Gunner. He gave her a slight nod.

"Don't look at him. My brother was talking to you." Freckles cuffed her, and she tasted blood as her teeth cut the inside of her lip. She scrambled into the truck and perched on the long bench, looking around for a weapon. She held off pulling her knife. She didn't want to show her hand too soon.

"No hitting the girl," Rings grumbled, "or I'll hit you."

"And that's why Da always called you soft. You, pretty boy, get your ass in the back," Freckles ordered with a thick jab of his finger.

"I'll grab the rope," Rings declared.

The truck jostled, and a peek over her shoulder showed Gunner clambering in, Rings behind him. And then Rings was flying!

Gunner kicked the man, who flew off the back of the vehicle, startling a yell from Freckles.

The truck bounced as Gunner jumped down, and then she couldn't see. Despite the orders, she scrambled from the cab in time to see the fight. While Freckles groaned on the ground, Gunner hit Rings, somehow dodging the knife he still held in his hand.

She gasped as a slice of the blade drew blood on Gunner's arm then cried out again when Freckles tripped Gunner, sending him down hard.

She should help him. She drew her knife and moved in to offer aid just as Gunner scissored his legs, toppling Rings. Freckles aimed his gun, about to fire. She opened her mouth to scream a warning, running with her knife out, knowing she'd never arrive in time, when Freckles suddenly flew forward.

The gun went off, but it hit nothing. She didn't worry about Freckles getting back up because help had arrived in the form of a large feline, currently chewing on the man.

"Kitty!" she squealed.

Then winced as blood spurted. She glanced at Gunner to see he'd subdued Rings. She didn't see blood, but the sightless eyes and the odd angle of his neck let her know he wouldn't be doing any of the vile things he'd suggested.

He stood and surveyed the scene before his gaze

went to her. His lips quirked. “I told you Kitty would find us.”

Relieved, she threw herself at him, and he caught her. She hugged him and laughed. “Did you plan this all along?”

“Well, once I realized they had transportation, it occurred to me to let them lead us to it rather than stumble around. I don’t know about you, but I’d rather ride than walk.”

“Where will we go?” she asked.

“That is a fine question.” He turned her around so they faced away from the forest. “It doesn’t look like the forest has much to offer. Which is why I’m suggesting we follow the road they drove in on.” He pointed to the faint rutted track.

She bit her lower lip. “Is it safe?”

“Nothing is safe, sweetheart. But staying here...” He sighed. “We could try and possibly survive. There’s water. Fish.”

“But you want to go back to your friends.”

“I want more than to just survive.” He shrugged. “I want a real bed. A blanket.”

“How will we find them? We don’t even know where we are.”

“No, and I realize we might never find my friends or Haven again. The wind and that flood may have taken us too far. But...” He turned her around.

"Together we can find a new place to call home. New people to be our friends and family."

The use of "we" had her heart stuttering.

"What do you say?" he asked softly.

Feeling bold, she lifted on tiptoe to brush her lips over his. "I say yes."

He groaned and wrapped his arms around her, lifting her off the ground, deepening the kiss.

Arousal flared inside her. He'd seen her. Seen her with her scar. Seen her with her hair a tumbled mess and mud coating her face, yet he still kissed her. And they might have done more if Kitty didn't meow.

She pulled away from him, breathless and tingling. "I should check on Kitty."

"You do that while I handle the bodies."

By handle, he meant drag them into the woods where they wouldn't be easily seen. He also stripped them of weapons, tucking the gun in his pants and putting the sword in the truck.

She spent a moment checking over Kitty. Her feline appeared in good health except for the gash along her hindquarter. A reminder of the soldiers they'd fought. It was healing well, but as soon as she encountered some ingredients, she'd make a salve to hurry it along.

If Kitty let her. The feline batted at her when she tried to inspect it too closely.

"Fine. But don't come meowing at me if it leaves a scar," Sofia grumbled.

"Scars are badges of honor," Gunner said, his stealthy steps bringing him close enough to startle.

"Not all of them." She didn't touch the one on her cheek, but she was aware of it.

"Are you ready? We should get going while it's daylight." The morning waned.

"I guess." She sighed, glancing behind her.

He murmured, "We'll find a new home. I promise."

Despite him holding the door to the truck open, Kitty jumped into the back. She didn't seem to mind the random equipment and made herself comfortable. Sofia climbed into the passenger's side, and Gunner swung into the driver seat.

He spent a moment fiddling with the dash, which had wires sticking out of it, holes that lacked buttons, and a general air of disrepair.

"Do you know to work it?" she asked.

"It's a truck. I'll figure it out." He gave her a quick smile. "If we're lucky, it will start when I press the button."

To her surprise, the vehicle rumbled to life,

vibrating the seat under her. "Speaking of luck, good thing Kitty showed up when she did."

"I knew she would. She's a smart cat. She was biding her time."

The reply had her blinking. "You mean you knew she was there?"

Gunner glanced at her and shrugged. "Yes. I saw her footprints around our camp. Didn't you? She marked it during the night to warn predators away."

"What do you mean marked?"

"She peed. All around us. Basically told anything out there that we're her pets."

She glanced in the back at Kitty, sprawled and already asleep as the truck continued to growl. The engine popped and shook, the whole machine shivering.

"If she was around, then why did she wait so long to attack?"

"Because I signaled for her to wait." He winked.

"I can't believe the pair of you planned that. You could have told me," Sofia grumbled.

"We didn't exactly have time. Once I knew they had a truck, we changed the plan."

"What's the plan now?"

"Drive until we find a place we can bargain for supplies."

"Bargain with what?"

He shrugged. "I'm sure we'll get lucky and find something of value on the way."

"We can't rely on luck," she insisted.

"Why not?"

"Because," she sputtered.

"What if I said that luck is pretty good? We're in the Marshlands? Which, if my information is correct, are part of the Sapphire domain, which rules by the sea." He grinned at her. "I've never seen the ocean. You?"

She gaped at him. "We can't just wander around in the open. What if we're seen? Maybe we should stay in the woods."

"But there's nothing in the woods. Aren't you curious at all?"

Yes, but what she said was, "There are rules about moving between the kingdoms. You heard those men. There are tolls to pay. Permissions to ask."

"So we go get permission."

"From who?" she blinked.

"Whoever's in charge, I guess. Our friends implied there was a city. And I'm wondering if it's the same one I've heard about that caters to the free folk."

"Free how?"

"No Enclave. No Emerald queen or her Centurions."

"You keep saying Emerald. Is that where you're from?"

"Gonna guess by the question that you're not." He went silent for a moment. "Which city were you banished from?"

"Ruby. But the Enclave rules us all."

"That they do." He glanced at her, ignoring the empty road. "Ever wonder what it would be like to live in a place where the Enclave isn't in charge?"

The question, spoken softly, hesitantly, mirrored an old fantasy of hers. "I want to believe there is somewhere you can live however you choose. Not be forced into a job. Not be told you have to serve people who disrespect you. A place where you can be friends with whoever you like." She didn't say the next part but thought it. *Be intimate with whomever you please.*

Even in an unknown place with danger lurking, she felt happier and more alive than she ever recalled being.

"For me, it's hard to imagine having my life so severely regimented."

Her lips quirked. "While I used to not be able to grasp how anyone could survive in the Wasteland."

"A trick of the Enclave because, by telling you what to believe, they control you."

"Not anymore," she said with a smile. She was free.

The idea had never fully sunk in before.

Free.

How absolutely terrifying.

It didn't escape her notice that they didn't have much. Then again, she'd had even less the last time she found herself without a home.

Now she had friends. She glanced behind at Kitty, who slept with her head on her paws, and then Gunner. The strong profile. The capable hands. The grin he tossed her. He also winked.

"We're going to take it one day at a time. Together."

The word repeated as she stared out the window at the flat plains they drove across. Most of it appeared dry without even stunted trees to adorn it. Only cracks, the kind that happened when the ground got so very dry that it contracted.

The track they followed had worn grooves into the hard-packed dirt. It still kicked up a bit of dust as they followed it.

Nothing else appeared. Not a single structure or other vehicle.

The landscape proved monotonous and dull

while the motion of the truck lulled. When she woke, it took her a bit to realize her head rested in his lap.

She bolted upright. "Sorry."

"Sweetheart, do not apologize. Your face down there totally made this ride enjoyable."

Her cheeks heated. "That is so wildly inappropriate to say." Even she knew that.

"But so much fun. You should see your face. I've never seen that shade of red before."

He teased, and it only served to make her blush harder. She couldn't look at him and chose to peek out the window instead.

He'd driven long enough that the late morning start had turned into waning afternoon. The flat plain was giving rise to random scenery. The crumbling buildings the distance, a speck flying in the sky. A bit of greenery began to appear, too. Trees with a few leafy branches, tufts of grass, the blades tall and thick.

"Where are we?"

"That is a good question. I haven't the slightest fucking clue." He shook his head.

"Then why are you driving?"

He shrugged. "This road obviously goes somewhere."

She snorted. "Don't all roads lead somewhere?"

"I've actually found one that goes off a cliff. So no. Unless death was your destination."

"The end of this road could also end in something bad. Freckles and Rings weren't exactly nice people."

Gunner eyed her. "Freckles and Rings?"

"It was better than calling them marauder one and two."

He laughed. "Ever heard of Hive City? Stories from travelers claim they're all assigned numbers at birth. No one has a name."

"A number?" Her nose wrinkled. "I might not have chosen the name I got, but it's better than a string of digits."

"I like the name Sofia."

"It's okay." She rolled her shoulders. "It's just that your parents named you. They gave you a name they thought would make you strong. They chose a name for you out of affection. Mine was randomly generated by a machine. I wonder what my parents would have called me."

He stopped the vehicle and turned to her. "I am an asshole. A serious asshole. I didn't mean to make you feel sad."

"I'm not—" She stopped, realizing that, yes, the thought of it did make her melancholy. She didn't like it. Regret wasn't something she'd felt in her old life. She'd not felt much of anything until the end before her banishment. As if her emotions had been hiding all that time.

"When you have a child, you'll be able to name him or her. Maybe with some input from the father." He stared at her so intently she couldn't hold his gaze.

"I would choose?" she squeaked. Her eyes widened. "What if I choose wrong?" What if she saddled a child with an awful name that they hated?

He laughed. "It's not that horrifying, I swear."

"How would you know? Have you ever named someone?"

He shook his head. "Nope. But I'm excited about it. I mean think of the possibilities if you name them right. Like Arrow. Fits a boy and a girl."

"You would name them after a weapon?" she exclaimed.

"Well yeah. Do you think Blade is better? Or maybe Star. I saw one thrown by this guy who was passing through, and damn, he could hit a target dead center every single time."

"In the ancient times, apparently parents named their children after those they considered famous or an elder in the family."

"You mean like after my mom or dad?" He

pursed his lips. "Hank and Patty. Interesting idea. And we can discuss it once you're pregnant."

She might have stopped breathing for a moment. "Pregnant?"

"You did bargain for a baby. I know I've been kind of remiss giving you one, but I promise, it is high on my list of things to do."

She shook her head lightly. "I don't know if it's the right time anymore."

"Now, don't be a quitter. Just because things look a little tough at the moment doesn't mean they won't have straightened out by the time the baby comes."

"We don't know where we're going," she remarked.

"Somewhere," was his reply as he got the truck moving again.

"We need more than somewhere. I can't be pregnant without a home," she declared. She wasn't even sure about having a child anymore. She'd mostly wanted one because a child would provide a cure for loneliness. She wasn't lonely anymore.

"A home. Got it. Anything else?"

"Are you asking if I have a list of demands before you can impregnate me?"

"Yes."

She laughed. For some reason, it struck her as silly. "Fine. Along with a home, I want a bed. With a mattress so soft I won't want to get up. And shoes." She stretched out her feet.

"I'll make sure you have several pairs." He sounded a bit choked. "Anything else?"

"I want to taste chocolate," she blurted out.

"You've never..." He trailed off muttering, "Of course you haven't. Why would they waste the good stuff on people they believe are beneath them?"

"I've heard it is decadent." The most intense thing she'd ever gotten to eat was a bowl of berries. The master received some as a gift, and he'd shared them with her. She'd never forgotten the tart and sweet burst of flavor on her tongue.

"I will hunt down all kinds of treats for you to eat."

"You're going to stay with me?"

"Of course."

"What about your friends in Haven?" she queried.

"Who do you think we're going to live with? We need a community if we're going to survive."

"How are we supposed to find them? We're not in your Emerald domain anymore."

"Nope, and I think we're just found the official edge of the Marshlands. Look ahead."

The road entered an area of growth. Long, mauve reeds poked from still pools of water, the top of it a brackish gray. Trees rose at random, the branches long and twisty, the fuzzy pink tendrils dangling from them touching the surface of the water, forming a filmy curtain. The bog appeared to extend for miles.

"Is it safe?" she asked.

He snorted. "You did not seriously just ask that."

The road he followed proved more a suggestion with rocks piled wide enough for the truck and nothing more. Dirt packed between the cracks of the stone somewhat smoothed the surface.

She wondered what would happen if the road crumbled. What lurked in the depths? And was that water even safe? This resembled her idea of the Wastelands and their supposed toxic nature. Seeing a ripple in the muck, she shuddered and looked away.

For distraction, she asked, "What is the Emerald domain like?"

"Not like this," he said. "The only marsh I've ever seen was small with gray reeds."

"There are no watery places like this in Ruby," she stated. "All lakes and ponds are protected by domes. Everything else is just barren."

"Emerald isn't that bad off. We have a massive forest as one of the domain boundary lines. It has a river that runs through it, and it gets rain often enough to keep it lush. Outside that forest, in the domain itself, there are a few lakes, but they aren't in domes."

"What do they do for water?"

"Depends on the dome. Some have underground wells they've tapped. Others keep replenishing reservoirs they've created."

"Why not build the domes closer to water?"

He shrugged. "Why have the domes at all? It's not as if the air is toxic like they claim."

"Maybe in other places, but Ruby still has issues with dust storms, especially the city. To protect the trees and other foliage, they have to be covered."

"Or so you've been told."

"I never thought of that." Her brow crinkled. "Given what I've seen since I left, it's more than possible. No one ever leaves and comes back to tell us what the truth is."

"In the Emerald domain, there is a strong push by the Enclave to keep the domes ignorant. A people who don't know and who fear are easier to control."

"It's pretty much the same in Ruby."

"And probably the same everywhere else as well. It's like no one cares."

Again, she couldn't help but recall how dead she felt in the city. "Because we're numb inside. I wonder..." She didn't finish the thought.

"Wonder what?" he asked, taking his eyes from their path just as the truck jostled.

"Watch the road!" she exclaimed.

"Well?" He returned his gaze to the front.

She finally said aloud what she'd wondered for a while. "I think the Enclave drugs the citizens. Makes us not want things."

"Why do you say that?"

"Because I feel so much now." She pressed a fist to her chest. "I cry. I rage. I feel happy. And proud. It's as if being away from the city has released me from some kind of stasis."

"It is my understanding, in Emerald at least, they feed the citizens a little something to make them more manageable."

"It's wrong. Who gave them the right to decide?"

"Their magical powers, according to them. Their psionics." He snorted. "If you ask me, that's a dumb reason to let anyone lead or make decisions."

His mindset reflected her own. She went back to something he'd said earlier. "You said you were looking for a place where your people could live freely."

"A place that might not exist. All I ever heard were second-hand stories," he replied. "Talk of a place where citizens have the same rights. Where work, not name, earns reward. And everyone is welcome. The thing that I couldn't understand was—"

"If it was so great, why would anyone leave?" she interrupted to finish his sentence.

He nodded. "You would think if this place was a Utopia, then they'd want to keep it a secret. Safe."

"Does it exist?"

"I think it does but have no idea where it might be."

"It sounds too perfect," she remarked, looking out the window at the sinking sun lighting the marsh with hues of mauve and red.

"Which is why it's the dream we're all looking for. If I could figure out its location, then I could tell my friends in Haven. Heck, I'd tell anyone who is tired of the Enclave making life harder."

"What happens if we can't find it?" she asked.

"Then maybe it's time we thought about making our own Utopia."

FOURTEEN

THE SUN WAS SETTING FASTER THAN HE LIKED, and still the hump he aimed for appeared far away. He knew better than to remain sitting on this strip of road after dark. He needed a more defensible spot. The moment the last rays of the sun disappeared, he flicked on the beam to light the road. A single headlight bounced and jounced, meaning he had to slow down.

"You're nervous," she stated. "What do you know that I don't?"

"Nothing. I've never been here."

"You've got the gun in your lap."

He fondled it. "This marsh has been too quiet."

Their passage was too easy. Not a single thing to get in their way. It could only mean one thing. The monsters would come out at night.

"Can't something be peaceful for once?" she lamented. "Why must everything always be about killing us?"

"The strongest survive."

She made a disparaging noise. "Then how am I still alive?"

"One, you're stronger than you think. Two, it probably helped you were friends with the biggest predator in that hidden valley."

"Kitty is pretty ferocious." She glanced back at her cat. Then turned a frown on him. "Kitty's watching behind us."

"Because Kitty is smart." Anything lurking out in the darkness would see them as fresh meat.

"It's all water, though. What could possibly attack? A fish?" She snickered.

Then she choked as something landed on the road in front of them. A fat creature with moist greenish skin, three bulbous eyes, no nose—just three holes—and a mouth full of teeth. It held a sharpened stick in a webbed-fingered hand. Given the many teats hanging from its torso, it appeared female. It also wasn't moving out of the way.

He slowed down the vehicle, the beam of light striking the strange creature. It hissed and ducked its face, obviously preferred the dark.

"Why are you stopping?" She dug her fingers into her seat and stared straight ahead.

"Because if it's more solid than I think, we could go off the road. I don't know about you, but I'd rather not lose the truck."

"I think it's a bad idea to be sitting here."

"Probably. More than likely the thing in front of us is the bait to spring the trap."

Sofia screamed as more of the creatures emerged from the muck, one of them slapping his webbed hands on the window and then licking it. The glass bubbled, and Sofia moaned. "This is not good."

"Nope, but now that they're all here..." He shoved the acceleration rod, and the truck shot forward, slamming into the body of the squat creature, splattering it over the hood. A few more flew off the sides. That made a couple less to—

"Duck!"

—throw rocks at the windows, but it was the jolt as something punctured a tire that worried him more. It slowed them down, allowing the monsters to catch up. Kitty growled in the back while Sofia stared out the windows, wide-eyed.

"They're coming!"

"We're going to have to fight," he advised. Even as it seemed unlikely they'd survive.

"Fight?" she gasped. "But there's so many."

He was aware. At least he'd gotten their weapons back. He pulled the sword from where he'd laid it at his feet. She followed suit and white-knuckled the dagger.

"Kitty, you make an opening for us. Sofia, you run and only slash if you have to. Follow the road to the hump. If we can get to higher ground, we can defend it."

"What about you?" she asked as a face pressed to the window, smushing between the bars to once more tongue the window.

"I'm going to give you time to run."

"I don't like that plan." She clutched the knife even closer.

"We don't have a choice. Ready?" He flung open his door and jumped out with Kitty right behind him.

He immediately slashed, his blade a touch dull but still slicing through flesh, splitting open moist skin, and spilling guts that steamed and reeked putridly. He kept swinging, aiming for the motion he could detect from the shadows, either slashing flesh or, in two cases, smashing crude spears before they could poke holes in him. It didn't take too long before the monsters showed a hesitant respect for his blade.

"Now," he said, keeping his eyes on the monsters forming a half-circle around them.

He sweated in the moist air, but his adrenaline was pumping. Plenty of strength left in his arms. He was saving the gun for when he couldn't lift the sword.

Sofia landed behind him, her breathing a panicked hitch. Kitty came padding from the side, a slow prowl that had the monsters shifting. What had the cat done to have them giving her a wide berth?

"Get ready to run," he advised.

He leaped forward toward the front of the truck, clearing the way. Kitty roared and bounded past him, pouncing on the swamp creatures, clearing a path.

He turned to see Sofia hugging the truck, eyes darting around fearfully. "Move!" he barked.

She focused on him then past him to her cat. Her lips flattened, and her shoulders straightened as she marched forward.

He guarded the rear, preventing the creatures from attacking by feinting and darting at those who dared come near. Kitty did a good job keeping them at bay in the front, but rather than thin the herd, more of them appeared, forming a loose, moving wave that kept darting close, working in tandem to force Kitty to defend one side or the other.

Sofia might be terrified, but she screamed and energetically attacked the monsters, sobbing as she stabbed. Against all odds they were moving forward, hopefully to the hump they'd seen before the sun set. The headlight barely provided any illumination at this point, the things swarm behind halting any chance at a retreat.

The ring around them grew so thick he expected them to rush and overwhelm. Only instead of pressing the advantage, the monsters suddenly disappeared.

What would make a small army of creatures flee?

Not something he wanted to meet. "Fuck me, something bad is coming. Run!"

He dashed for Sofia and grabbed her free hand with his, tugging her into flight. Their legs pumped as they pounded along the road that had turned pitch-black as something blocked out the light of the truck. They couldn't see a thing, and yet there should have been starlight at the very least. Sofia stumbled, and he halted lest he throw her off balance. He turned and saw it, a hulking, amorphous shape of water and weeds that constantly undulated as it leaned for them.

It writhed as if alive and stank of rot, of meat gone bad and water turned rancid. It shot out tendrils of fluid, vine-like and whip quick. It grabbed Sofia.

"It's got me!" she screamed.

Even though he couldn't see her in the darkness, he had to do something to help her.

Kitty bolted past and threw herself at the monster. Took a great big bite. Gagged and spat.

The smell of it roiled his own stomach, but he darted in close enough to slash at the creature, knowing it wouldn't do a damned thing. But he still dug his sword into the monster. It sliced easily but didn't bleed. How did you kill the marsh itself?

The hump of bog rolled for him, and he kept ahead of it, knowing he couldn't stand his ground and kill it. If only he had fire. Fire tended to even the odds.

Tendrils of muck shot for him, and he sliced them one after another, only it had no effect. The edge of the road reared behind him as it turned slightly without him noticing. His foot splashed in water.

Water. Behind him the marsh was dormant. So what was different about the marsh in front of him?

Something must control it. Monster. Magic. Machine. It didn't matter. Once he realized the water itself wasn't the enemy, he charged it. He slammed through the weeds and decay, the slime and chunks. He popped into a bubble inside the strange threat, where he found Sofia strapped to the wall with reeds. A strange man stood beside her, naked, muddy, and crazy-eyed. The orbs lit as if from a demonic entity inside.

Gunner had seen that look once before. The insanity was unmistakable, making him very dangerous, especially since he obviously wielded magic.

"Die, fucking wizard!" Gunner swung his sword.

The naked man shrieked. "Get out of my house!"

"Make me," Gunner growled.

He ran for the guy, ignoring the reedy mess, but the man proved more agile than expected. However, the space wasn't very large. It didn't take long to stalk the wizard down, slicing deep enough to distract the magic. Then Gunner sliced again.

The wizard shrieked, and the space they were in suddenly shifted. Moving and rolling and regurgitating on land. Sofia yelped as she landed, whereas Gunner cursed because his sword arm hit the ground first, the impact jarring the sword free.

He sprang to his feet and pulled one of his small knives, aiming for the wizard, who struggled to his feet, still snarling. Gunner's dagger sailed through the air and was batted down by a burst of water.

Sofia was shrieking as she slapped away the reeds that bound her. He kept his gaze focused on the wizard, pulled the gun, and aimed.

The wizard opened his mouth. The hole in his head dropped him before a sound emerged.

Gunner watched the light go out of the wizard's eyes just as something stabbed him.

He looked down to see a spear sticking from his side. "Fucker!"

He meant to kill the creature that attacked him but got poked with another pointy stick. It shouldn't have been enough to fell him.

He sank to his knees. It had to be some kind of poison. He heard a roar, and a body soared past him, killing those that stabbed him. Not that it mattered anymore, as his vision blurred into darkness.

FIFTEEN

Sofia could only stare and blink as shock held her. The hole in the strange man's head leaked sluggishly, black ink in a night that remained dark except for the fading headlight on the truck. To the side she could hear Kitty growling and the wet chewing sounds of a kill.

A little too late.

It happened so fast. The creature had risen from the muck and pulled back its arm. Gunner had been so intent on the naked psionic that he'd never seen the attack.

The second spear hit him in the leg, but by then, he was already going down. And he didn't get back up.

Sofia dropped to her knees beside him. His eyes

were closed, his breathing shallow. She swallowed hard as she saw the spear still sticking out of him.

"Gunner." She moaned his name and looked at him helplessly. This was beyond anything she'd ever tried to heal. No amount of mud could fix a bleeding hole. "I don't know what to do."

She wasn't a doctor. They knew how to stitch and set wounds. She just provided the remedy to remove the scarring. But she knew she had to remove the spear and apply pressure.

Removing it, though, would make the bleeding only faster, yet it couldn't stay in him. The sight of it was so wrong. She fluttered her fingers a second before grasping it.

"I'm sorry," she murmured, her voice thick before yanking.

He might be unconscious, but he still bucked when she pulled free the weapon. The wound gushed. She tossed the spear before slapping her hands on it to stop the bleeding.

"Don't die," she muttered. He couldn't die. She needed him.

Needed him to open his eyes and say "sweetheart" in that low, husky murmur she'd come to enjoy. He didn't regain consciousness, and his breathing began to stutter.

She pressed harder on his wound, sobbing. "Don't go. Please. Don't leave me."

As if to mock her wishes, his breathing grew even more shallow, and the light from the truck dimmed. Soon she'd be in the dark. Alone.

If only she had something to use to stop the bleeding. But she couldn't remove her hands. She couldn't stop the pressure, or he'd die.

He'd also die if she did nothing.

Vaguely she heard Kitty snarling, and it got brighter around her even though the truck remained dim. There were splashes. A few whistles and bellows.

She didn't care. She only focused on the hot blood spilling from him. A killing wound that needed a doctor, or at least a master apothecary. Not an assistant with no ingredients and barely any skill.

But Gunner seemed to think she didn't need those things. He was convinced she could heal. If there was ever a time to find out...

She flattened her hands on him, biting her lip as he twitched, feeling the pain even in his deep sleep. His breath wheezed. His blood squished wetly between her fingers. She closed her eyes and willed every bit of intent she could manage. Heal. Heal. He had to heal.

She needed him alive. Not just because he knew

how to fight and live in this wild world but because she liked him oh so very much and wanted him to live.

Live. Damn you. Don't you dare leave me alone.

Her hands heated, hotter than she'd ever managed for any potion, and yet she continued to hold them on his skin.

Live. Because I need you.

Tears leaked from her closed lids. Hot streaks down her cheeks that dripped from her chin.

Live. Please.

The heat in her hands should have burnt the flesh from them both. It was intense and painful. So intense she forgot to breathe.

And then his chest heaved. He took a deep, unhindered breath. Then another. But she didn't know how to stop. Her hands remained hot. She wavered on her knees.

Gunner suddenly exclaimed, "Sofia, you need to stop." He pushed at her, breaking the contact.

Sucking in a deep breath, she choked. Gasped for air. Her chest rose and fell as she stared at him. He looked better than she felt.

"Did it work?" she asked, her lashes fluttering.

"Yes, sweetheart, it did."

"I'm so tired."

"I know. Come here." He reached for her, and she fell into him, exhausted.

Someone whistled. "The pair of them are going to sell high. The fellow beat Pedronias with only a shit sword and a gun and the woman can heal."

"Don't touch her," she heard Gunner exclaim, standing with her in his arms.

"Look at you, acting all protective."

"You saw what I did with that swamp wizard. I can take you on, too."

Such a brave statement. She wished she could say something, but everything inside was too heavy. The final thing she heard was, "Dart them both, but make sure you get him twice."

And then nothing until she woke in a strange kind of prison. It appeared as if she were contained in a woven basket, the braided pieces stiff enough to form bars that curved overhead to form a cone-shaped top. The spaces between the twisted fronds gave her peeks of her surroundings. A lichen-covered wall, parts of the rock peeping through. The light blue-green of the moss tempted the apothecary in her, who'd only ever worked with the dried red kind.

Turning slowly so as to hopefully not draw attention, she managed to form a picture that was better left unpainted.

She found herself in some kind of settlement,

which was being kind. There were no real houses, just primitive frond-woven tents—some of them emitting smoke—next to tumbling stone walls. The ruins still had enough shape to form a barrier, all the better to protect the people.

A people as she'd never seen before.

In the Ruby Kingdom, the only people she'd ever seen were human. Meaning no extra limbs, scales, fur, anything that was considered deviating from the baseline. Only Wastelanders, poisoned by the land, suffered such from the Deviant syndrome, and even those were more legend than reality.

She couldn't help but stare. Not in repugnance, but fascination. Everyone was so different. A man with a flat nose and webbed hands, patrolling with an axe in hand, his gaze always moving to the walls, looking for commotion. The mother hustling her children. The only thing different about them were the tails peeking from their backsides.

But the thing that struck her most, the biggest difference, was how free they seemed. They talked among each other. Called out, shouted, slapped each other on the shoulders. Hugged.

She tucked her knees to her chest and rested her chin on them. In the city, she had a few people she talked to. Not much or often. A citizen had to work for the privilege of living there. Funny how the

Enclave, supposedly the most valuable of them, barely appeared to work at all.

The people in this settlement all had their own tasks, but they did them freely with serious mien or good humor.

What she didn't see was Gunner or Kitty. Had they escaped? The last thing she recalled the newcomers had wanted to take both her and Gunner prisoner. But what of her cat?

Had Kitty managed to stay out of their reach?

Did she really heal Gunner?

Or had he died from his wound?

No. He had to have lived. She refused to believe anything else until she saw proof otherwise.

Glancing to her left and right, she looked for another woven cage like hers. Instead, she saw a pen of men packed together behind a fence.

Before she could examine each face, a pair of legs moved to stand in front of her. Someone wearing short pants like Freckles and Rings crouched and leered at her, his teeth pointed, his eyes strangely milky and lashless. He also didn't blink.

"You are a healing witch," he stated, gargling the words.

"No. Not a witch." Those were the evil entities in stories written by the ancients.

"Yeah, you are," the stranger argued. "I seen you. Healing your companion."

"I merely applied a balm to his wounds," she lied.

But apparently this man knew the finer details of what she did. "You lay your hands on him and then chanted. Brought him back to life."

"It wasn't a chant." Just her rocking back and forth, wishing he'd heal.

"Doesn't matter what you call it."

"What are you going to do with me?" The fables she knew usually had witches dying in horrible fashion.

The man grinned, his teeth utterly fascinating and terrifying all at once. "Witches are valuable. We will sell you."

The very idea had her blinking. "Sell me? But I'm a person, not a thing."

"And?" He seemed genuinely perplexed.

She hugged her knees tighter. "Can't you just send me home?" Problem was when she said home, she didn't mean the Ruby City but the valley she desperately missed.

The request made her captor laugh. "You are going to a new home."

The idea he'd sell her and not give her a choice

chilled her right through. “What of Gunner? What did you do with my companion?”

“A fine warrior like him has his own buyer.”

“He’s alive?” She wanted to close her eyes and bask in the relief.

“The dead man rose from the ground out of a huge puddle of blood and fought like a beast to try and protect you. Killed five of mine before we managed to dart him enough times. Took six before he stopped swinging those knives of his.” The man sounded positively gleeful. “He’ll fetch a fine price. Maybe even better than you if you keep saying you’re not a witch.” The implication being she might not be worth much. Which made her wonder what would keep her safer? She didn’t know. This wasn’t a city with set rules.

What should she choose? Deny she had any power and claim that her captor was mistaken or embrace the witch thing in the hopes it led to a better situation.

“His injuries? They’re healing?”

The man snorted. “What injuries? Never seen such pretty skin on a warrior. If it weren’t for his skill, I’d have thought him pampered Enclave.” He spit on the ground. Apparently even in these ruins, the elite weren’t well-liked.

“He’s not Enclave,” she reassured.

"I already knows that." He sneered. "A Wastelander from Emerald. A rare thing. Means I can hike his price."

"He'll never agree."

"As if he's got a choice." Her captor snorted.

"Don't hurt him."

"Not planning to. Can't sell a dead man. Or woman." He leered at her.

"Let me see him." She grabbed at the braided reeds on her cage, unable to stem her desperation. "Prove he's alive."

"I ain't doing shit. He ain't your concern no more."

"But—But—" She sought a reason why they had to stay together. What would this man accept? "He's the father of my child." No need to mention the child hadn't actually been created yet.

He eyed her belly. "You're not breeding."

How could he tell? "Why can't you sell us as a pair?" She didn't know if it was ever done.

"Get more apart."

Every answer only served to frustrate. "What about the feline that fought with us?"

"You mean the cat?"

"Yes, the cat," she growled through gritted teeth. "What happened to her?"

"Nothing yet, but not for lack of trying. Hunters are looking for her. The fur will fetch a fine price."

"Don't you dare touch Kitty," she yelled, tugging at the rigid frond bars. "Leave her alone."

"You are loud." The man frowned at her. "I won't mention that to the buyer."

"You can't sell me."

"Not that again." He actually rolled his eyes at her. "You talk too much. Good thing I'm selling you. We leave for the city in the morning."

"What city? Who are you selling me to?"

"Anyone with something to trade. Don't worry. Next time you wake up, you'll be in your new prison."

His grin didn't reassure, but she was very disturbed when he inserted a reed tube between the bars. She couldn't avoid the dart.

When next she woke, it was to a pungent aroma being waved under her nose. The acrid mist made her eyes tear, and she flung herself forward with a gasp.

Women in filmy green diaphanous gowns with veils over their faces stood around Sofia. They peered at her with eyes lined in shades of rainbow makeup.

It took only a quick glance to realize she wasn't in a cage anymore. She appeared to be sitting in a bathing chamber of some sort. Of more concern, she was nude. Completely. And now that she was awake, hands tugged at her, pulling her toward a bath made of stone, steam rising from the surface. With accented words and gentle shoves, she was told to get in.

"Stop." Sofia shook her head, resisting their tugs, her red hair dangling and dirty down her back. "I want to know where I am."

The smiles made her wonder if they were genuinely happy or plotting her demise. Especially when one of them said, "You are in the paradise city known as Eden."

Sofia frowned. "Never heard of it." Even as the name seemed vaguely familiar.

"You are in New Eden, the beautiful garden of the ancient gods," said a woman dressed in a drape of light blue fabric, her wrists jangling with bracelets.

That was why it sounded familiar. It was a fable of a city from defunct bibles that were old even in ancient times. "Whose home am I in?" she asked, looking around the lovely chamber.

"You are an important guest of the castle," declared another of the ladies, the burnt orange gown offsetting her glossy skin. Her hair was coiled in intricate braids crisscrossing her head.

It made Sofia want to hide her own dull and

knotted locks. The gowns would have been nice as well, loose and airy. She wasn't comfortable being naked. "What's expected of me?"

"We're just here to help you bathe and dress."

"I can do that on my own."

The women smiled, but one sassily said, "Obviously not." She eyed her. "We're going to need lots of soap."

Heat filled Sofia's cheeks. She didn't enjoy being filthy. "I'll take a bath alone, please."

"I wasn't going to climb in with you." The woman with braids grinned, her dimple teasing.

"My name is Sofia," she offered.

"We know. You're the witch."

"I'm—"

The woman continued, "I'm Josette, and this is Stefany."

"I'm not a witch," Sofia huffed.

"Are you sure? Because around here, they're in high demand."

"To do what?" she asked, taking a step forward toward the still steaming tub. The water was scented, too. Sweet and tempting.

"Depends on your skill. What kind of witch are you?"

"If I were—not saying I am—a healing one." She

reached the bath and dragged a finger over the surface.

Hot. So, so tempting.

"Healing?" Stefany sounded skeptical. "Eh, it's a good one. Steady work. You good at it?"

"Doesn't matter if she is or not," admonished Josette. "She needs to get in that tub because he's waiting on her."

"Who is?"

Stefany's smile turned mischievous. "The most eligible mate in the city and for hundreds of miles around."

Knowing they weren't possibly talking about Gunner and getting his face out of her head at the word eligible were two different things. And suddenly she knew what she needed to know next.

She lifted a leg into the tub. The water proved warm, languorous. She relaxed in it with a sigh and soaked for a minute before casually asking, "The warrior that was brought in with me. Is he nearby?"

"We don't know anything about a warrior. What does he look like?"

"He is tall, broad of shoulder, with a square jaw, blue eyes, and he likes to jest quite a bit."

"Sounds handsome," Josette replied before shoving Sofia's head underwater.

She rose, sputtering. "What is wrong with you?"

"You needed to get your hair wet."

"You could have asked."

"I could have," Josette said.

No apology was coming, but Sofia couldn't find it in her to care when the fingers lathered her scalp with soap. The fragrance relaxed her, and she tilted her head as she closed her eyes. Basked in the massage of the fingers through her tresses.

She expected the second dunking and had her mouth closed and breath held when she went under. She remained there while Josette swished the hair to rinse it. When she rose, she'd barely blinked when water poured over her head. She looked over her shoulder to see Stefany aiming a handheld hose. The mixture of rustic and modern should have been jarring, but she rather enjoyed it.

"Stand," Josette ordered.

Sofia rose, the hot spray as Stefany rinsed her keeping her from shivering. The towel they rubbed her with fluffy soft. Embarrassed, she tried wrestling a towel free. It resulted in her getting snapped on the butt.

"That wasn't nice!" Sofia was getting mighty tired of Josette.

"Not for you maybe."

The pair of women seemed determined to drive

her insane. Nice one minute, kind of mean the next. But nothing truly malicious.

Dunking and towel snapping weren't horrible things, just not something that usually happened in an Enclave-controlled city. She'd also never been taken care of before.

They rubbed lotion on her, brushed and dried her hair, then coiffed it before dressing her. She kept trying to protest their ministrations. She wasn't sure she liked it. They didn't care how many times she insisted she could care for herself.

By the time they were done tugging and stroking and even plucking, she appeared as an elegant lady. Someone fancy enough to be mistaken for Enclave.

That couldn't be good.

"Am I ready now?" she grumbled when they tossed slippers at her.

""You're presentable. Think she's his type?" Josette asked her friend.

"Maybe." Stefany canted her head. "Hard to know what his type is. He never seems to pay attention."

"Tell me about it. Even my brother couldn't get a read off him, and he tried."

"With or without his shirt?" snickered Stefany.

"What do you think? If Armand can't get a rise

out of him, then I doubt she can." The women eyed her and found her lacking.

But she'd finally gotten the gist of their conversation. "I am not going to whore myself."

Josette snickered. "You should be so lucky."

A knock at the door led to Stefany announcing, "The guards are here to take the witch."

Sofia didn't argue the title. She might need its protection. She certainly wished she was as brave as those she'd read of in books. Her knees practically knocked when she exited into a hall lined with windows overlooking an enclosed courtyard.

Not knowing what to expect filled her with fear, and the guards—older, serious men with weapons prodding her along—didn't help. The flowing skirt, layers of pink filmy material, kicked out as she went halfway around the circular hall until they reached an elevator.

It sped down a few floors before spilling them into a grand space finished in polished tile, white and gleaming. The walls, plastered over and a pale cream, showcased exquisitely rendered paintings. Although she had to wonder at the subject matter. The images were quite impossible, such as the half-woman, half-fish. What of the beast with the upper body of a man but the hindquarters of an animal?

Perhaps these images were reproductions from

ancient times or artifacts themselves. As her guards escorted her across the vast space, she noted giant metal embossed doors, currently open and yet partially screened across with bars, leaving only a narrow entrance. It was guarded by men in breast-plates holding large guns with swords strapped to their sides.

If she didn't know better, she'd think she was in a castle. But only the Enclave lived so grandly. As she kept following, she couldn't deny the opulence of the finely carved furniture. Real wood, not a hard polymer composite. Its grain gleamed while the seat cushions looked plush.

She was brought to a pair of golden doors twice as tall as her and four times as wide. A grand entrance. Not that they were opened for her. Hidden in the carvings was a smaller door through which her guards indicted she should go.

She balked. "What's inside?"

"Get in and you'll see."

"Why can't you just tell me?" One of them sighed, and the other yanked on her arm before shoving her through the door.

Stumbling, she recovered quickly enough and eyed the area around her. Golden-hued floor, the shine muted. The carvings in the floor were intricate and darkly lined. The room was rectangular in shape, narrow through the middle but long, an alley leading to a dais. Many tiers rose to a platform and the ostentatious throne sitting upon it.

Once it drew her gaze, she couldn't look away. It was the biggest chair she'd ever seen. It appeared as a sinuous creature with body twining to form a seat. The head was a vicious, snarling thing with clear stone teeth, a place for the man wearing a simple circlet to rest his hand. As if he petted the carved monster.

The man appeared alone. She'd yet to see another person in the room, just the two of them, and yet, she'd never been more frightened in her life. There was something cold in his gaze. Assessing and predatory as he fixed on her, not speaking a single word.

She tried to root herself. Her feet moved in spite of her wishes. She found herself approaching him, each step making her breath stutter and her heart pound. Attempts to lean back, to pull free, failed. Something pressed on her, a heavy weight that demanded she come.

What if she didn't want to? She pushed back. Tried to shove the impulse to obey out of her head.

She finally managed to stop as she made it to the bottom step of the dais. She panted as if she'd exerted herself. In a sense she had.

The presence poked at her, trying to find a way to shove her again. She focused her gaze on the stairs in front of her. She was not climbing those stairs.

Nope.

Never.

The onerous weight withdrew, and the low chuckle that followed tickled the skin and raised bumps.

"You are an interesting woman, just like Jakori promised."

"He might have overstated my finer qualities." There was no point in ignoring whoever sat on that throne. Angering him might make her situation worse.

"Your Highness."

"Excuse me?" She finally glanced upward and caught the strong planes of his face. The dark wing of his hair. The gold circlet that rested atop his head was slightly askew. His outfit appeared to be all black. Black tunic. Trousers. Boots. Not a bad-looking man; however, that didn't ease her trepidation.

His lips twisted. "When you speak to me, I am to be addressed as 'Your Highness,' although I will also accept 'master.' I should add, failure to do so will result in punishment."

The cold threat meant her hands trembled as she

gripped her skirts and dropped into a curtsy, hastening to say, "So very sorry, Your Majesty." It didn't occur to her to push this man. There was something much too deadly about his manner.

"Come closer. Let me see what I'm buying."

The nonchalance bothered. What would he do if she turned around and marched away?

"Are you deaf?" The words rang, piercing and sharp, causing her to exclaim in pain.

She clapped her hands over her ears and glared. "Are you always this arrogant?"

He eyed her with a gaze that almost seemed amused. The tone was anything but. "Come here before you truly say something I'll have to punish."

She pressed her lips to avoid more trouble and climbed to the top of the dais, which had a platform big enough for her to stand a pace away from the man on the monster chair. A big man. He sneered as he looked at her.

"Jakori said you were a healer. Obviously not much of one. Your face is marked."

"Your skills of observation must be so handy in ruling your kingdom, Your Majesty." She should have bitten her tongue.

"You are impertinent."

"Sorry, Your Highness. Being held in a cage does that to a person."

"If you don't want a cage, then you need to show you have some worth. Let's see if you are as talented as Jakori claims."

He snapped his fingers, the sound slight, and yet a door opened and in came two guards holding a man between them. His head was shorn to the scalp, his jaw slack, his body limp.

"Slice him." The king waved his fingers.

The guard obeyed, a sharp blade slashing across the prisoner's arm. The blood flowed fast, not that the man noticed. He kept gazing off in the distance.

"Bring him to her." No need to point.

The guards carried the prisoner close enough to toss by her feet. The injured arm flopped, and the blood pooled. She caught the metallic odor of it. But more than that, felt it calling to her. Tingling against her senses. That was new.

"Heal that man," the king demanded. "Let's see what you can do."

"I can't." The king appeared much too cold to trust. The answer as to what she should do became clear. *I can't let him know what I can do.*

He leaned forward and said softly, yet firmly enough that she heard him, "Heal that man."

In her head, she also heard, *or else.*

She clasped her hands in front of her. "I don't have any supplies. He'll need a salve. The fresher, the better. And bandages. Most likely some stitching, which is a task for a doctor."

"Put your hands on him and fix his wound."

"I'm sorry, but I don't have that kind of skill." She decided in that moment it was better to pretend ignorance. Who was this king? She'd thought she knew the names of all the domains, but she'd never heard of Eden. And a king in the Marshlands? Not something she'd ever learned. Then again, she didn't know much of anything outside of the Ruby domain.

Could be he truly was a king, and Enclave. In which case, what would happen if she claimed psionic abilities? Would he offer a place in his castle? Ha. The best she could hope for was to be put to death.

"If you don't heal him, he dies."

Because the king's guard had cut deep and true. The man would bleed out. Sofia stood over the stranger, wringing her hands. She had no idea what to do. Where to start.

What she'd done for Gunner in the marsh she'd accomplished out of desperation. Even if she wanted to repeat it, she wasn't sure she could. This man meant nothing to her. And he meant nothing to the king. Was his life worth hers?

If she did rescue this man, what then? What would this king want of her?

"I can't help him." She shrugged. "You should bring him to a physician."

The king leaned away and smiled. Not reassuring. "So that's how you're playing it? Fantastic. Kill him and get him out of here." The king slashed his hand.

The guards moved in, and she gasped, "You're not going to even try to save him?"

"Why would I? A convicted criminal is useless to me. He was slated for the fights and, given his skill level, would have died anyhow."

The callousness appalled. "Why must you kill?"

"Because I will not waste resources and food on criminals. People convicted in my kingdom either earn their keep while incarcerated by entertaining, or they die."

She didn't ask what he meant by entertaining because she understood. He had his own version of the Enclave court. "Will you kill me, too, since Jakori lied to you about my abilities?"

"Kill you? My dear Sofia, I have too many uses planned for you." He purred the words as he descended the steps, bringing a heavy presence with him. It smothered. He didn't hide his power. He stood on the floor, and yet he towered over her.

She leaned away. "I'm not useful. Not one bit."

"You better hope you are because the Marsh

kingdom has no use for people who don't provide for the greater good."

"Doing what?"

"You know what I expect. My kingdom could use more healers."

"If you bring me ingredients, I can make some salves."

He snorted. "I don't need creams. Perhaps you need a little bit of time to think about your decision. I'm going to give you a taste of what life could be like if you choose to be a productive citizen and obey your king."

"You're not my king. I'm a Ruby citizen." Her chin lifted.

"No, you're not." His teeth gleamed. The smile didn't reach his eyes. "You were banished. Tossed out for crimes against an Enclave citizen."

"I was wronged." Her lips pursed.

"I don't doubt you were, but that is the nature of the game. And now you are in a new game. My game. Obey the rules and you will earn privilege. But disobey..." He shrugged. "Try it and you'll see what happens." The king looked past her and ordered, "Take her to the pink tower room. Guard her door. Make sure she's fed."

A rough grip around her arm saw her high-stepping quickly to follow. They practically dragged her up some steps and tossed her inside a room that was probably nicer than anything she should be enjoying.

The king had called it the pink room because it oozed that shade. From the palest of pink rugs on the floor to the bright pop of it on the massive bed. She'd wager it was soft. There was an oversized window, which she immediately checked out. It exited onto a balcony overlooking a river that wound through the town. An eclectic mix of old and new, the windows of them strung with fronds for curtains, fabric in others. Plaster and stone. Gleaming mirrored surfaces set off by dark and pitted stone. A city reborn it appeared.

And she was in the tower. Gripping the railing, she glanced down. The drop was too far. She wouldn't be escaping in that direction.

She turned back to the room and explored further, discovering the bathroom with a tub that had faucets running hot water.

Not warm.

Hot.

And on the lip of the tub, scented soaps and lotions. The thought of taking a relaxing soak without someone trying to scrub her tempted.

She bit her knuckles and tried to think of Gunner. She'd just been bathed. Who knew where he was or what he suffered.

Stepping back out into the bedroom, she tried the main door next. No surprise, they'd locked it against her. She ignored the books stacked by the bedside and the carafe and glass sitting on a tray. It didn't feel right to enjoy the amenities while she didn't know what had happened to Kitty or Gunner.

The day waned into night, and she stood on the balcony watching as the sun set. The beauty of it actually took her breath.

"Gorgeous, isn't it? I demanded this view when I had the castle rebuilt."

Sofia whirled at the voice and beheld the king in her chamber, looking more confident than he had the right to.

"What are you doing here?"

"My castle. I go where I like."

She stepped back inside. "What if I'd prefer some privacy?"

"That kind of thing is earned. And you forgot to say, 'Your Highness.'" There was mockery in the words.

"Far be it from me to show disrespect." The same way she'd once shown it to Citizen Jezebelle. She'd end up beheaded for sure.

He smiled. "Perhaps for this evening, you can call me Roark."

She blinked in confusion. Was the king flirting with her?

A commotion at the door showed someone wheeling in a cart with several domes sitting on it. The woman pushing it wore the loose belted tunic and trousers that ended at the knee. Her sandals wound up her calf. Her hair was short, too short to even brush. She also kept her gaze down as she uncovered all the dishes.

Sofia couldn't help but stare at the food. She'd never seen some of the things on the plates other than in pictures. She'd definitely never eaten any of them.

The king waved. "Sit and eat."

She shook her head.

"Why not?"

"Because I don't know if Gunner has food. And your friend Jakori said he was going to hunt down my cat and skin it. So no, I am not going to eat your food." She crossed her arms and turned her head to the side, expecting to feel him pressure her. To use his psionic ability to force the issue.

"I'll pay Jakori and his men to not hunt your cat."

The reply took her by surprise. "You will?"

His lips quirked. "Why not? After all, by agreeing to pay them for prisoners, they no longer eat them."

She gulped. Perhaps there was something worse than being sold. "What about Gunner? Did you buy him too?"

"I did."

"Where is he?"

His expression went flat. "He is no longer your concern."

"What if I insist?"

"Insist and I will remind you who is actually in charge here," he growled, and the force of his presence bore down on her so strongly she leaned away. "Sit your rear end down and eat."

"No." She barely managed to whisper the word.

"Are you going to make me have a guard hold you down while another force-feeds you? Because I will."

Looking at his cold expression, she didn't doubt it. She sat down and stared, overwhelmed by choice and guilt.

"Guilt about eating. Because of your companion." Roark chuckled as he murmured, "I assure you this Gunner you're so concerned about might not be eating as well as you, but he's being fed."

"You know where he is."

"I do." The king served himself a variety of items, not just the meat.

She took a small portion of some fluffy white

mixture. A piece of battered meat. The food was a medley of color and texture from crispier bits to blue leafy things drizzled in sauce she discovered as she took a bite. The sweet tang and the crunch were delicious. As was the battered meat. The fluffy white stuff was bland, but there was a sauce to solve that and a drink. A flavored water that had a bit of an aftertaste she couldn't place. But she couldn't help herself. Once she started eating, she couldn't stop.

By the time she did, the king leaned back, looking all too satisfied with himself. They'd not spoken much during the meal, but once they were done, he eyed her.

"You were a Ruby citizen."

"Yes."

"Ranked as?"

"Apprentice apothecary."

"We call them druggists here," he remarked, leaning back in his seat, drinking a glass of red liquid. Wine, he called it. She took a sip and made a face. She stuck to water.

Water she spat out as he said, "Did you know that only psionics attuned to the healing arts are allowed to work in the Enclave city pharmacies?"

She choked while he sat there looking quite composed. "I am not psionic."

"Not true. You are not an Enclave member, but

you are most definitely a psion. Like me. Like so many others."

"That's not—"

"Possible?" he said, interrupting. "Oh, but it is. I and my others are living proof. Which is why the Enclave is going to have to recognize me and accept that I'm king."

"They'll never make you Enclave," she blurted out.

"I don't really care if they do, but they will respect my kingdom and my authority."

"Or else what?" she said.

"In ancient times, we would have gone to war."

She gaped at him. "Are you insane?"

"Not yet." He stood and paced her room, the size of it impressive until a large man entered.

"What are you going to do to me?"

Rather than answer her question, he went off on a different tangent. "Do you have family, Sofia?"

She shook her head. "Not really. The only thing close would have been my master." Whom she'd not even seen in her final days as he'd been gone on business. She'd been making her own meals when everything happened.

Roark's lip curled. "A master is not family. He's the man who bought you to serve his business."

"Bought?" She shook her head. "We are chosen."

"Bought," he firmly insisted. "With the price depending on your skill level."

"How would you know?" she exclaimed. "You're not even Enclave."

"Because some of us actually take the time to find out more about our neighbors. Your Ruby city for example. It's a bit looser on the morals than other Enclave-controlled places. They don't forbid sex, but they do feed parts of the populace contraceptives. Can't have the wrong sorts making babies."

She couldn't argue because the former was true, and the latter she'd suspected. "I was taken care of." The only rebuttal she had.

"Of course, you were, because you had value. Did everyone you know get the same care?"

She pressed her lips rather than reply. He knew the answer and was trying to make her say it.

"The Ruby queen and her predecessors have been lying to its citizens for a long time, now. Did you know there's a second city only an hour away that has no dome and is a veritable paradise? The Queen's Summer Palace is what they call it."

"You lie."

He shrugged. "Believe me or not. That is your choice."

"Why do you care what I believe or not? Do you

think telling me something I know will help you somehow?"

"I'm trying to convince you to try something different."

"Meaning?"

"I am inviting you to live here. As the king's witch."

"I don't have any psionic abilities," she muttered, realizing even as she said it how stubborn she sounded.

"Jakori is telling the truth of what he saw. I could use a healer of that caliber. Spend the night thinking before you answer." Roark moved past her, and the table still laden with dishes, to the door. "You could do worse than live here under my rule."

"I won't agree to anything without Gunner."

"Unfortunately, he's needed somewhere else."

"Then no deal."

The king paused at the door. "I would strongly advise you rethink that position."

The king could threaten all he liked. Her decision wouldn't change.

SIXTEEN

There were a few things that made a man feel inadequate. One of them was getting into an epic battle with a swamp wizard, only to then be captured and sold.

He'd not even gotten to fight his way out. He'd spent most of his captivity drugged. At one point, partway through their trip, he'd woken tied to the lumbering back of some animal that reeked. He'd been unable to discern if Sofia was anywhere near him. Had she even survived their encounter in the swamp?

He didn't understand how he'd survived. He clearly recalled dying, bleeding, the pain, and then the blessed darkness.

Sofia must have saved him, which surely meant she lived. But they'd been captured. By whom?

Turning his head side to side, he tried to discern how to escape.

Someone noticed and bellowed, "The foreigner is awake."

"Dart him."

Someone stuck him with a pointy object laced with drugs. Gunner fell asleep and woke inside a stone block cell. The door was a set of floor-to-ceiling bars set deep into the structure he'd wager.

Shaking his head, he approached the bars, feeling his body fighting off the effects of the drug. He needed to wake up and figure shit out and soon. Being in a cell didn't bode well. And he was not happy that he didn't know what had happened to Sofia.

"Sofia!" He shouted her name in case she answered.

Jeers met his cry. Kissing noises, too.

The bars jolted him the moment his fingers came in contact with the metal. He snatched them free yelping, "Fuck me!"

"Don't touch the bars," said a gravelly voice.

"That bit of information might have been more useful earlier," he snapped, shaking the tips of his fingers.

"It's not a lesson you soon forget."

The voice seemed familiar, and Gunner

approached the bars once more, remaining just far enough away to avoid electrocution. He peered across from him, trying to discern details despite the current dimness in the place. "Titan, is that you?"

"Depends who's asking."

"As if you don't know. Where you been? We've been wondering where you got to." Gunner could barely see the other man. Titan appeared tucked in the corner of his cell, the light overhead not functioning.

"Here and there."

"We were worried about you."

"I left a message."

"Saying 'gone, see you soon' isn't exactly self-explanatory."

"I went looking for something."

"And found it in a cell?" Gunner said lightly.

Titan snorted. "Apparently I'm good at getting captured, given this is my second time in as many months."

"How did you get arrested?" Gunner queried. "What happened to you?"

"I might have taken a wrong turn and gotten here."

"Where is here?" Gunner glanced at the stone wall, old and pitted, but the bars appeared more recent. "Last I recall I was in the marshes, fighting."

"You are still in the marshes. In the want-to-be kingdom of Roark the First."

"Who? You're gonna have to give me a bit more info."

"Roark, the king of the Marshlands, self-proclaimed, I should add. He's a nobody. Came out of nowhere, barely educated, unmarked, but powerful, apparently. Somehow, he convinced the marsh clans to stop fighting each other and the Enclave and band together."

"Hold on," Gunner interjected. "You mean we're not dealing with an Enclave member?"

"Nope. Roark and the united Marsh clans rebuilt this old city. Rumor says he wants the Marshes to be recognized by the Enclave and declared a sovereign nation so they can build some trade channels."

"What does that have to do with us?"

"Nothing," Titan replied. "We're simply for entertainment. The Marsh king employs the use of tournaments as part of his justice system. Meaning fighting matches with lots of blood."

"So we're under arrest?" he asked. "But I haven't done anything."

"It doesn't take much to be arrested. Turns out Roark is a good ruler, because there aren't enough criminals anymore to please the crowd. So they started conscripting trespassers."

"I wasn't drafted into this fight club. Someone sold me," Gunner remarked.

"Because they found you trespassing. Perfectly legal according to Marsh law."

"That is severely fucked up."

"I don't know. It's brutally efficient from what I've seen." Titan appeared to admire it.

"How long have you been here?"

"Too long," Titan grumbled in reply.

"I wish we'd have known you were a prisoner. We thought you'd left and needed time to deal with the accident." Titan might have returned sporting a metal arm and leg, but his mind and emotions remained scarred. "We would have come to rescue you."

"I don't need rescuing." Titan shifted, as if agitated. "But I have needed time to come to grips with the fact I'm not dead."

"Does that mean you'll come back with me to Haven?"

Titan snorted. "Still trying to be funny I see."

"I'm serious. We are not staying here."

"Maybe you don't want to stay, but I gotta say, this place ain't half bad."

"It's a prison."

"It's easy," Titan said softly.

Meaning what? "Have you tried to escape?"

A low chuckle floated from the cell across from him. "Why would I? I have everything I need here." The words were flat.

Did Titan speak truly or because he knew someone listened?

He might have chatted with Titan some more, but there was a commotion. Boots stomped in cadence and were met by the catcalling of prisoners. But the sound abruptly halted. The reason came into view a moment after the soldiers split to either side of his cell.

A man dressed in black, a few decades old, but no silver yet in his dark hair. They stared at each other a moment.

It was a soldier who broke the silence first. "Kneel for the king."

King? This must be the famous Roark he'd heard of. The man who'd bought him. Who might know where the fuck Sofia was.

"My knees are kind of sore. I think I'll stand." He leaned against the wall.

Kneel.

The command didn't come from any lips, and yet he slammed to the floor anyhow.

"That's better." The king smiled. "Must get these things out of the way if you and I are going to have a chat." He waved at his guards. "Move along. I can handle our guest."

The tromping of boots moved away, and the silence between Gunner and Roark lengthened.

They'd never met, and yet, given the arrogance oozing in front of him, if he'd not talked to Titan, he would still have guessed the man was someone important, an Enclave-level dick for sure.

The nostrils of the king flared. "I have to admit I'm less than impressed. She keeps asking about you, and I really don't see why." The man eyed him, but Gunner reacted at the words.

"What have you done with Sofia?" Gunner reached for the bars, too late remembering the electrical charge. He gasped and shook his hurting hands again while Roark shook his head.

"You and Sofia, both lacking manners. You will address me as 'Your Highness.'"

Gunner would have preferred the term 'pompous prick,' but he knew to play the game for now. "Where is Sofia, Your Highness?" he muttered through gritted teeth.

"Enjoying my hospitality. She's quite the looker. Powerful, too, according to the blood work we've completed. She'll make good breeding stock."

Gunner growled and fought the temptation to reach through the bars. He wanted nothing more than to throttle the man who stood within reach, a cool smile on his lips.

"Don't you touch her."

"Or what? What exactly will you do? You're in a cell."

The observation cooled him. "What do you want with me? Why are you here?" Because Roark wanted to speak to him alone. Well alone except for Titan, who had to be listening.

"Tell about the place you come from. Emerald demesne, correct?"

"Don't know what you're talking about. I'm a Marshlander. One of your subjects as a matter of fact. Which means I demand you respect my rights," Gunner said with a grin.

"You are not a Marshlander. You belong to a group of people led by a man who talks to animals."

Gunner pressed his lips tight. How did this king know so much?

Roark remained undaunted, and uncanny. "I know these things because it is my business to investigate matters that might affect my kingdom."

"I'm no threat to your kingdom."

"Never said you were." The king smirked. "You're what I call an information source. There is a treasure trove available. Your mind is wide open."

The very idea his mind was being rifled without him knowing chilled. “Leave my head alone.”

“Don’t blame me if you’re going to broadcast everything you feel and know.”

“I’m not doing it on purpose, trust me,” Gunner managed through gritted teeth.

“Tell me about Emerald.” Roark pinned him with a gaze.

The urge to spill everything he’d ever experienced in his life had him biting his tongue. He closed his eyes hard and tried to not see the land he knew but didn’t always love. The Wasteland with its cracks and sparse pockets of habitation.

“Not a very nice place. No wonder they’re always trading for more and more food. A good thing the mine hasn’t dried up,” the king muttered.

Gunner couldn’t make any sense of it. Gunner tried to focus on something other than thoughts about his home. “Is it true you’re going to make me fight?”

“I hear you’re quite good at it.”

A man had his pride, and Gunner’s swelled at the praise. “Maybe. Does it make a difference?”

“It does if you win.”

“What does a winner receive?”

“That depends. Win big enough and I will grant a boon.”

"Anything I want?" Gunner asked.

"If it's in my power."

"What if I asked for my freedom?"

The king canted his head. "The most obvious choice, of course. And you could demand it. I would recommend, though, that a warrior of your skill, who is perhaps in need of employment, request to serve in my guard."

"Why the fuck would I want to work for you?"

"Because I pay very well," Roark explained. "Given it is also considered an honor, I've had many former arena winners ask for it as their boon."

"Titan didn't."

"Titan enjoys self-flagellation," the king said dryly.

"Bite me," was the grumbled reply from the other cell.

"I am not here to negotiate with Titan but the one called Gunner. Second-in-command of the Wasteland group known as Haven. Renowned for his skill with guns and knives. I hear you took out an infected bog magus."

"You mean the guy inside the muddy puddle?"

The king's lips twitched. "Yes. It is an unfortunate ailment that hits some of those born with a strong affinity to it. The wild overtakes the man."

"That wild tried to take Sofia from me. It didn't end well."

"She means something to you, this woman?" Roark bluntly asked.

It occurred to him to lie, but he couldn't. "Sofia isn't to be harmed. If I win in this fight you want me to have, then she walks free with me."

"You and the witch? That would require two boons. Alas you can have only one, and it must involve you. Sofia has her own task to accomplish."

The words didn't reassure. "What do you want in exchange for her? You need information? I'll tell you about Emerald. Not that there's much to say. A rather sizeable portion of it is barren, with the majority of its people living in domes ruled by the Enclave, overseen by a queen."

"Which is common knowledge. I want to know more about you and Haven, a tiny group of non-citizens managing to live free and evade the rule of the Emerald queen."

"I don't know what you're talking about." He played dumb. He couldn't have said why.

Titan snorted. "He already knows all about us. He reads minds."

"I do," Roark affirmed. "Some of them more boring than others."

"Stay out of my head." Gunner scowled.

"I will if you tell me what I want to know," the king pointed out slyly. "I hear Emerald lost a dome to rebels recently."

"You don't say. That would be pretty brazen." He neither admitted or denied.

The king smiled as if he knew. "It would be, but then again, Emerald has been struggling for a while. Rumors are they're having problems thriving. Citizens are disappearing, the Incubaii tanks keep failing, and given their laws banning actual natural procreation, they are in a spiral that will lead to extinction without change."

The stark prediction had Gunner shaking his head. "You're lying."

"Am I? You have seen their corruption. Have yearned to put a stop to it."

A familiar frustration welled within. "So what if I have? What am I supposed to do? I'm just one man."

Roark's expression turned cold. Icy cold. "I am also one man, and I started in a hovel. Born in mud, living in mud. Eating mud when my parents were killed. Now I'm king."

No mention of what happened in between, but Gunner couldn't help a grudging admiration. "Does a self-proclaimed king count, though?" he mused aloud, being an intentional shit.

Roark didn't grab the bait. "Tell me about Haven."

"I don't know a Haven."

"You really shouldn't lie to someone with empathic psionic ability."

A what of the what? "I don't give a flying fuck if you're a mind wizard. I am not ratting out my home."

"The Emerald City does not consider you a citizen."

"I wasn't talking about them. Stay out of my head." He closed his eyes and tried to think of anything but Haven.

It had the opposite effect. Images of the bunker they'd lost flashed in his head. A few years of stability and a place that was thriving and growing, lost in an Enclave attack. He tried to focus on something else, anything else, like...Sofia.

She appeared in his mind and in ways he hoped that mind wizard couldn't see, her lips parted and full, her cheeks flushed, his name spoken in a soft throaty whisper. Once he started, he couldn't stop thinking about her. It amazed him she seemed to like him, too. Dare he say maybe even love? She'd saved his life.

He needed to get out of here and find her.

I know how you can see her. Come here.

He didn't even question the demand, just

stepped closer to the bars. Hands reached in to grab him by the cheeks and drag him close. The bars didn't zing him this time, and yet he still jiggled as the king held on to him. His thoughts churned, and he caught more than a few glimpses of himself, how he looked, his arms, legs, other parts.

When the king released him, Gunner gasped and fell to the floor.

"Well, that was interesting," Roark said. "And now that I know everything I need, what do you say we pay a visit to Sofia?"

SEVENTEEN

The next day, the king returned, striding into Sofia's room without a single knock. He didn't exactly surprise her. She'd been awake for hours.

Roark wore only a button-up shirt tucked into leather pants with thick boots. To her surprise, a cat followed on his heels. A tiny, sleek, two-toned creature with an arrogant face.

The king paid it no mind as he leaned against the doorframe. "Have you come to a decision?"

She chose to delay. "Good morning, Your Highness." She curtsied and held it long enough that he snapped, "Get up already."

She rose and eyed him. He looked frazzled and impatient. "It's a beautiful day." It actually was; she'd seen the sun rise over the city, an incredible sight without a dome. She found that facet fascinating.

"You are trying my patience. Will you heal for me or not?"

"I told you. I don't know how."

"I see you plan to keep lying. Very well. Have it your way. You will remain in this room until you cooperate."

"I can't cooperate. I am not a psionic, just a simple apothecary, and not even a full one but an assistant."

"You will have this morning to rethink your stance."

She almost yelled after Roark as he slammed the door shut, only narrowly missing the tail of the cat as it slipped in and chose to nap on her bed.

The day passed. Long. Boring. Without food. The carafe of water long empty.

The king thought to manipulate her. She feared it might just work.

Around dinnertime, and hours after the king left, she lay wide-awake on top of her sheets when there was a commotion. She sat up, heart pounding, as the door opened and someone wearing a hooded cloak slipped in.

"Who is it? What do you want?" She brandished a book, her only weapon.

"It's me." The voice froze her.

"Gunner? Is that really you?"

He shucked the hood as he moved close, the parting of the cloak showing he wore a loose tunic and pants like the servants here. His hair appeared a touch disheveled, his jaw showed a bristly shadow, but his eyes were clear.

He'd never looked better.

Sofia scrambled out of bed and into his arms, taking him by surprise. He staggered but recovered quickly, his arms coming around her.

"You're alive!"

"Of course, I am," he said with a chuckle. "Did you really think a dungeon could hold me?"

"I was so worried," she admitted, leaning to look into his eyes. He seemed taller than before.

"You can relax now. I've come to rescue you."

"Thank you." For some reason that made her deliriously happy. She rose on tiptoe and pressed her mouth to his.

He didn't react at first, and when he did, it was to give her a quick kiss then set her away from him. "We don't have time for that. It won't be long before they notice I knocked out the guards."

"You fought your way here?"

"I didn't have a choice. The king is planning to make me fight to the death. Thought we should get out before that happens."

"How will we escape?"

"You leave that to me. Give me a second and we'll get going." Gunner grabbed her sheet and tore a strip from it.

"What are you doing?"

"Just bandaging up my arm." He flicked the cloak, and she noticed the blood soaking his sleeve. "I got nicked by a blade. Don't worry, it's only a scratch."

"Let me see." She reached, but he angled away.

"It's nothing."

"Give." She grabbed hold of his arm, frowning at the lack of awareness she usually felt when they touched. There was something odd about...

The idea slid away before it could form, and she pulled his arm close.

The slice went across the bicep, deep enough that it bled steadily down his arm.

"Told you, it's nothing. A bandage will fix it," he remarked.

"Don't be foolish." She placed her hands on it. "We can't escape with you dripping like this." She didn't allow doubt or a lack of cream to stop her. She could do this. Had done this before. But she wasn't panicked this time. Not desperate to heal him.

She squeezed his arm, felt the firm muscle, the tear in the skin over it. The tips of her fingers heated. She felt it going after the cut, the warmth sinking into his flesh, and because for once her mind was clear, she actually got a deeper look at him.

And quickly realized it wasn't Gunner. The heat shut off immediately.

There was a pleased chuckle. "Was that so hard?"

At the change in timbre, her gaze flew in shock to see not Gunner but Roark, wearing a smirk and his own face.

She released him and backed away. "What are you doing here? How?" How had he worn the visage of another?

"Doesn't matter how I did it. What matters is you can heal."

"No, I didn't. Your arm is still injured." Indeed, it still looked slightly angry, but the flesh had pulled together, and it no longer bled.

"Only because you stopped."

"I won't do it again." She tucked her hands behind her back.

"Heal someone for me, and I will give you a position in my kingdom. A home, wages—"

She interrupted. "You should find yourself a real doctor."

"Someone save me from stubborn woman," Roark growled. "I am tired of your arguing. Come with me." He wrapped his hand around her arm and pulled.

"Where are you taking me?"

But the king wasn't answering. The lithe feline followed them out of the room, the tiny body enough to have guards jumping out of the way. It sauntered quite saucily, and Sofia wondered why they allowed it so much liberty.

She was marched from the castle to a vehicle, a rare thing in Eden she realized, which sped through cobbled streets with channels running down the sides. She had a chance to see the strange medley of old and new, the stonework of some ancient place still providing a framework, with patches of newer stone filling in the gaps.

The king saw her watching. "It's still a work in progress."

"Your city has no dome."

"Because we know it's possible to live with the land. For the rare times the air or the foliage tries to poison us, there are remedies."

"What about the dust storms?"

"We don't get those here, although it does rain. Hence the trenches in all the roads. It's said a long time ago, when the city was new, that the water ran through the streets and the inhabitants boated everywhere. But that was before the world tilted again. The city spent some time after that abandoned."

"Why did the original inhabitants leave?" Despite herself, she was curious.

He shrugged. "No one is quite sure what happened, although most of the stories blame the marsh."

"Yet you still chose to live here."

"Because I always wanted a castle."

She blinked at him. "That's a little crazy."

"You'll discover I'm a man who gets what he wants."

Meaning she should stop fighting him. Yet to give in might prove even worse.

"How did you get people to agree to help you?"

"Because many of those who live here had nowhere else to go. It seemed easier to restore than start from nothing."

"And they helped you?" she asked.

"Yes."

"Why?"

"I offered them a better choice. A chance."

"That involves serving you," she said.

"You should join them. They seem quite happy."

The vehicle stopped outside an amphitheater that no man or woman had built. The stone bowl appeared melted in rings and then carved, the tiers forming balconies for the crowd. There were stairs chiseled into the melted and shaped rock. At the very bottom of the pit, a pair of giant archways, currently sealed by bars, and a few smaller ones. It reminded her of the Ruby City Court but with no roof overhead. The jubilant air also proved a change.

At the arrival of the king, the crowd chanted and cheered, "All hail the king, master of the marsh." There were no boos or jeers. Then again citizens of Ruby never dared either. People were attached to their heads.

Yet it wasn't fear that made them enthusiastic. There was something different in this crowd. Something boisterous and emotional. The king stood at the edge of the terrace and said nothing, did nothing. He had his hands tucked behind his back. The people roared at the sight of him.

She hung back, trying to understand why they had come here.

After a moment, the king turned his back to the ongoing noise and pointed her to a seat that flanked the larger one meant for him. Once he sat down, the cheering finally stopped.

An announcer bellowed out a greeting. "Welcome one, welcome all. It's time for the weekly justice fights."

"What's about to happen? Why am I here?" she

asked, because the title of the event didn't inspire confidence.

"You have repeatedly asked to see your companion. I'm granting your wish."

She turned a glance on him. "You're making Gunner fight."

"I am. Against my champion in the final round. A champion who has yet to lose by the way."

The words did their job of giving her a chill. "That's because whoever it is, he's not yet come up against Gunner. He's an excellent warrior."

"I guess we'll see. Unless you've changed your mind about working for me."

"I can't." She said it softly, even as she had a sinking feeling she'd just lost. It was one thing to ignore the plight of a stranger and keep pretending she had no power, but now Gunner's life hung in the balance.

A horn blew, and an announcer spoke, excitement in his every word as he introduced the criminals, detailed their crimes. The crowd took to booing often during their segment. She noticed the crimes weren't petty things. Assault. The luring of a child. Theft.

The cases had been decided beforehand. Those in front of her were actual criminals facing their sentencing, and the crowd roared with excitement as the man convicted of luring a child was torn apart by a swarm of small animals that covered him so thoroughly only his screams emerged. There was the man who assaulted a woman who got to go up against a different woman armed with knives. A champion hired to mete out justice on behalf of the victim. When the warrior woman was finished and flung the hunk of meat that would hurt no one again to the ground, the crowd went silent for a moment before it screamed.

Brutal. Sofia glanced over to see only callous disregard in the king's face. He watched and didn't care. His court was a bloodthirsty place.

She didn't belong here. She couldn't stay.

When Gunner finally appeared in the arena, fear filled her, especially when his gaze sought hers. The idiot even winked.

The king finally deigned to speak to her. "The moment has come for your Gunner to face my champion. A champion who will only stop on my command. The choice is yours, Sofia. Will you be my witch, or does he die?"

EIGHTEEN

After the king left Gunner—wearing Gunner's face the fucking prick!—he'd railed for a while. What if the charlatan fooled Sofia?

He grabbed the bars, yelled as the electricity once more ran through his hands, and cursed some more.

"Fuck me, you're being loud," Titan complained.

"I think I've earned the right. That asshole is wearing my face like an outfit. He's going to use me against Sofia."

"Your fault for pissing him off. You should have told him what he wanted. He's a mind reader. It's not like you can hide anything from him."

Gunner grimaced. "Axel can." But most people didn't have the kind of mental shield necessary to block someone with true power.

"You're not Axel. And neither am I. Fucker's good at using our weaknesses against us," Titan grumbled.

"What did he use against you?"

"Nothing. It didn't work."

It sounded as if there was a story there, but there wasn't time to talk about it. Guards appeared, and the prisoners were carted off, a few at a time, being prettied for the upcoming fights. Gunner ended up bathed, his hair trimmed, his beard shorn until only smooth skin remained along his jaw. They oiled his body and dressed him in form-fitting breeches. No shoes. No shirt. No armor.

It was ridiculous. Yet he fit in with the others. Because it wouldn't do for the gladiators to show poorly when they entered the ring against the criminals.

When it was his turn, there wasn't much surprise they pitted him against Titan. They were the only two left.

His friend wouldn't look at him as he loosened his body. Gunner noticed the metal limbs, a result of intensive injuries Titan had suffered. He'd not been the same since the attack by the wild animals and loss of his arm and leg.

"What's the plan?" he murmured to Titan.

"Win."

Against his friend? Then again, he hadn't forgotten the king's words. Prevail and he could have a boon.

What would he ask for? Freedom seemed the most obvious. But surely there was a way to ensure Sofia came, too?

Exiting from the cool tunnel to the noisy bowl of the arena wasn't what caused him to stumble. His glance around the stadium only barely took note of the jeering crowd. He had eyes only for Sofia, standing in the grandest box of all, wearing a filmy gown with her hair pinned back. She stood from her seat and stared at him. Sitting beside her, the king who smirked.

Gunner could have sworn he heard Roark's voice in his head, whispering, *Win and you can use your boon to see her.* An interesting idea. If he saw her, then maybe they could escape.

Her worry showed, and Gunner winked at her, trying to show reassurance even as he muttered to Titan, "I need you to throw this match." Because he wasn't entirely sure he could beat his friend, not with the modifications to his body.

"I can't." Titan's jaw shifted. He kept glancing upward, not at the king but to his left, where another woman sat. She appeared to be ignoring the proceedings, more interested in a tablet she held.

"I need to win this for Sofia."

"I am not losing. You don't understand. I need this win to make Roark promise." Now Titan's gaze flicked to the king. What was it he wanted to win?

"I'm sorry, but I'm gonna have to knock you out." Because Gunner had learned the fight didn't have to be to the death.

Titan slid a glance at him. "You can try."

The announcer's voice rang out, offering an embellished intro. "From the barbarian Emerald lands comes a marauder without compare. He is called the Lucky Rat because he always seems to get out of trouble. But will he prevail tonight against our current champion? The man who is part machine and all killer, our very own Tin Man."

The crowd went wild. Gunner glanced across at Titan and tried to remember all the weak points he'd learned during their training time together. There wasn't much, and it had been a while. The one thing he did recall was Titan could handle a lot of abuse.

They were given no weapons. Not unheard of. Sometimes the crowd liked a sweaty and slick wrestling match, one of strength and dominance. They also cheered to see grown men crying when twisted a particular way.

As Gunner walked away from Titan, he limbered up discreetly, keeping an eye on Sofia.

Noticed the king waiting. Waiting to see what he'd do.

He had to win. Against his friend. Which meant taking Titan out without killing him but in a way that would satisfy the king.

He stood, head bowed, hands loose by his side. The crowd grew quiet, and he listened, reached with the senses he'd honed while blind, and leapt straight up as Titan rushed in, his silent run a thing of locomotive power.

Gunner remained safely out of reach as Titan charged past. Titan took a moment to slow his momentum enough to flip around. Meanwhile Gunner landed in a crouch, one hand on the ground, his eyes on Titan.

With a bit of luck, he'd put Titan on his back.

He rushed for his friend, who charged. They hit in a thud that shook them both. Their hands reached and their legs twisted as they grappled. Hard and fast. Heaving and panting.

Straining as best as they could. This was where Titan would beat him. He had the strength, whether it be natural or machine-based. Gunner could feel Titan gaining the advantage, bending him. It wouldn't be long before something snapped.

And then suddenly he wasn't losing. Gunner achieved the upper hand, flipped his friend onto his back. When Titan heaved under him, he let the guy get to his feet before he slugged him again and again. He felt bad for hitting his friend, but only one could win.

Might as well be him.

The last uppercut took Titan on the side of the jaw and snapped him hard enough that he wavered on his feet. When Titan fell, Gunner could have sworn the floor trembled. The crowd lost its mind.

Sofia stood and clapped. Her joy obvious.

He waited for the king to acknowledge his win. To ask him what he wanted.

Roark stood and placed his hands on the parapet. He gazed down. "Congratulations on winning. It seems your luck is holding. I'll see you at the castle for your prize."

Gunner wanted to argue, but perhaps this way was better. Making demands of a king in the middle of an arena filled with his people might not be best.

There was time wasted with those escorting him insisting he bathe. Then they dressed him in pants, a shirt, and even shoes. He felt like a winner, which boosted his confidence as he was led through a place that displayed a grandeur and wealth he'd not ever actually seen. Sure, he'd come across ruined remnants of greatness. But the castle and then the throne room showed opulence.

A wealth and prosperity Roark supposedly built. What kind of man inspired that kind of work and loyalty?

Gunner tried to keep his awe to himself as he was shown into the presence of the king. It took control to keep from running when he saw Sofia stood at the bottom of the dais, hands clasped, the tension in her evident through the stiffness of her posture.

"Hey, sweetheart," he called out.

She didn't move or reply.

That kind of worried him. "Are you okay? Has the king treated you well?"

That merited a slight nod.

"You didn't agree to anything, did you?"

No reply.

He stopped in front of Sofia, and instead of looking at the king, he took her hands. "I won't have you promising anything on my behalf."

"Promise what? I can't do anything," she whispered stiffly. Her eyes were wide and full of fear.

"That's the right answer," he said softly. "Don't worry."

"I am worried, though." She clasped him tight.

She'd yet to figure out luck wouldn't kill him. Not here. Not yet.

"If you're done making false promises, we have to settle your prize," the king interrupted.

Gunner cast a heated look at the king. "You know I want my freedom."

"Then you can have it. But just so we're clear, while you can leave, Sofia stays here."

Immediately, Gunner shook his head. "Like fuck. Sofia comes with me."

"That requires a second boon. You won only once. Your choice. Your freedom or hers. You can't have both."

He spoke without hesitation. "You will free her and never bother her again, nor will any of your people, for so long as she lives."

Despite it being a multi-part wish, the king snapped his fingers. "Agreed. Sofia, you are free to go."

Her mouth rounded. "Go where? I have nowhere to go."

"Not my problem," Roark said. "Now move away from the rat."

"Why?" she asked, blinking up at the king as soldiers grabbed hold of Gunner and pulled him away.

"Let me go," he growled, shaking free.

The guards blocked him from approaching Sofia.

She and the king still spoke. "Your companion

chose to save you over himself. Altruistic of him. Also stupid. Someone shoot the man. He's selected his prize."

"No!" Sofia yelled. "He won. You can't do that."

From his position behind the soldiers, Gunner's blood ran cold. The king planned to use Sofia's affection for Gunner against her.

"You agree then to work for me?"

"Yes, I'll heal for you. Are you happy? Now leave Gunner alone," she yelled.

"I think you're lying. Shoot him." The king flicked his fingers, and Sofia, expression horrified, screamed.

NINETEEN

Sofia winced at the loud crack of the firing gun, but Gunner recoiled, his shoulder flung back by the impact of a bullet. Red stained his chest, soaking his shirt. He went down to his knees, expression incredulous as he bled out.

Her heart stopped.

She took a step, but the king barked, "Don't touch him."

If she didn't do something, he would die in front of her. "Why would you do that?" she screamed, turning on the king. "I told you I would do what you wanted."

"But would you have done it properly? Or would you have held back? I can't have you holding back. There is too much at stake."

"Why are you doing this to me?" she sobbed.

"Why won't you leave me alone?"

"When are you going to let go of what the Enclave hammered into you over and over? When will you realize the good you can do? Why do you insist on hiding your ability?"

"Because..." She looked at her hands, flexed her fingers. "Because I am afraid."

"Afraid of what? Being great? You could save him." The king pointed to Gunner, who appeared dead on the floor, and yet it was almost as if she could also see a shadowy version of him standing there yelling at her.

The king said nothing as she stumbled to his side. "You're cruel." She dropped to her knees beside Gunner. Poor dead and dying Gunner.

"Hey, sweetheart," he whispered, his eyes half shut.

"Gunner." She breathed his name.

He took one last breath. His body heaved a final time. Then he died, and for a moment, she wanted to die with him. Then she reacted, slapping her hands to his chest, only they went right through his body. His entire frame disappeared, and she was left staring at the floor.

Her vision warped as reality snapped back into place. Gunner stood off to the side yelling at her. "Ignore what you see! He's playing with your head."

No, what Roark had done wasn't playing. He'd shown the possibility through a vision. What might happen. "He'll kill you if I don't help him."

"Fuck him. You don't have to do shit."

Yes she did. Gunner had not seen what could—would—happen. Not felt the crushing despair. She wouldn't let him die.

Whirling from Gunner, she tucked her hands in front of her stomach and stated, "I'll do it. I'll be your witch."

Gunner yelled, "No. I won't let you trade yourself for me. Get the fuck out of my way, assholes." Gunner fought the soldiers, and while he might not be injured, there were plenty of them converging on him.

"Don't hurt him," she exclaimed, pleading with the king. "I said I'd help, but you have to promise you won't hurt him."

"Put him to sleep." The king snapped his fingers.

Gunner bellowed. His body heaving, his eyes wild, his step wavering as the drugged darts took effect. He sank to his knees, reaching for her. "Don't."

Didn't he understand? For him, she'd do anything.

Gunner was caught before he hit the floor. The king gave his orders. "Take him somewhere he can recover." He joined and then surpassed her, a tall ominous figure drawing a cloud around him that licked the senses.

"Follow me," Roark commanded.

It no longer occurred to her to refuse. The horror at seeing Gunner die clung to her still. She didn't want to feel it again.

The path they took through the castle brought them all over the place until they ended up in a tower similar to hers, but they went higher, the steps winding around and around until they found themselves in the peak, where there was a massive open space with windows all around.

The room was bright and white and so very clean. The windows were closed, the white drapes hanging without a flutter or speck of dirt. The shelves running the length of the wall underneath appeared quite tidy with perfectly aligned books and objects. There was a round table surrounded by a few chairs. On it was a partially completed puzzle. She'd received one once as a present. She'd never had time to actually complete it. Who did puzzles in this childish place?

There was a swing with a cushioned seat and a rocking chair with a rounded base. The bed she avoided looking at was massive, with four posters rising to form a frame from which draped a canopy.

The light pink fabric panels hanging from the top rail were drawn.

Beside the bed was a trolley covered in bottles. The smell of sickness filled the air and worsened when the drapes around the bed retracted, tugged open by ghostly fingers. Sofia heard a slight wheeze.

She looked down upon a child. A small girl child with long white hair pulled to the side in plaits. Her features were sunken, a sign of malnutrition or dehydration, maybe even both. Except Sofia didn't think it was from lack of food or water. She noted the carafe beside the bed, the bowl with fruit in it and, beside it, wafers of some sort.

"What's wrong with the child?" Sofia asked, moving away from the king and closer to the bed.

"She has the Marsh sickness."

"Meaning?"

"Lack of appetite. Aches and pains. Convulsions. It varies from child to child. Those that survive never get it again."

"Do most survive?"

"Not once the fever turns to chills." Said in a low monotone, even though the child slept.

She put her hand on the girl's forehead. It was cold. Too cold. Yet her skin felt damp. "I've never seen a sickness like this," she had to admit.

"You have to help her."

Sofia glanced at the king. "Why didn't you tell me it was a child who required my help?"

"Would it have made a difference?"

The answer should have been no. Yet, looking upon the frail body, she realized it did matter. She remembered a few other kids while growing up who got sick. One of them—apprenticed with her—fell ill, left, and never returned. It never occurred to her until now to wonder if that person died.

"I don't know what to do." The truth.

"Help my daughter." The anguish in his words almost excused his behavior. He obviously loved this child, like she loved Gunner.

People sometimes made hard choices to save those they cared for.

"I will try, but I can't make promises." Sofia placed her hands on the girl, one on her forehead, the other against her midsection. She closed her eyes and concentrated, forcing some intent. *Heal.*

Her hands didn't warm. The child moaned, and her father shifted, grabbing the girl's hand, bowing his head against it.

Why wasn't it working? It took some inward looking to realize she still feared. Feared that she'd fail. What if she wasn't special after all? In some ways, that might be the worse thing of all.

She looked at the wan face of the dying girl. She

had to try. What if she could do good? What if...what if she could be a person who made a difference? Who saved?

The heat started, pulsing from her fingertips then infusing her whole hand. The girl stiffened, and her breath halted. Stopped and didn't restart.

The father uttered a broken word, but Sofia no longer listened. She *felt*, aware of the child in a way that showed her what was wrong. Showed her the illness attacking.

For a moment, as she hung suspended in a place that wasn't here or there, she agreed with Gunner when he called it magic. The warmth streaming from her was more than just an ability she wielded; it was an indescribable force that understood how to repair. It swept in and killed the bad. Slammed into it and burnt it to nothing, and then, that same power, her magic, reinforced the good.

By the time Sofia pulled away from the child, she was shaking and breathing hard. Opening her eyes caused her to see dancing spots, and she realized the only reason she didn't fall was because she'd landed on her knees.

"Papa." The little voice, hoarse and high-pitched, brought a sob strangled by laughter.

"Is that you, my stinkweed?"

The giggle was enough to bring a wan smile to

Sofia's lips, as did the hugging between the king and his child. She'd done it. She'd saved a life.

And now she felt as if she'd pass out.

She stood and wavered on her feet. "I need to rest."

Roark turned to face her, the child on his hip, a genuine smile on his lips. "Thank you."

She wanted to ask him what happened next, but she teetered on her feet as exhaustion sought to make her its next victim. She barely noticed when she was picked up and carried to her room then practically dumped on her bed.

She couldn't have said how long she slept. When she woke, she realized she wasn't alone. Someone spooned her body. The frame at her back hard and big. It felt right, familiar, and she tingled, but what if it wasn't him?

"I know you're awake."

She relaxed. It was Gunner. "How are you here?" Was this another horrible mirage where the king made her see things?

"The guards brought me about an hour ago. I tried to wake you, but you were sleeping hard."

"I was tired." An understatement. Lethargy still clung to her but more the type that happened when lying abed too long.

"You healed someone for him."

"I did."

"I told you not to."

"I had to. I couldn't let him hurt you." That earned her a squeeze and his warm breath caressing the shell of her ear.

"You're not supposed to need to save me."

"What if I want to? I don't want you to die."

"And I don't want you to be forced to do things. I want you to be free."

The very idea seemed outrageous. "What if I wanted to heal?"

"Do you?" he asked.

"I don't know. For so long I've been scared to admit that I might be different."

"Something has changed with you. Who did you heal?"

"His daughter," she admitted softly. "She was dying. I don't know if she would have made it another day. But I had the power to help her."

"A sick child, eh?" Gunner grunted. "Might explain why the king is acting a little crazy."

"A little?" she retorted. "He killed a man in front of me for not doing what he wanted."

"In the Wastelands, we call that being brutally efficient."

"He could have just told me. He didn't have to

play games," she complained, and yet, at the same time, she had to wonder at his earlier accusation. Would she have tried as hard if Gunner's life weren't at stake?

"The man hasn't managed to make himself king and a force to be reckoned with by being too open and nice."

"I guess," she said with a sigh. "How come you are here? I thought you'd be far from here."

"You asked I not be harmed, not for my freedom."

She grimaced. "I should have worded my request better. I'm sorry. I—"

"Don't you dare apologize." He covered her, his body heavy, his gaze intent, his words soft as he murmured against her ear, "Be careful what you say. We're probably being watched."

She didn't care if they saw her hugging him. "I'm so glad you're not dead."

He grumbled, "It would have been better if you let me die. Now the king will use me against you whenever he wants something."

"I couldn't let you die."

He reared back enough to grin at her. "Which I'm good with. What I don't like is the fact you had to save me in the first place. I won't let you be a slave to that prick who calls himself king."

Her mouth rounded. “You shouldn’t call him names.”

“I’ll call him whatever I like.”

“He was doing it for his daughter.”

“Which is super chill for him. But he’s still a dick.” He rubbed his forehead against hers. “I missed you.”

She hugged him. “I wish...”

“Wish what, sweetheart?”

She eyed him. “Wish we’d had a chance to be together.” Now that she’d cured the king’s daughter, would she have her freedom? Would Gunner go back to his cell to be used every time the king wanted something from her?

“Fuck me. If only I knew they weren’t watching.”

“Are you sure they are?”

His lips quirked. “How do you feel about being undercover?” He tugged the sheet over them, even their heads. “Now they can guess but can’t see.”

“See what?” she asked.

“Shh. We probably don’t have much time.” He kissed her, his mouth hot and hard.

It brought a moan to her lips, a sound of need that he swallowed as his hands fumbled to yank at the gown someone had put her in. He wore only a shirt and trousers.

She yanked at his top, pulling it over his head until his skin rubbed against hers, providing a sensual friction. His lips meshed hotly with hers, igniting her blood and making her wonder how she'd ever believed that fake version of Gunner. Only this man set her alight.

His mouth moved over hers, tugging and teasing, while his hands tucked the sheet behind and under her head. With them fully covered, he knelt under the makeshift tent. She wondered his intent until he leaned down and grasped the tip of her nipple in his mouth. She made a sound and arched as he sucked, moaning and moving, the sensation of his mouth on her incredible.

He switched breasts, sucking and tugging anew on her other nipple until she squirmed and gasped his name. "Gunner."

"Yes, sweetheart?"

She didn't have a reply, just more squirms and moans as he lavished attention on her breasts, teasing them until she gasped and ached for something more. Something to soothe the pulse between her thighs.

He kissed her, his body crouched over her, meaning he had room to slide his hand between them to toy with the flesh between her legs.

"Fuck me, you're wet." He stroked her, teasing

her sensitive flesh, stroking until her hips gyrated, and she moaned.

Only then did he position himself over her and kiss her again. She pulled hungrily at his mouth, feeling that tension inside her, that need.

He pressed against her, the tip of him huge. But he stopped rather than penetrate her. Took a moment to whisper, "Do you want this?"

She did. More than anything. "Yes."

With her consent, he slid into her, thick and long, stretching her in a way she'd never imagined. She gasped into his mouth, clutched him as he moved inside her, rocking and pushing, drawing her tension higher and harder, faster and faster, until she sobbed as her body sat poised on the edge.

"Come for me, sweetheart," he murmured, and with those words, she climaxed.

Cried into his mouth, her body undulating in pleasure. He shuddered against her, his big body trembling, his shaft pulsing inside her.

"I love you," he whispered against her lips. "I love you, and I promise we will find a way out of this."

"How?" she whispered.

It seemed hopeless. Now that the king had seen what she could do, he'd never let her go.

Before he could reply, an alarm went off.

TWENTY

The strident ringing of bells had Gunner rolling from Sofia and pulling up his pants. Never rush out into possible danger without trousers. It was distracting.

As he prepped himself, he held off from swearing about the poor timing of the bells. Then again, he'd kind of been expecting them. His luck wouldn't let him down.

"What's happening?" she asked, doing her own squirm under the sheets as she struggled to get her gown over her head.

"Something's wrong."

"Obviously," she grumbled, sliding out of the bed.

The fabric covered her body down to her ankles, and yet she looked beautiful. Her hair tumbled around her shoulders. He reached for her, needing to hold her.

The door to the room slammed open, startling a cry from Sofia. A pair of guards entered, one of them opening his mouth. "The king said—"

He never finished that sentence. Gunner leaped, moving faster than they expected, ramming into the guard's midsection. The momentum slammed them into the wall, with the guard taking the brunt of the abuse.

He *oomphed* and sagged in Gunner's grip. But he wasn't quite out. Gunner placed his hands on the guard's head, took it in a firm grip, and bounced it off the wall. The impact sent the guard to slump senselessly to the floor.

"Stop it. I'm not here to hurt you." The other guard held up his arm and yelled at Sofia, who kept grabbing books and tossing them.

When she ran out, she grabbed a pillow and shrieked, "Don't you dare touch me."

It worked surprisingly well, offering Gunner the precious seconds he needed to charge the second guard. A hard jab to the gut, an uppercut to daze him, then a knee in the gut again to get him to fold, followed by a yank to the head and an elbow to the back of the neck. The guards lay on the floor, unconscious.

"Help me." He quickly divested the larger guard of his shirt and boots. The pants were similar enough.

The smaller guard's tunic hung on Sofia, and the pants wouldn't stay up, but tucking her gown in them helped.

While Gunner divested them of their weapons, she grabbed the belt off the pants of the bigger one and used it to tie the wrists the guards. It showed she was thinking and not in shock.

With them dressed and him at least armed, Gunner held out his hand to her. "Let's go." Before more guards arrived and made things more difficult.

The bells still rang, a discordant clanging that he hoped would distract anyone they encountered before they looked too closely at the pair of ill-dressed guards.

Entering the hall, he noticed several ornate doorways. "Where are we?" he asked as he began tugging her down the hall.

"Castle."

"I realize we're in the castle. Any idea of how to get out?" They'd reached the end of the hall and entered an open gallery that was more of a walkway circling around a lofty space. It was open to the floor below with a staircase down, and yet, if they followed the railing and remained on this level, across from them appeared to be a set of glass doors leading outside.

"I never saw much outside the bedroom. I don't know how to get out."

He'd not gotten to see much either. The guards that fetched him had hustled his ass upstairs. More concerned about Sofia, the most he'd done was glance out her window and quickly surmise they wouldn't be going out in that direction.

"Spread out. They're around here somewhere!" someone yelled. There was the thud of many booted feet, and a squad of men went running across the floor below, all of them armed.

Avoiding them seemed best. Gunner tightened his fingers on Sofia's, and hugging the wall, they followed the inner circle balcony, too intent on the far end to pay much mind to the splendor displayed below.

They reached the far side and the doors, which opened onto a balcony. Only a few paces deep, it overhung the scummy river running through the city. The gray line of it separating the castle from the opposite shore gave him an idea.

"Do you trust me?" he asked.

"Do I have a choice?"

The reply made him grin, and he cupped her

chin. “We will get out of here. My luck’s feeling pretty good today.”

“Mine’s not.” Her shoulders rounded.

Concern filled him. “Are you not recovered from the healing?”

“If you’re asking if I’m tired, then the answer is yes.”

He glanced down at the river. “We won’t get a better chance to escape.”

“I know. And we need to leave.” She took in a breath.

Gunner glanced at the door in time to see people coming up the steps. They didn’t have long. He glanced back down at the waters sluicing past. He had no idea of the depth, but it was wide enough they’d hit it if they jumped.

“Don’t be stupid and suicidal. Step away from the edge. You don’t want to go for a swim. The river monsters aren’t kind to outsiders,” announced Roark.

Gunner glanced over his shoulder to see the king had joined them on the balcony.

“Says you.”

“Don’t believe me, then jump.” Roark waved his hand.

“We won’t jump, but we’re also not staying,” he announced.

"Why not?" the king asked. "It's not as if you have a home to return to."

"I'm not living in a cell fighting in your petty games. And Sofia isn't going to be your slave."

Roark tucked his hands behind his back. "What if I said you'd be citizens?"

"I'd say your offer comes with terms."

The king's expression proved aloof. "Of course, there are terms. My kingdom, my rules."

At the claim, Gunner snorted. "I've been hearing about you and your rules. Anyone that doesn't follow them gets put in a ring to fight."

"Not just anyone. That particular honor is reserved for the truly criminal. It's better than coddling those who don't contribute to the greater good. We only provide support to those who can't care for themselves. If you stay, you will be expected to provide a service."

"And if we don't?" Gunner asked

"Then this won't be your home for long."

Despite himself, Gunner admired the king's methods. For a society to work, people had to contribute, big or small.

"What kind of jobs could we even do?"

"With your strength and skill, you could probably find security work. The castle guard is always seeking recruits, as is the City Task Force. I should mention, thieving is not tolerated nor is wanton violence against others to acquire their things."

The guy seemed to talk a good deal, but Gunner knew the number one question that would expose him. "Sounds great, but what if a person wants to leave? What happens to them?"

"What makes you think anyone ever wants to leave?" Roark had a half-smile on his lips.

And he finally felt a push against his mind.

Leave and go where?

The pushed query echoed in his head, and suddenly, it was as if he saw a fast-paced movie in his head, one that showed him this city. Eden. Old and new, the streets full of people. Safe. Plentiful. Protected.

A nirvana for someone homeless for so long. Given the images didn't come from him, though, it could be a lie. He closed his eyes and braced against the images.

"Get out of my head."

"Try closing it off a bit. It's quite distracting having you both shouting."

As if sharing his discomfort, Sofia huddled close to him. Roark had just reminded him of his power. He'd not actually used the force of it on them yet. Not unleashed his true strength. Gunner didn't know why, nor was he waiting to see if Roark just toyed with them. He flicked a glance to the river below them. He didn't doubt for a moment it had monsters. The question was, which would be worse? The king in front of them or the river below?

As if reading his mind, Roark frowned. "Still thinking of jumping. Why would you leave? I am offering you a home. A safe place. Isn't that what you want?"

Gunner's lips pressed into a line. "I won't be forced."

I haven't forced you. Yet. Take the offer.

It was Sofia who replied. "Let us go. I did as you asked. I healed your child."

"But we don't know if it's permanent. She might need more healing." The anguished father said those words, but it was a king with a cold gaze who remarked, "I will not let you leave."

Return to the room.

The push at his free will showed Roark's true colors, and Gunner made a choice. He pulled Sofia close and whispered, "Close your mouth and hold your breath when we hit the water. And whatever you do, don't panic."

"You, idiot. *Don't jump.*" Roark roared the command.

Gunner had been waiting for the moment when a mental shield would be most effective. He wasn't good at holding them, not for long, but it was enough to ignore the command. He swung his legs over the railing, but felt Sofia resisting.

Roark growled and reached for them, his brow drawing into a mighty frown. The hammering against Gunner's mind shield brought a wince. He could feel himself trembling with the pressure, wanting to succumb to the urge to climb back onto the balcony, get on his knees, and lace his hands over his head.

He panted as he fought the suggestion while, beside him, Sofia whimpered. "Get out. Get out. I can't stay."

Just as he was about ready to bend a knee, there was an explosion that rocked the castle, drawing the king's attention. The pressure on his head eased.

Gunner didn't waste any time. He looped an arm around Sofia's waist, swung a leg over the edge, dragging her with him, and jumped.

Sofia's strident scream followed as they plummeted, and he hoped she had the sense to close her mouth before they struck the water. He managed to hold on to her despite them hitting hard. He tucked her close, fear trembling in her limbs, but she didn't thrash out of his grip. He kicked them to the surface and didn't stop until their heads were above water where they could breathe. She gasped for air, and for a moment, he just held on and bobbed in the current carrying them rapidly. To his surprise, no one was yelling behind them. No one appeared to be in pursuit. The bells had begun to ring again, and he smelled smoke. Never a good thing in a place where people lived in close quarters.

He let the current carry them past the main part of the castle, far enough that he noted the castle was surrounded by water, the river and the channels cut into the rock forming a sort of moat.

As they left the sheer wall of the keep, they drifted into the town proper. He kicked toward the opposite side, aiming for the many docks running along the edge of the channel, the boats tied up for the night and no one guarding them. He managed to grab the wale of one. Sofia understood and gripped tight to the boat. He gave her a heave, and she tumbled into the flat-bottomed craft hard enough it rocked, and she almost tipped back in.

When it stilled, she peered over the side. "I don't like this."

He grinned as he clambered in with her. "We haven't even started moving yet."

She moaned. "Don't say move."

She sat clutching her stomach, whereas he went after the ropes mooring it. He then pulled the long paddle from the bottom and put it against the dock to push them into the current just as someone yelled at him.

"Fucker. Get your ass off my boat." A corpulent fellow dressed in knee-length breeches and a stained shirt ran for them, closely followed by other angry faces.

Using the oar, Gunner pushed again against the dock to give them distance, but in a surprise move, the fellow dove and grabbed hold. Even though it threw the man off balance, he wouldn't let go. The owner of the craft tumbled into the river, yanking the oar from Gunner's hands. And there wasn't another to be seen. The current caught them, and it didn't much matter.

The river moved swiftly, and yet the boats chasing moved faster, the setting of the sun not daunting them in the least. They hung lanterns from their prows, shouted as they stroked after Gunner and Sofia, but despite the fact they had no oars or pole to move them any quicker, nor even a sail to catch the wind, those pursuing had the worst luck. A capsizing craft snarled their pursuers, giving them a chance to move ahead.

No matter how good his luck though, it seemed inevitable they would be caught, which was why he knelt by Sofia and grabbed her hands. They were cold, and she stared blankly with her eyes wide. Shock had finally hit her.

"Look at me."

She focused on him.

"I need you to stick with me. I need your help."

Some of the wild panic subsided. "What do you need from me?"

"They'll probably catch up to us soon. Which means we will have to fight."

"There's too many of them!" she exclaimed.

"We can even the odds. Can you fire a gun?" He offered her one of the ones he'd pulled off the guards.

She shook her head. "You're probably better off using it. I wish I had a knife."

"Sorry, no knife, but keep in mind, you're not defenseless," he said, suddenly inspired. "Your magic, if it can heal, I'll bet it can harm."

She stared at him.

"Think of it as healing in reverse. If someone lays a hand on you, hit them with a pox, or stomach cramps."

"We're about to be murdered and you want me to give them runny stools?" Her nose wrinkled.

"If you don't like that, then trying something else. Anything will help. They're catching up to us."

He turned from her, only to realize those chasing had halted and turned around. The river drew the boat past the city limits, and they encountered the first tendrils of a green-gray fog.

"Why are they stopping?" Gunner mused aloud. Could it be because night fell? Or something else? The fog crept closer, an ominous thing with seeking tendrils. "Cover your mouth."

Rather than ask why, she did her best to pull the wet tunic over her mouth and nose. He did the same, but the fog thickened, permeating the fabric he used as a mask, getting into his mouth. His lungs.

He could feel his mind getting cloudy. His vision blurred. He reached for Sofia, whose eyes bulged.

He wrapped his hands around hers and got her to stare at him and not the mist. "Calm down."

"Poison," she croaked.

"Yup." His body began to cramp, especially his lungs. "Use your power. You can." He gasped for air, only it burned. "Heal."

Her fingers tightened around his, and her gaze focused, steadied from terror to concentration. His skin heated where she touched him. His lungs eased, and he took a breath. It didn't feel like fire being poured down his chest.

He smiled at her. "Keep doing it."

Sofia nodded and kept the magic going, the warmth only concentrating on their chests. The fog didn't seem to cause any other harm.

It felt like forever before the river carried them past the mist. When the air no longer tried to kill them, she released her grip and collapsed. He only just managed to catch her.

He placed her in his lap, cradling her head, the woman he'd risked everything for. The king had offered him his freedom, and yet, without Sofia, he had no interest. As far as he was concerned, he'd found his mate. The woman he'd ask to promise. The one he'd have babies with. Grow old with.

If they survived.

As the boat floated down the river, Gunner remained awake. He heard monsters that night. Big things that splashed around. Little things that squeaked when caught. Shadows flew overhead, blotting out stars, but his luck held. Their boat kept trundling along the current.

In the morning, it rained, turning the ride wet and miserable. He lifted his face and let it wet his tongue. The sun emerged in the afternoon and dried them. He used his tunic to form a shielding tent over her face. She slept still. Her breathing even, but not stirring at all. Evening fell again, and he was tired. So tired. But did he dare fall asleep while the boat drifted to who knew where?

His luck gave him one last bump, literally. The boat snagged on something and turned sideways then stopped moving. A glance over the wale showed a chain, as the culprit, the heavy links, stretched across the river.

The horizon glowed with the last rays of the setting sun, and through the weeds lining the bank, he could see docks on either side of the river, old stone and rotted wood, almost hidden by the reeds. A place to stop for the night and finally get some rest if they could find a place to barricade.

Grabbing hold of the chain, he pulled them along, arm over arm, until they reached a dock. He wrapped a rope around a rotted post. Only once he'd secured both ends did he lift her from the bottom, keeping track of the quiet, broken by the occasional splash, the hum of insects, the rocking of the boat against the pier.

Pure silence would have meant something lurked. The trees by the edge of the river had formed a filmy canopy that hid the shore. Once he'd made his way off the pier without falling through any rotted spots, he found himself past the curtain of branches and in a village.

Several structures greeted him, reminding him of Eden, given they were mostly made of stone. They didn't have the many more modern touches, though, that he'd seen in the city. The buildings' roofs had ben thatched, some of them still sporting layers of reeds. Others gaped open. Unlike the ruins they'd seen their first night in the marshlands, this place had an abandoned feeling to it.

Only as he carried her through the overgrown village did he realize that it had been in use more recently than he first thought. Most of the thatches remained in decent shape. He chose one that seemed intact with its windows and doors shut tight. Inside, he found it still furnished if covered in a layer of grime. The humidity in this pace made a soft fuzz grow on many of the surfaces.

After he chased the bugs from it, he laid Sofia in the bed he found. He re-barred the door and checked the windows. He took the knife he found in a cupboard and went through every corner, starting in the bedroom. Only once he'd killed the bug population and ensured there was no other living being did he sit by the bed, knees to his chest, the weapons he'd stolen within reach.

It was a long night. And he was tired.

So very, very tired.

TWENTY-ONE

SOFIA WENT FROM SLEEPING TO AWAKE, TRYING to make sense of what she sensed around her. Last she recalled they were in that horrible fog. It was poison. Pure awful poison, and it attacked them, forcing her to use her magic. Use it until she felt like a candle, a melted puddle with nothing left to burn.

She was no longer in the boat that rocked just enough to make her stomach queasy. This bed didn't move. The air she breathed was damp and musty. She could hear the soft breath of someone nearby. She rolled enough to turn her head and look, but the room was dark. Too dark to see. She heard a slight creak. Barely a sound really, but she went stiff.

It might just be the normal sounds of a building settling. Still, it didn't hurt to hold her breath. To feign sleep and watch through the tiniest of slits.

She heard the scuff of a shoe. The swish of fabric. They weren't alone.

Friend or foe? Odd how she'd so easily adopted that concept. How she'd shed everything she knew and embraced a new truth. A new reality. With Gunner.

"I don't see them." The voice was not one she knew.

The bedroom door was only partially ajar. Not enough for her to see, only hear. Although she did appreciate the soft glowing light, as it let her see Gunner, sitting on the floor, leaning against the bed. Surely he wouldn't sleep if he feared for their safety. Unless he was exhausted. It appeared to be dark outside. Was it still the night they'd fled Eden? It felt longer. Which meant they might have been traveling for a full day.

The poor man. He'd finally succumbed to sleep. She hated waking him. She didn't make a noise as she reached for him. Her fingers brushed his hair. He didn't move. His breathing continued, slow and steady.

It might be up to her to defend them. Yes, defend, because only a foe wouldn't knock before entering, especially a bedroom.

The door swung open, and the light brightened. She kept her eyes closed and listened.

"The nap bomb worked. I told you it would put them to sleep," a male voice crowed.

A what? The implication it was some kind of drug made her realize Gunner didn't sleep naturally.

"Don't celebrate so quickly." It was a female this time. "I doubt it will last long. The scent is faint in here, which means they might not have gotten much of a dose. Tie them up. Start with the big one first."

"The rope's in the boat."

"Of course, it is," the woman sighed. "Go grab it while I watch them."

There was no attempt at being quiet as the male of the pair left.

Only one person to handle. All Sofia had to do was attack. She opened her eyes and started to move, which was when she discovered Gunner wasn't sleeping.

From his spot on the floor, he dove at the woman and shoved her out of the way. Their nap bomber's partner screeched as she flew through the door and landed with a crash.

Gunner turned and mouthed, "You coming?"

Sofia slipped out of the bed, and her first step wobbled. How long had she been sleeping? Her legs refused to straighten, and her head swam.

Gunner caught her, sliding an arm around her waist to steady her as they went through the door to a different room with a table and chairs, as well as a wide couch with moldy cushions of fabric. The woman groaned, pushing up from the debris left behind from the broken chair.

Gunner ignored the main door and half carried Sofia to the opposite side of the house, exiting via a smaller portal set beside a counter and sink. They found themselves in a jungle of green, the foliage growing thickly, and yet it wasn't entirely dark.

A light shone somewhere nearby, enough to give them some idea of their surroundings.

"Who was that?" she hissed as they ducked under a tree and its veil of mossy strands. With each moment she was upright, she found herself getting stronger and more alert.

"No idea. Probably sent by the king."

Her lips turned in a moue of annoyance. "I am surprised the king hasn't come himself."

"Doesn't matter who he sent. We might have to fight to escape."

"What do you mean 'we'? I don't even have a knife. How am I supposed to fight?" She hung her head, feeling useless.

He grabbed her hands and gave her an earnest stare. "Remember what we talked about earlier. Healing and hurting. Opposite sides of the coin. If you can do one, then it stands to reason you can do the other."

"What if I can't?"

He rolled his big shoulders. "If that fails, kick the guy in the balls and punch her in the breast."

She blinked. Almost snorted. "That's your advice?"

He leaned close and kissed her. "No, my advice is do whatever you have to and stay alive."

"I won't let them hurt you."

"Ditto." He gave her another hard kiss and whispered, "Stay here while I handle it."

"Handle what?"

But he was gone, stepped out of the protective shade of the tree. Gone to face danger alone, once more protecting her. Who would protect him?

I will. She was the only one who could.

She stared at her hands. Could they be her weapons? Time to find out.

She shoved through the tree's veil and grimaced as the sticky strands tried to adhere to her. Gunner wasn't immediately in sight. She had to walk past the end of a house toward the bright light.

Staying tucked behind a corner, she found him standing in a mossy square, facing off against two people in cloaks. The woman from inside, her hair turning gray, the ends of it cut chin length, her expression flat. By her side, a young man, his expression eager, a sneer on his lips.

"Where is the healer?" the woman asked of Gunner, and Sofia noticed the blue highlights in her gray hair.

"I don't know what you're talking about." Gunner spread his hands. "I'm the only one here. Just stopped for the night."

"Don't play stupid. A moment ago, you were both sleeping inside that house."

"And now we're not." She could hear the smile in Gunner's words. "Which means you're in a heck of a lot of trouble if you don't leave. And when you do, take a message to Roark, would you, and tell him to fuck off."

The younger man brayed with laughter. "You think he sent us? That marsh rodent is nothing but a pretender, and the true king of these lands will soon put him in his place."

It surprised her to find out these people weren't sent by Roark, especially since they knew of her, called her healer. Why did everyone want her so badly?

"I'll tell you the same thing I told *King* Roark. You can't have her." Gunner's statement warmed her heart.

"No one is asking permission. Fenlin, take care of

him, and then we'll hunt down the woman," the female said.

Sofia realized she'd have to act. Even though she saw no weapons on the man and woman, she recognized their confidence. They thought they could take Gunner, which meant they were probably power wielders of some sort.

Gunner oozed confidence as he said, "Enough of the posturing. You are not the one in control of the situation." He pulled the gun from his belt, finally taking aim.

The woman smiled. "If you're going to threaten, at least make it believable. I know that weapon went for a swim."

"Does Roark know he has spies in his city?"

A sly expression crossed her face. "Do you really think he'd let them live if he did?"

Fenlin took a step forward. "Why are we still talking with him? I'd like to get out of this place. It's creepy. I swear I still hear them screaming."

"Who?" Gunner asked, even as Sofia also wondered.

"The pretender in the Marshland knows who died here and why." The woman wore a haughty smile. "And why people will keep dying if he doesn't take a knee to the true king."

"Whatever your problem with Roark, it doesn't involve us."

"No, it doesn't. But you are in my way."

"Let me ask you, how's your luck?" Gunner sounded ever so nonchalant.

Sofia thought it an odd question.

"My luck is fine. But yours doesn't seem so good according to my sources."

"Ah, but that's the thing about luck," Gunner noted. "If you get enough bad, the balance eventually swings, and you can count on some good to come your way. As you noted, I'm overdue."

"Take him out," the woman ordered her companion.

"About time," Fenlin grumbled, raising his arm.

Sofia saw no weapon in his hand, and yet Gunner recoiled as if punched.

"Fucking wizards," Gunner grumbled. He aimed his gun, but it didn't fire. He staggered as Fenlin neared.

Gunner turned and threw his weapon, hitting the thatch of a nearby house, which caused something nesting in it to jump in the air with a mighty flap of wings. Fenlin startled, and his foot slipped, his aim went awry, and the bird overhead squawked. It also pooped, the mess of shit landing on Fenlin's head. The boy looked less than impressed.

Sofia smothered her mouth to hide a laugh.

"Stop playing with the Emerald rat. Finish him," yelled the woman with a distinct lack of patience.

Fenlin's expression twisted, and he flung his hands at Gunner, who suddenly darted to the side, scooped up something from the ground, and tossed it. The rock hit Fenlin in the forehead, and he went down hard.

The woman snapped, "Must I do everything myself?" She narrowed her gaze and focused on Gunner. Flames appeared at her fingertips, but rather than aim at Gunner, she went after the buildings, lighting the thatch on fire, illuminating the night.

The thing about flame was it spread to anything it could find. It jumped from the roof to a vine then zipped along until the tree Sofia sheltered under began to smoke. Her throat tickled. She covered her mouth, but the air quality worsened. The reasoning behind the fire became clear—flush the presence of anyone else around.

And it worked.

Needing to get out of the smoke, Sofia stumbled out and heard Gunner yell, "No."

She looked and saw him running for the wizard woman, paying no mind to the flaming balls she flicked at him.

Before Gunner reached her, something launched itself from the shadows. A sleek four-legged body with a sinuous tail.

"Kitty!"

Her feline knocked into the firewoman, grabbed her in mighty jaws, and bounded away.

Rather than follow, Gunner sank to the ground, and Sofia ran for him. She smelled the burned flesh before even reaching his side. She grabbed at him and eased him down before he could topple.

"Hold on," she murmured, finding it easier and easier to pull forth that kernel of heat inside. She pushed her magic into him, but her rest hadn't replenished all her power. She fizzled before she was done, but at least he breathed more easily, his burns now spots of pink healing skin instead of open raw flesh.

His eyes remained shut.

"Gunner." She leaned over him, and her tears fell. Would they always have to fight to survive?

"With luck, he's dead," snapped Fenlin, having recovered without her noticing.

With a brutal grip, he snared her around the neck, cutting off her air supply. Her fingers dug at him, her eyes wide and startled, her mouth a gasping O.

Fenlin dragged her off her feet. "Thank you for

getting rid of that annoying hag. Now I won't have to split the reward when I bring you back to Seaside."

"No." The word barely whispered past her lips, but the horror swelled within. This man was going to sell her. He had no right.

A booted foot kicked Gunner as Fenlin stepped over him, dragging her along. "As if you have a choice."

Choice.

There it was again. That thing others seemed determined to take from her. Except, what gave them the right?

Was she going to let this Fenlin, a puling excuse for humanity, actually make decisions for her?

Her hands still gripped his where he hung onto her neck. Skin to skin. Could she really turn her healing gift into something else?

Time to find out.

She pulsed her intent. *Die.* Her hands turned icy cold.

TWENTY-TWO

Gunner's eyes opened to the dancing flames on the roofs of the houses. They lit up the night sky and reminded him of the pain when the witch flung fire at him. An agony that now proved to only be a cringe-worthy memory. He sat up and saw his hands pink with new skin rather than charred. His face...he slapped his cheeks and found them intact. He'd been healed. Only one person was capable of that.

Sofia! He stood and whirled, seeking her, but the bright flames blinded him to the shadows, and the smoke stung his eyes.

"Sofia!"

Instead of a reply, a furry shape padded from between two buildings. Kitty shoved her giant head against his hand.

"Hey, big girl. Have you seen our Sofia?"

Kitty remained by his side, which surely indicated Sofia didn't need their help. She probably bided her time. She had more courage than most, even if she didn't recognize it.

The cat meowed and then hissed, her fur standing on her back. Gunner realized he heard a strange rumbling, but not that of a motor or anything that drove on land or in the air. By chance, he glanced toward the river and saw it rise over the rim of the trees, a wave of water, readying to soak.

Kitty yowled at the sight, and Gunner braced himself as it came crashing down, heard it splash, and the hiss of fires being put out, only he remained dry. Opening his eyes, he noticed the area around him and the cat remained untouched, but everything else dripped. The flames had been extinguished so thoroughly they didn't even smolder. The night turned dark once more, except for bobbing little lights moving toward him from the path leading to the pier, as if tiny bugs carried lanterns. Or more likely they were just glowing sort of insects, he amended, as they appeared a few paces ahead of the Marshland king. Roark wasn't dressed like a monarch, though. He wore battered leather pants and molded tunic. His boots went to his knees, and he'd left the crown at his castle.

Gunner growled and pointed. "I knew you were behind the attack."

"You know nothing," Roark spat. "I have only just arrived, too late again apparently."

"You followed us."

"More like I took a guess I'd find you here. This is the last town the river passes through before branching."

"You aren't taking her back," Gunner stated. He might not have a weapon, but he would fight.

"I wasn't planning to."

"Liar."

"As if I care what you think. I have more important matters to deal with. Spies in my kingdom. A rival monarchy attacking my people." Roark glanced around him. "A pair of runaways is the least of my concerns."

"Yet here you are."

A voice spoke in his head. *If wanted to force you to obey, I could.*

Gunner set his jaw. "I'd fight you."

You could try. And yet, with just a push...

Without meaning to, Gunner hit the ground on his knees.

Shall I make you beg? Dance? Throw yourself in the river?

In that moment Gunner understood the king

could do all those things. The power he felt pulsing against him...

It suddenly released, and Gunner popped to his feet. "You've made your point."

"Good, and now that you understand what I can do, I will add that I am here to tell you I won't force you to stay."

"Says the man who had me and Sofia locked up."

Roark shrugged. "I won't apologize for what I've done. I'd do anything to protect those in my care. Kill. Imprison. The good of many is worth that of a few strangers." Roark's expression remained uncompromising, and once more, Gunner understood his position. More than once, Axel and the Haven gang had been in untenable situations, where they had to make a choice for the greater good. A leader had to make hard decisions.

For some reason this reminded him of what Titan had said after their battle when they'd been returned to their cells. *"I wish I could have found this place before my life went to shit."*

"Why?" Gunner had asked.

"Because it's a good place. A place I could have called home."

Bloody Roark read his mind. "Ah yes, Titan. He escaped the same night you did. But he didn't go alone. I take it he's not with you."

"No." And he hoped wherever Titan went he found peace.

Before Roark could reply, a body staggered into view. It was Fenlin, but with a face swollen to the point that he couldn't use his mouth or see from bulging eyes. He sank to his knees and gasped, reaching for the king.

Roark eyed Fenlin with no compassion in his eyes. "You! Did you really come back to the scene of your crime?"

Gunner might not have felt what the king did, and yet there was no denying the panic that suffused Fenlin as he choked and clawed at his face before rising and stumbling off in the dark. But of more interest than the suddenly stricken wizard was Sofia, who emerged from the same shadows as Fenlin and advanced on the king, hands outstretched.

"Walk away or you, too, shall suffer my wrath."

A bit over the top, but the confidence was sexy, if aimed at the wrong guy.

Roark didn't budge. "I won't offer apology. When it comes to my daughter, I'll do anything to protect her."

"I won't let you force me."

"Wasn't planning to," the king replied.

"If you're not here to drag us back or apologize, then why did you track us down?" Gunner asked.

Moving to Sofia's side, he laced his fingers with hers, feeling the chill in her skin. The tremble she fought to hide. He doubted she had the power to do anything, and yet she bluffed. Showed such courage.

"I'm here to make you an offer," Roark claimed.

"I don't want to make a deal with you," she huffed.

"Are you sure? Perhaps you should hear me out first, for I was going to name you Duchess Sofia, which comes with the position of master pharmacist."

She tilted her chin. "I am not a master of anything."

"You may call yourself whatever you like. I am offering you the opportunity to have your own practice."

"Serving you?"

The king shrugged. "Serving the kingdom."

"She can't heal everyone." Gunner couldn't even begin to imagine the toll it would take if she constantly used her powers.

"I wouldn't expect her to, but perhaps we could have the understanding that you will, at your discretion, use your healing abilities if there is great need."

"And I would decide?" she said, chewing her lip.

Gunner could see she was tempted, and honestly, it was more than he had to offer. He wasn't even sure he could find Axel and the others. And even if he did...did he expect her to live in a dirty camp, struggling to find food?

The voice whispered in his head again. *What if you could give your people a home?*

Gunner's gaze focused on the king. "Stop poking around in my head and spit out what you want already."

"I want you, Haven, everyone you know, to join me."

"Join you?" He laughed. "What kind of fucked-up request is that?"

"You've seen Eden. The beauty."

"And squalor," Sofia added. "It isn't all beautiful."

He agreed. "It is possible for any city to not have its dark places?"

"You killed a man," she declared. "In front of me."

"A convicted criminal who would have died anyhow."

"You mean if I'd saved him—"

"He would have still been executed. I told you, we don't abide criminals."

"You tolerate your Marsh people selling folk."

"I thought we agreed that was for their own good. The old recipes are still in use in many spots."

The grin helped, but it was the lack of pushing on the mental shields that intrigued.

He no longer tried to force their will.

"Why us?"

"You're a capable man. The kingdom could use more capable citizens."

"To live in the city?"

Roark rolled his shoulders. "Maybe. The city is getting full, but I am sure we could figure something out that would accommodate you and the rest of Haven."

For some reason Gunner's gaze was drawn to the ruins. So many buildings. So many possibilities.

The king probably read his mind, because he said, "Before you ask, you should know this hamlet was destroyed by my enemies. They attacked without warning or provocation."

"Did you avenge them?"

"I couldn't until tonight." The king looked to the shadows. "I am not always as free as I'd like to travel outside my kingdom. The mantle of responsibility keeps me anchored."

"Why were they attacked?" Gunner asked.

Roark stared him straight in the eyes. "Because there is evil in the world."

Not the answer he expected. "Do you think that evil might return to this place?"

"Honestly? Maybe. Probably." Roark shrugged. "At the same time, the previous inhabitants were few and perhaps no longer as tough as the wilder villages. Domestication tends to soften people over time. This outpost town requires strength."

"Also needs a shit-ton of work," Gunner remarked, looking around. Benny would kill him if he didn't bargain, because that was what was happening. They bargained for something that Gunner was scared to believe.

The king smiled. "Indeed, it does require some rebuilding. Given this town is an important line of defense along the border with the hostile territory of the Sapphire domain, aid in rebuilding could be requested from the crown."

"And who rules us?"

"Ah, that's a little more complex. Your Haven could keep Axel and its current people in their positions; however, they will abide by the law of the land."

"Which is your law."

"Don't forget to say 'Your Highness.'" Roark's smile was cold, but Gunner recognized the firm will.

The question being, would they be ruled fairly, or would they trade one despot for another?

If it were just Gunner... The king was offering a

home for Haven. The one thing he couldn't turn down. He needed to let Axel and the others know.

"What's the catch?"

"The Marshlands become stronger." The king didn't even bother to lie. "Your friends need a place to live. I need someone to guard our borders."

"That's a pretty big job. You're at war with the Enclave and pretty much anyone who won't recognize the Marshes as a kingdom."

"Yes." Still no apology.

It brought a smile to Gunner's lips. "If you don't stop, I'm gonna start liking you, I think." He sobered. "If I say yes, it has to be understood I might have to spend time in New Haven helping out."

Sofia straightened and added, "Me too."

The king sighed. "If this is your way of saying you want to be together, in this same village, then so be it. I would ask one promise."

Sofia didn't even ask him what it was, just replied, "I'll help her if needed, but your daughter won't die. Not of that marsh sickness at any rate."

Roark visibly eased. "Now that we've clarified our positions, you should make all due haste to your Haven group before the Port City Enclave realizes you've bested their spies."

"Is that who they work for?"

A small smile touched Roark's lips. "Not anymore."

It was then that Gunner had to admit the flaw in their plan. "I'll give Axel and the others your offer, if I can find them. I don't know how to get to Emerald from here."

"And here I thought your plan to follow the river was intentional and brilliant." Roark snorted. "The river forks. Follow it south and it leads to the beaches and cliffs that border the ocean. Take the branch to the east and it will lead you into the woods that form the border between us and Emerald."

"Getting to the forest does me no good. There's a crack running through it that can't be crossed."

Again, the king smiled. "Yes, it can. You just need to search a little harder. Now, since we're done here, you should know that there is a truck or two that was left behind in one of the outbuildings. Supplies too. Take what you need."

"What if we leave and don't come back?"

The king didn't bother replying. Why would he? He'd just given Gunner the best chance at a future. The Eden they'd been looking for, though they would still have to fight the land and the Enclave, their enemy. As expected, keeping a home wasn't going to be easy.

Which was kind of how he preferred it.

TWENTY-THREE

THE KING LEFT THE SAME WAY HE ARRIVED, wrapping himself in the water from the river and essentially disappearing. A man of incredible power, and not Enclave born.

"What a pompous prick," Gunner muttered.

"He is. But..." She hesitated to say it.

"He's offering us the chance of a lifetime. I know." Gunner snorted. "Which is why we need to find Axel and the others to tell them. But first..." He drew her close and kissed her then rested his forehead against hers. "Thank you."

"For what?" she said, not feigning surprise.

"Saving me. I keep trying to come to your rescue, but you don't need me."

What a silly thing to say. She cupped his face.

"On the contrary, I do need you. Need you to love me. To teach me. And most of all give me the baby you promised. I think I saw a cup in that house."

For some reason, he found that outrageously funny and laughed. He was still chuckling when he found the truck the king had mentioned. It took only a little fiddling to get it running. She spent that time scrounging in the houses, Kitty keeping watch over her, until she'd found a medley of items to aid on their trip, including a knife. Not that she needed a weapon. She was deadly on her own. Or she would be once she had a nap.

They set out by midday, and Gunner held her hand and smiled as they travelled, following the river, Kitty napping in the back.

The water engine choked and gasped and made all kinds of awful noise, but having it beat walking, and it proved easy to fuel. It turned out there were waypoints along the river. Also abandoned, like the town, but they offered safe spots to rest.

Kitty, having slept all day, took their stop as an opportunity to stretch her legs and hunt. Whereas Sofia stretched her limbs and smiled. She'd napped in the truck and felt her strength returning. It was an unmistakable feeling, and she couldn't help but recall that dulling of her senses when in the Ruby

City. What was in that drink the master made her every morning? What would happen if everyone in the city woke up?

They took turns watching for predators as they bathed, with Gunner spending more time watching her than the landscape. She laughed at one point and splashed him. Which resulted in him scooping her into his arms, soaking his clothes to kiss her. With the sun setting, they made haste to get inside, where they locked the stone and mud hut against the outside world.

Gunner had made them a bed of spongy branches with a blanket she'd scored from a derelict house covering it. It wasn't the finest of linens or softest of beds, but she didn't care, not when his lips pressed so sweetly against hers. His hands made quick work of the motley arrangement of clothes she wore. She stripped him just as quickly.

They came together in a hot clash of breath, teeth, and flesh, with her legs parting to welcome his hard thrusts. Her body undulating to meet the rising pleasure only he could give. To reach that pinnacle where everything was perfect.

And just when she thought it couldn't get any better, he stroked her body again.

When she awoke the next day, the hut alight

with the sunshine peeking through the cracks, it was to find him grinning as he watched her.

"Why are you so happy?" she asked, rising with a stretch.

A soft smile pulled at his lips. "Because I love you." And then because teasing seemed to be their thing. "I don't think I put a baby in you last night. I think we should try again."

They did. And then to be sure, they made love each time they stopped. Quick encounters when they had a short stop to stretch their legs and replenish the engine's tank. They kept their longer sensual exploration for at night. Except the evening it rained, and Kitty joined them inside. In their makeshift bed. Between them.

They spent days travelling before they made it to the edge of a daunting forest. The trees were so tall, but Gunner appeared excited to see them. They had to ditch the truck, parking it under the boughs, hoping it would remain there until they returned.

It took three days of hiking to hit the crevice that split the forest, too deep to climb down, too far to jump across. According to Gunner even the quickest of drones couldn't span it. Something oozed from the crack and killed almost all electronics.

Taking the advice of the king, they followed it.

Another two days of walking until they found the massive tree that had fallen across.

"It's big enough to drive over," she remarked.

Gunner eyed it, and the freshness of the wood where it had split from its rooted base. "This happened recently."

"How lucky."

For some reason he found that extremely funny.

The wolgar found them the first night they camped on the other side of the gorge. They appeared from the shadows, and Sofia stuck close to Gunner, who, in turn, murmured, "Kitty, be nice. These are our friends."

Not according to the large feline. Kitty had her ears flattened and her lip raised in a snarl.

The wolgar didn't attack, but they did keep track of them, and Gunner seemed convinced they were herding them in a certain direction. That evening they made camp up in a tree—because of a nearby nest of blood biters—with Kitty standing watch. It wasn't until hours after nightfall that a voice from the ground startled them.

Startled her at least. Gunner appeared to be expecting it.

"I knew you were too annoying to be dead," said a voice with dry sarcasm.

"I came back just because I knew you'd miss me."

Gunner helped Sofia out of the tree, and she stood in front of a big guy who appeared undaunted by the wolgars sitting at his heels.

"Looks like you've got quite the story to tell," said the man she found out later was the infamous Axel.

"Actually, it's more than a story," Gunner said. "I found Haven a home."

EPILOGUE

THE OUTPOST PROVED JUST THE RIGHT SIZE FOR New Haven. The fact it had been raided before and the population sent fleeing or dead didn't daunt them one bit. For one, Haven had more people, people willing to fight for their home. Plus, they had some magical talent of their own. Let the Seaside king try attacking again.

At times, Sofia was convinced Gunner and the others were eager for it. Anxious to do anything to show the Enclave they were done playing their petty games.

No one really wanted to fight, but they would. Because freedom was at stake. The truth needed to be heard. And lives had to be protected.

Her hand went to her belly, and she smiled as she watched Gunner outside with Kitty. He'd decided it would be cool if the feline could do tricks like Axel's wolgar. It wasn't working out too well.

Kitty was much too amused by the human who kept telling her to fetch. With reason.

"When I say attack, you look where I point and go nuts. Like this." Gunner jabbed a finger at the reed figure he used for sparring practice and ran for it, fake snarling. He tackled it, hit the ground, and rose. He brushed himself off saying, "See, how easy it is? Your turn." He pointed. "Attack!"

Kitty eyed him, padded over, rose on her hind legs, and licked him.

At the expression on his face, Sofia couldn't help but laugh. Laughed so hard she missed Gunner sweeping close enough to grab her in his arms and swing her off her feet.

"You think that's funny, eh?" he said in a mock growl.

There was only one answer to that. "I love you," she said and then whispered the secret she'd just uncovered. "Daddy."

RIGHT BEFORE THOSE BELLS WENT OFF IN THE Marshland dungeons...

Titan sat on his cot, feet flat on the floor, his

hands on his knees. Eyes closed. But he could hear. Heard the tap of her heels as she came down the hall. Smelled her perfume. Still the same. The effect on him hadn't diminished.

She stopped in front of his cell.

He didn't look. Wouldn't.

"Hello, Titan." She spoke his name softly. As if she had the right. Yet she'd betrayed him. He had only to put a hand on his chest and feel what they'd done to remind himself.

He closed his eyes tighter and whispered, "Go away."

Because she was a reminder of what had been done to him. How she'd been a part of it. How he'd changed.

"Let me help you. Please," she offered.

At her request, something in him snapped. His focus shifted.

The next thing he knew, he was running through the night, away from the dungeon that couldn't actually hold him. A body slung over his shoulder.

Fuck. What had he done?

He tossed his burden onto the ground and, in the cresting dawn, could have groaned as he saw who it was.

Riella, with her flaming red hair, freckled skin, and lying lips.

Why did he take her? The king would have given him his freedom. A place to live. A purpose.

Instead, he kidnapped Riella.

The daughter of his enemy.

And despite knowing they would come after him with everything they had, he wasn't giving her back.

Stayed tuned for Twisted Metal Heart, where Titan must overcome his anger if he's ever going to find peace in his heart.

For more Eve Langlais books visit: EveLanglais.com

TOXIC DUST
EVE LANGLAIS
WASTELAND TREASURE
EVE LANGLAIS
TWISTED METAL HEART
EVE LANGLAIS
CATASTROPHIC ATTRACTION
EVE LANGLAIS
IRON PIRATE
EVE LANGLAIS
ASH PRINCESS
EVE LANGLAIS